# FIERY SPIRITS & VOICES

# FIERY SPIRITS & VOICES

## Canadian Writers of African Descent

AYANNA BLACK, EDITOR

HarperPerennialCanada
HarperCollinsPublishersLtd

FIERY SPIRITS & VOICES

For information address HarperCollins Publishers Ltd., 55 Avenue Road, Suite 2900, Toronto, Ontario, Canada M5R 3L2.

http://www.harpercanada.com

HarperCollins books may be purchased for educational, business, or sales promotional use. For information please write: Special Markets Department, HarperCollins Canada, 55 Avenue Road, Suite 2900, Toronto, Ontario, Canada M5R 3L2.

First HarperPerennialCanada edition

This HarperPerennialCanada edition is a reprint of both *Fiery Spirits*, originally published 1994, and *Voices*, originally published 1992, and includes updated biographical information and a new preface by the editor.

Canadian Cataloguing in Publication Data

Main entry under title:

Fiery spirits & Voices:
Canadian writers of African descent

Previously published independently under titles: Fiery spirits and Voices

ISBN 0-00-648521-9

1. Short stories, Canadian (English) – Black authors.*
2. Canadian fiction (English) – 20th century.*
3. Canadian poetry (English) – Black authors.*
4. Canadian poetry (English) – 20th century.*
5. Black Canadians – Fiction.*
6. Black Canadians – Poetry.*

I. Black, Ayanna.
II. Title: Fiery spirits and Voices: Canadian writers of African descent.
III. Title: Voices.
IV. Title: Fiery Spirits.

PS8235.B53F54 2000
C813'.0108896071 C99-932416-0
PR9194.5.B55F53 2000

00 01 02 03 04 KRO 6 5 4 3 2 1

Printed and bound in Canada

# Contents

## *Preface to the New Edition*

*Art expands history as it affirms identities; it creates new songs, new histories and new beings as it apprehends the future.*
*We are who we make ourselves to be.*

Nkiru Nzegwa, theorist writer/artist

*Not everything that is faced can be changed, but nothing can be changed until it is faced.*

James Baldwin

Here I am at Potsdamer Platz, in Berlin, having a glass of wine with a friend. It's ten years since the wall between East and West Berlin came down. I remember watching this event—this victory—on TV. I can still envision that sea of people crossing triumphantly over to the West. I imagined I heard the words of Martin Luther King: "Free at last, free at last, great God Almighty, I'm free at last!" That was a day of liberation.

Sitting here today, I am also reminded of the time when Cecil Foster, the Toronto writer, and I sat at the Four Seasons Hotel discussing the original edition of *Voices: Canadian Writers of African Descent* over a glass of wine. Some walls—some barriers—are not made of bricks and stones. In order to be a published writer in Canada, I had to break down many invisible walls. *Voices* was an important anthology for this reason; it was a good catalyst in the breakdown of the racial barriers dividing the Canadian literary establishment. It consequently pushed the works of its writers into the mainstream.

That was in 1991. It was invigorating. It was a time of enlightenment, a time for social, political and cultural change. As artists of African descent, we felt that we could empower ourselves. We came to an understanding that we must speak for ourselves if we wanted to be heard...that no one could sing, dance or talk for us. No one said it better than Langston Hughes in "Note on Commercial Theatre" in the *Selected Poems of Langston Hughes*:

...someday somebody'll
Stand up and talk about me,
And write about me—
Black and beautiful—
And sing about me,
And put on plays about me!
I reckon it'll be
Me myself!

Yes, it'll be me.

In the late 50s and 60s, a wealth of Canadian writers of African descent existed, sprinkled in different regions of Canada but practically unheard of, although all had between one and six published books. Anthony Phelps, John Hearne, Samuel Selvon, Jan Carew, Gérard Étienne, Frank Fouche, Lennox Brown and poet Anna Minerva Henderson all contributed immensely to the development of an African-Canadian literary form. But during this period, the only recognized black Canadian voice in English literature was Austin Clarke, the literary stalwart and a major mentor to many of the writers in this collection. He articulated his feelings of isolation in an interview with Stella Agloo Baksh that was printed in her book *Austin C. Clarke: A Biography*: "All this time there was no black presence and no black aesthetic, no one to whom I could go to explain the essence of my anger...I had to search for it in America..."

In my opinion, Clarke paved the long and winding road for all of us, interfacing with the publishing establishment and the art councils, helping to reduce racial barriers and, thus, enabling institutions to be more receptive to writers like Dany Laferrière, George Elliott Clarke, Cecil Foster, Dionne Brand, Claire Harris, Lawrence Hill and the next wave of writers: André Alexis, Nolo Hopkinson....

This volume presents the reissue of two anthologies, *Fiery Spirits* (1994) and *Voices* (1992), in one seminal volume. The contents remain as they originally appeared; and I chose not to rearrange the works, but rather, to maintain the integrity of each anthology. Since 1992, much has happened. Austin Clarke was awarded the 1999 W.O. Mitchell Prize, which goes to a Canadian writer who has produced an outstanding body of work and has served as a caring mentor for other writers. In 1992, he was honoured with a Toronto Arts Award for Lifetime achievement in Literature. Dionne Brand won the Governor General's Award for Poetry in 1997 and the Trillium Award in 1997. She was also shortlisted for the Chapters/*Books in Canada* First Novel Award in 1996 and the Trillium Award in 1996. Yvonne Vera won the Swedish Prize "Voice of Africa 1999." She also won the Commonwealth Prize for Literature in

1997. Claire Harris was shortlisted for the Governor General's Award in 1993 and 1996. Rozena Maart was awarded the Journey Prize for Best Short Fiction in Canada in 1992. Paul Tiyambe Zeleza has received many literary awards, including three of Africa's most prestigious book award, the Noma Award for Publishing in Africa. Honoured as a poet and as an activist scholar, George Elliott Clarke has received several awards, including the Archibald Lampman Award for poetry in 1991, the Portia White Prize in 1998, a Rockefeller Foundation Bellagio (Italy) Residency in 1998, and the University of Waterloo Arts Alumni Award in 1999. Sadly, the passing of John Hearne in 1994 has deprived us of much significant work.

Yes. We have seen an increase in the recognition granted to Canadian writers of African descent; but there is still a need and desire for English translations of francophone works. For example, Gérard Étienne is the author of eighteen books that have been translated into several languages, including Russian, German and Spanish. Yet, there is no comprehensive volume representing his work in English. There is also a crying need for English writers to be translated into French.

Still, we can take heart when we see old barriers being torn down. The writers in this anthology are tangible proof of the richness that is evolving from the removal of invisible walls. As we enter the millennium, these writers have created an important expectation...a benchmark for current and future writers.

Ayanna Black
Berlin, Germany
December 1999

# FIERY SPIRITS

Speak, memory speak
Our loins ache
To deliver

—Harold Head

Thank you, Harold, for your generosity, passion, and love of African-Canadian literature.

# Preface

*. . . inspite of jim crow.in spite of lynchings.in spite of laws against them speaking their tongues, playing their drums — in spite of the rules against their religion.in spite of.in spite of in spite.they creating . . .*

*—Marlene Nourbese Philip,*
Showing Grit: Showboating North of the 44th Parallel

Historically, from the days of slavery, people of African descent have forged our pathways. Africans, captured and shackled in chains en route to the New World (the Caribbean and North American colonies) spoke several languages, all of which originated in the Niger-Congo family located in West and Southern Africa. When African slaves landed in various colonies around the globe, ruling colonialists separated those who spoke the same language to prevent insurrection; additionally, they forced their slaves to learn and speak the language of the European colonizers. Margaret Bushy, in her "introduction" to *Daughters of Africa*, explains:

> *The linguistic versatility demonstrated by people of Africa and the African diaspora is in itself a remarkable testament to survival of vicissitude in a history that has weathered subjugation and colonization by the powers of Europe. Those Africans transported to the New World in the course of the slave trade were forbidden to speak in their own native tongues, whether Yoruba or Asante Twi. . . .*

The synthesis of African (Yoruba, Igbo, Asante Twi, Kikongo and others) and Western languages (French, Spanish, Dutch, Portuguese, English, etc.) proved most confrontational and, as a result, produced an extraordinarily complex language born of cultural resistance — and denial of cultural expressions (language, belief systems, religions, and values). It provided a necessary conduit between master and slave; it allowed for a communication of survival; and, most importantly, it enabled the collective to plan individual escapes to freedom.

In his "Introduction" to *Talk That Talk: An Anthology of African American Storytelling*, Henry Louis Gates Jr. points out:

> *The stories that we tell ourselves and our children function to order our world, serving to create both a foundation upon which each of us constructs our sense of reality and a filter through which we process each event that confronts us every day. . . .*

In ancient times, highly esteemed women of the Ebo, Akan, Mende and Yoruba cultures represented the life-giver and creator of human culture still central and essential to our societies. Like men, women storytellers (or *griots*, or town criers) are the librarians and the historians, an information storehouse that ensures the proliferation of African culture and reinforces our heritage.

Like archaeologists, we investigate and excavate both political and personal (or external and internal) landscapes in an attempt to understand place in the context of an Old World while confronting dislocation in the context of the New (in order to tell our stories).

*Fiery Spirits* gathers writers from diverse cultural and geographic backgrounds. It includes African Canadian writers whose families have lived in Canada since the 1700s, the new and not so new people of African descent who have been transplanted from the Caribbean since the 1950s, and writers who have recently immigrated from Africa to Canada. And, more recently, civil war and tyranny, exasperated by a terrible and vicious famine that the war caused, have brought refugees from Uganda, Ethiopia and Somalia to seek political asylum in Canada.

These writers retrieve and borrow elements from the painful and complex history of experiences born of slavery and colonization, cultural genocide, famine and civil war, and tyrannical dislocation. Although steeped in African literary tradition, African Canadians incorporate diverse cultural, ideological and geographic references in our works and further represent various literary influences ranging from western classics to the literature of developing countries.

This collection presents new works of short fiction, poetry, monologue and epistle from both new and established authors. It spotlights authors writing from the centre of their being with confidence, maturity and an extraordinary sense of socio-cultural impact vis-à-vis linguistic and aesthetic experience.

I chose to begin the collection with Carol Talbot's mythical and multi-layered short story, "The Crystal Cave," an appropriate piece since, in many ways, the cave symbolises a kind of womb of memories, a place of collective consciousness depicting past, present and future. A memory recall — sharing of stories — an essential element of African oral tradition, a healing place. Pauline Peters' monologue, "Dryland" depicts a lost language and identity, but it also celebrates our survival.

Others writers explore issues currently under discussion in various communities. Archie Crail, for example, reflects on subtleties of power, institutional politics, and individual racism in "Affirmative Action" while Sylvia Hamilton evokes an air of indifference in her poem "Shoes." Paul Tiyambe Zeleza cites the struggles of mixed marriage in "Foggy Seasons." Gérard Étienne reflects on love and the betrayal of a dying country in "La pacotille". Kuwee Kumsaa cites the hypocrisy of living in North America and yearns for reunion with her country in "Lamentations: A Letter to My Mother." "Why," Stefan Collins's deeply moving piece, examines the invisibility and isolation within AIDS communities and toasts the strength he has discovered in his struggles. Jan Carew's, "Canopus," "Nocturne For Roots" and "Africa — Guyana!" remind us of the lives of mothers in ancient Africa. John Hearne in "Living Out the Winter" shares the complexities and confrontations of living in the Caribbean amid an atmosphere of violence.

These pieces, confront issues both painful and joyous, a fact we cannot avoid because they are part of living and part of society's ritual. Courtnay McFarlane's "Catharsis/One," Charles C. Smith's "Atavism," "Between Destinies," and "Daydreaming About My Father" and Minister Faust's

"The Brown Moth" reflect on death. Dee September in "Grief" also examines lost ones, but in the poems "Weight of War" and "In a Breath" she evokes the determination and the joyful experience of the human spirit.

Others look at women's lives. The characters in Yvonne Vera's "A Woman is a Child," Leleti Tamu's "Town" and "Every Goodbye Ain't Gone" and Dionne Brand's "Three Passages from Elizet" all live different lives, but the pieces all affirm and validate women's lives, inventing new worlds that instill courage to strive for liberation, courage to be assertive, the courage to laugh, play, and cry and finally, the courage to love.

Rudolph Allen ("My Grandfather and I"), Richardo Keens-Douglas ("Moonface") and Jane Tapsubei Creider ("The Woman in the Pit and the Elephant's Trunk") write with wit and charm and capture the creative minds of young adults.

These stories are moulded in 5,000 years of African literary tradition, while offering a shared history with shared traditions interconnecting diverse contemporary realities (feminism, racism, homophobia, love/identity and death). *Fiery Spirits* celebrates the unique and inventive *griots* of African-Canadian literature who will take us into the twenty-first century.

Ayanna Black
September 1994

# Carol Talbot

## *The Crystal Cave*

The limbs of the trees were twisted and gnarled, dark shadows etched against the sky. The roots lay withered on the ground, scattered among the brittle brown leaves. Sixteen-year-old Alonia lay in a sodden heap, the bright colours of her robe defiled with caking blood, stones and mud. Strands of hair, pulled loose from once neat braids, partially screened her face, as if to keep the secret of her agony to herself. Her hands lay relaxed at her sides contradicting the angry imprint of her own nails in their palms.

As she cradled her daughter's dark head in her lap, Magdela felt her grief as a bottomless well with no promise of healing waters. Hers was an agony of silent tears.

In a distant memory, the scene from the village came back to her . . .

*The ugly crowd of hecklers — children too — the whole of her village, it seemed, through the shocked haze of her horror and shame, was there shouting taunts of "Slut! Harlot! Desecrator of holy beliefs! Witch! Whore! Wanton one!" The leering Mordu at the lead watching and goading. But even at the time there was a lascivious light in his eyes — a grim pleasure shining perversely as he engineered the rape of her pride. His was not the gentle spirit of his father, the healer, but the malicious spitefulness of the jealously inadequate who revels in the telling of twisted tales on the innocent or naive. And there at the back, her other self no longer, Dragonian stood, a tall shrunken man enhancing her shame with his silent condemnation. Righteous indignation was properly mirrored in the mask that had become his face.*

She remembered thinking, bitterly, that her own parents were probably there too if their feeble legs would carry them that far. Even if they hadn't come, what could they have done against the lies and insinuations of the healer's own son?

My shame lives on, she thought. My shame lives on. So reverberated the mindless chant in her head.

Alonia's hollow eyes carried the shadows of dark below them. Magdela shuddered under their relentless gaze and saw her future and her past stretched out before her and behind her in the silent reflection of her daughter's shame. They had to go on. She coaxed Alonia to her feet and turned her towards the road.

Heavy mists shrouded the hills as they trudged onward, day after day, dragging their few belongings behind them. Alonia walked stolidly beside her mother, sometimes stumbling, her hand held firmly in her mother's grasp. No word or even sigh of complaint crossed her lips. She walked, her sightless eyes fixed on something in the distance.

In the nights Magdela was often awakened by muffled moans from her daughter, followed by anguished writhings whose soundless pitch reverberated off the walls of Magdela's shattered heart. Other times the moans exploded into screams and then melted down to the distressed keening of a hurt and frightened child. At those times Magdela could sometimes see the madness gleaming in her daughter's eyes. All she could do was hold her close and rock her, crooning sounds of comfort, saving the pain of her own broken heart for some future time. Locked inside was the hatred stored and building against he who could have prevented this torment to her and her daughter.

Why hadn't he understood?

*Magdela cupped the egg in the palm of her hand musing over its pearly essence — subtle blue effervescence at the edges that seemed not edges but endless curves in orbital illusion. Her other hand was cupped lovingly over that other barely perceptible curve which pushed tentatively against the loose folds of her homespun skirt.*

*Abruptly, her reverie ended as Dragonian burst into the room. Cold drafts from the outside night swirled around his feet and rose up to violate the room's cosy warmth as he struggled to get the heavy door closed without dropping the load of firewood he was holding in his arms. Magdela rose to help him, pausing just to lay the egg carefully on the mat on the table. The man dropped the wood by the fireplace. The energy of the storm was in him — contained. The woman raised her lips eagerly in greeting, snuggling contentedly into the comfort of his arms, when the moment was suddenly shattered.*

*How could it be? The egg lay strewn on the cold stones of the floor, the yolk bleeding indiscriminately into the cracks. Magdela broke from the man's grasp and fell to her knees, tears welling up uncontrollably in her eyes. She picked up a few of the sticky fragments and held them close as the tears slid silently down her cheeks. The man knelt down beside her, concern dominating his face, and put his hands on her shoulders. Magdela looked at him briefly, but then jerked her body away, anger suddenly flashing fire in her dark eyes.*

*"How could you? How could you!"*

*Dragonian recoiled in shock.*

*"It was an accident! I'm sorry . . . But, Magdela, it was only an egg! Why are you upsetting yourself so?"*

*"You don't understand! You just don't understand!"*

*And she turned away from him, sobbing uncontrollably.*

*Dragonian stared at her back helplessly, anger beginning to creep into his face.*

*"You're being silly. I don't see why you have to get so upset over an egg. Grandmother Tatta has many more where that one came from. I know your time is coming near, but, Magdela, you can't let little things take over your senses like this."*

*Magdela was crying quietly now, but still she refused to look at him. She couldn't understand herself . . .*

Did some of the blame belong to her? Could she have tried to get Alonia back among their own people? Should she have accepted the often proffered hand of male partnership and protection? Sometimes in the night, after Alonia had had one of her nightmares, and Magdela had held her trembling body close until she fell into a more peaceful sleep, Magdela's doubts would assail her and further sleep for her would become impossible. They were in trouble and Magdela prayed for the healing cave . . .

*Could the healer help? Somehow she was cut off from Dragonian. A cold fear clutched at her heart. They had been together such a short time — not even a year yet. She did not want any barriers or beginnings of barriers . . . maybe they were not hers . . . could he want barriers? Was this coming child somehow a threat? She didn't know, but the egg was broken and could never be mended. Could the healer help?*

*Her troubled spirit dragged on her as she approached the cave mouth. Fragments of light glanced off its edges — pinpricks of knowledge for those who dared to believe. Then she was alone in the dancing light of the crystal cave, but its song held no meaning for her. She tried to catch the teasing flickers of meaningless subterfuge. Her soul reached out, her heart cried, and in her mind she heard the words: "Don't try. Trying is too hard. Wait and the light's vision will be. See with the heart and let the soul be. Light will speak."*

*Then, in her and through her, she felt a pulsing rain bathing her soul in images profane: all her frustrations of misunderstanding, all the deaf ears and blind eyes, all to whom her tongue must be dumb — a world full of shadow forms admiring their own reality. Shards of light pierced ever deeper and she feared the pain relived: moments of uncontained anger, hollow tears in an empty shell. She felt cast alone on her own sea of emotion, the lifelines dangling and drifting away from her as she lost herself in her unreal reality.*

*The light was merciless.*

*"Healer, help . . . it's too much for me!"*

*But he too must have turned away.*

*The cacophony continued, and the shards of light splintered yet again. Then the light stopped.*

*Magdela sat unto herself alone. The world's edges had been washed away and the tears of time lay dried upon her cheeks. She would be content to wait or to come back another time. And so the sea of peace lapped at her feet and the winds of destiny rang round her head — a soft blessing on her brow and then a cool touch on her hand, each one in turn. She slowly lifted her heavy body and turned to re-enter that other day . . .*

That memory and the memory of the early days of mother hood would bring her comfort. It was a golden time — a celebration time — when the child close to the mother is embodied in her spirit through the long days of earliness. Baby words become ideas of loving, caring, warmth and beginning otherness, continuing the eternal circle of bonding between mother and child.

And Magdela had woven the spirit of this time into her cloth, twining the pastels of the spring meadow with the vibrant shades of the summer berries and the soft earths of the fall roots, singing the rhythms of childhood remembered and childhood revisited while the little ones of the village stopped by with their mothers. And in this way they carried on the harmonies of the generations before them. They talked of many things and seeming nothings — quiet hums peppered with the children's laughter and occasional squeals of play. And those had been the early days of Alonia's childhood: precious days held sacred in the patterns and rhythms of her mother's ever busy hands.

Magdela could hear again the voice of the old woman: "*Go to the dark caves of your memory; Magdela, fear them not. Wisdom often hides there and you must patiently coax her to come out. We must learn to keep the playmates of our heart, not deny their existence just because they cause us pain. Unacknowledged, they may storm and fume creating havoc for us in our outer lives.*"

Spinning could suspend the wracking frustration of a mind in conscious whirl caught up in an endless wheel of unproblem-solving. When soul cried out for relief, its quiet rhythms could soothe and comfort and the oils of the yarn be a balm for the troubled spirit. Or, from that quiet oasis, one could sometimes dare to venture into the darker reaches of life's experience and not get lost. So on she would spin, rocking gently, spinning in the soft rays of the sun and the sweet rhythms of her baby's rising and falling sleeping breath.

*Her hands were scratched and bleeding: dirt was smeared on her face and torn clothing.* Magdela started awake, frightened and ashamed — another time, another place — past or future, past and future. She knew not which this time, but of one thing she was sure: the dreams would always go on, must always go on.

The mist of the morning's dawning dusted her face and glow of its glory reflected softly on the mirrored surface of the small lake. Carefully, Magdela moved away from Alonia's sleeping body and walked to the water's edge. She dipped her hands in the cool water and splashed her face and body, watching the rivulets drip over her breasts. She could not help herself. The night had not washed the memories away. That other morning crashed into consciousness yet again . . .

*She was at the edge of the morning bathing pool. Impulsively she had shed her clothes unself-consciously and waded into its crisp coolness, nerve endings tingling in memory of the dancing light of the healing cave. Then she dipped her hands in the cool water and splashed her face and body, watching the rivulets drip over her breasts. She leaned back and felt the sun play in dappled patterns on her face . . . peace unto her peace . . .*

*When, suddenly, a noise from the shore had brought her to her feet. Someone was crashing clumsily and heedlessly through the brush. Magdela felt panic and fear. To run for her clothes? Hide in the water weeds? What to do?*

*She saw the flashing robe of the intruder, a slightly built person of medium height. It was Mordu, the son of the healer — a loner crashing through life the same way he was crashing through the bush. He preyed upon the unsuspecting and then carried bad tales to the elders. He was disliked but custom would prevail and wrongdoers he reported would be punished according to the laws of the tribe. And she — Magdela — married and with child had been out naked in the bushes at high noon. Oh how the hungry Mordu would feed on that!*

Images ebbed and flowed . . . The gleam of Mordu's eyes burned into her memory, reviving the old humiliation of that time and touching on the undercurrent of grief that came when she thought of Dragonian. Lost husband, lost life . . .

*Her exile had indeed been lonely, but Magdela had been too busy with survival to dwell on that fact. She had no idea how far she had travelled nor even for how many days or even weeks, but this day she had paused to gather late berries. Their dark juices stained her fingers and lips and she was almost happy.*

*Then, without warning, her pain was upon her. The dull aching of the morning had become an insistent stabbing in the middle of her back and the light trickle between her legs became a warm but frightening gush. Involuntarily, she crossed her legs, her eyes clamped shut in pain. Forgotten was the dappled light falling through the heavy branches of the fir trees and the lacy canopy of the maples and birches. Her makeshift basket toppled to its side as she hastily dropped it — succulent fruit scattering among the leaves and twigs already dropped as harbingers of the next season.*

*Light seared her eyes behind her closed lids, and lost was she in her pain and distress. Finally the pain eased and awareness returned. What to do? How far had she come? The morning dew had long dried on the grasses and weeds around her. The lazy buzzing of a bee penetrated her senses and the quiet emptiness of the afternoon spurred a sudden feeling of aloneness. Automatically she stopped to right her basket and scooped the spilled berries back into their temporary home.*

*Then another pain stabbed at the centre of her being and she gave in to it, collapsing against the rough bark of the nearest tree. The haze of pain lifted again and Magdela faced a new thought. Something was wrong! Shouldn't there be hours of less intense pain before this mind- and body-wrenching ordeal she was now enduring?*

*She forced her mind back to the innumerable conversations among the women at the wash pit and the more personal conferences she had had with her own mother and aunts. Other memories came only as agitated fragments as she tried to hang on to conscious intelligible thought.*

*Another stab of pain. Thought left, and the effort to think as well, as she gave herself over to this inexorable battle within. She held the mound that was her stomach — crooning and swaying — willing her baby to be comforted and okay. Why had she been left so alone? Where were the old wise ones of the tribe now in her time of need? It felt hot and sticky under her heavy skirt. Carefully she lifted her clothing to inspect herself. A dark stain pooled at the entrance of her birth canal and anguish filled her soul. She wanted to cry — to give in like a forgotten child and sob mindlessly for a mother to come and take care of her.*

*She stumbled to her feet and managed to break some branches from the soft-needled tree she was leaning against. She hugged them to her breasts as the next wave of pain crested over her, then dropped them deliberately by her feet as she stumbled to search for some clean mosses and grasses. For the next pain she was ready and leaned heavily against another tree, praying for a little more time. All her energy was now focused on bringing her tiny one alive into her world. A few more forays would have to do. Single-mindedly she panted through the pains and used the intervals between to gather more branches and moss and to sustain herself with berries and sips from her water bag. So little time, so little time . . . She forced the insistent chant from her inner ears.*

*And then there were cool hands on her forehead and she wept warm tears of relief. As the next pain surged through her being the joy of birthing engulfed her, suppressing the agony with the ecstasy of life. Magdela lay back on her rude bed, eyes closed against the day. Into her own being she was swallowed up — a moment in time precious — the union of two lives becoming mother and daughter. The tiny head emerged and gasped its first breath: two lives merged and she knew it was done. Quiet tears slid down her cheeks, the awful loneliness of the empty forest gone, forgotten in the grasping need of tiny spastic fingers and grabbing lips. The infant lay peacefully against her body, quiet comfort in its small sucking sounds as Magdela instinctively massaged the birthing fluids into the tender skin warming and stimulating the tiny form. The old one moved with quiet experience helping her body finish its job and tidying their small space under the trees.*

The birds began to cry raucously, pulling Magdela abruptly out of her reverie; the wind picked up insistently and the sky darkened. Magdela hurried back to Alonia and tried to soothe her with quiet tones even as she urged her to her feet and hastily gathered their things together. Alonia's sightless eyes darted nervously and agitation and fear were mirrored in their dark depths.

"It's all right. It will be all right," Magdela murmured.

The gnarled roots of the trees became more tortured as they pushed deeper into the bush. Magdela's eyes searched desperately for some sort of comforting shelter. Great drops of rain began to splash on and around them and flashes of lightning seared the sky. Finally, as the rain began to fall in earnest, Magdela pulled her daughter into the meagre shelter of a clump of tall bushes. Thunder clapped abruptly in their ears and Alonia shuddered up against her mother, bravely fighting off the hysteria that threatened to envelop her.

"It's only a thunderstorm," Magdela intoned, "only a thunderstorm."

They sat huddled close together and waited out the whipping wind and lashing rain.

And so they toiled onward, Magdela following her inner guide, the past hounding their trail with its ghostly memories and the future only a glimmer of inner faith. Magdela knew they should not go back; back along the pathway would be to retrace the past and there would be no going forward that way. She began to see the meaning in the old woman's words. The journey into the cave of self would reflect their present journey; Magdela knew that was so and the knowledge strengthened her steps. Other times her mind would try fruitlessly to wander over to Alonia's life experiences. But she could not take her daughter's journey for her. Each one has her own path to live. She came to realize that she could only hope to meet the meaning that was Alonia's journey where their paths truly intersected, or more intensely, where they walked in unison. But even then, the meaning would only be as it was specific to her life sense. This knowledge frustrated Magdela and generated deep anger within her.

What then was the real nature of seeing or not seeing? Yes, in one sense, Alonia was blind, but in another, what was the vision of her journey? What horrors tormented her to wrack her body with wrenching tears and cause her to cry out in anguish from her dreams and memories?

Mostly Alonia's was a silent struggle. In the first days, Magdela had tried to distract her, to bring her out with chatter — idle chatter, perhaps, when she thought about it — the weather, the sights, the sounds. But pain would flicker across Alonia's face or shadow her bright unseeing eyes with their secrets hidden in their depths and Magdela would feel afraid. Afraid to probe. Afraid to venture into the shadows haunting her daughter's memories and dreams. Afraid to talk to her of her life's journey or even to share her own — all so intensely private and painful. Must their journeys be so lonely?

Not once did Alonia ask where they were going. Perhaps that was a good thing, because Magdela didn't know what she would say.

And then, after many many days and longer nights, they came upon an almost overgrown trail. Magdela felt an odd tingle of anticipation as they worked their way through the undergrowth. The path was narrow and steep; the sunlight a shimmering haze as they arrived at the cave's mouth. The birdsong was muted, the squirrels and chipmunks silent. Only a light breeze sighed through the trees and flitted lightly over the upturned faces of Magdela and her daughter.

Magdela stopped and pulled Alonia close to her side. In silent harmony they set down their packs and Alonia hesitated as Magdela stepped across the edge of the cave mouth and was engulfed in the wonder of its glory.

Rays of light from across the spectrum glanced chaotically off the thousands of faceted edges. Magdela moved deeper into their welcome and found her hands moving in the familiar dance of the weaver. Her fingers encircled a thread of indigo and another of rose and drew them out taut . . . then another two threads, and another . . . and another.

Then she sensed her daughter's hands on hers and together they danced more threads over and under . . . over and under . . . and through others stretched taut. The cave's lights sang past the pain behind Alonia's eyes and beyond the agony of Magdela's memories. Each was at peace within the harmony of the healing cave and each would be at peace whenever they danced its healing rays. Magdela would weave the colours of the lights and in those patterns Alonia would speak the visions of truth and healing.

And the old woman would send others — the lonely, the heartsick, the weary — to find their own harmony in the dance of three. And destiny, if one believes in such things, would be fulfilled for those who can see the reminders of the dance of be: the past, the present and future, one reality linked for eternity.

# Pauline Peters

## *Dryland: In My Village*

This story begins beneath the skirt of Mantis-She who sits like a giant praying mantis, just at the edge of Dryland. She is a mountain whose long thin arms reach down to the valley. Her colour is high green.

They say that Mantis-She was once a woman who had lived so well that Spirit made her into a mountain — but that's another story.

This story begins beneath the skirt of Mantis-She, and though it is true that she has never moved, there is a feeling about her that she is only waiting for someone to walk into her arms so that she can pick them up and carry them back to the bright green star she comes from — but that's another story too.

Beneath the skirt of Mantis-She, there is a woman sleeping. What she does not know is that there, inside the curve of her foot, is an old man. He lives there within the curve of her foot. The bones of her body are his instrument. The bones of her body have no marrow. The old man plays her bones like a flute. What she does not know is that her breathing in rustles the soft leaves of his brain. What she does not know is that her breathing out is the sound of his memory.

In the beginning
We lived in a small place
And there were many who
We did not know

And my eyes were a village.

At the middle
Was the big tree
The baobab tree
With all her children around her.
Each one connected
By a thin line
To the grandmother

To the grandfather
To the woman
To the man
And to the child
And we searched for water
To bring home to the child

And there was no word for I.

We pounded the earth
And we did not know
That the place where we lived
Was like the head of a pin
On the back of an elephant.

Some travelled
And brought home stories
That made our eyes big
And stretched our minds
Until they hurt.
But we were satisfied
Although there were long days
When it did not rain.

And there was no word for God.

It stayed that way
Until the Spirit came
How can I tell you?
I didn't see it
Nana, she didn't see it
We slept it
We dreamed it.

The Spirit said:
You are a good people
And I bring you a gift
It is a dangerous gift
And you must be careful with it
This gift is the Word
And I warn you
You must use it with care.

The Spirit stayed
Seven years
Teaching us how
To use the Word
How to plant it
How to reap it
And how for each one thing we learned
There was a shadow.

We learned how it could bless or curse
Help or hurt
Soothe or trouble

And we learned our names

The Spirit stayed seven years
And we were never the same
We learned how to smithy in our fires
Heavy words,
Light words
Sweet words
Bitter words
Lying words
And true things.
And after seven years the Spirit left.

Then this happened:
Travel and trade for one thousand years
And we rose high
To sit on the back of the elephant
Seeing further than an old man could dream
And crossing waters
Wide and deep
And full of salt.

And we carried the Word with us.
Used once it made you strong
Twice it made you sure
Three times you were certain
And four times never wrong
Never wrong.

And back home
Beneath the baobab tree
Those who gazed in the water
Saw what was coming
How the Spirit had warned us
How we forgot
And how across the water
Above our heads
Enemies smithied in our own fires
Out of a jealous word
Would sell us.
And how the buyers were coming even now
Coming to take us
Take us in boats
To a cold place
Where they would beat us
And breed us
And take away our names.

But what they did not see
Were the children
Of the children
Of the children
Who would take new names
And learn new words
For God.

*

Some say that there is a great woman in the sky. There is a great woman in the sky and the world is inside of her mouth. There is a great woman in the sky and the world is the word inside of her mouth. Inside the body of the great woman in the sky, memory is turned into salt, so that when the great woman cries and her tears fall to the earth, the ocean and the soil are full of memory, each grain of salt holding the memory of one soul. But that's another story too . . .

# Kuwee Kumsaa

## *Lamentations: A Letter to My Mother*

Dearest of the dearest, beauty of all beauties, tenderest of all hearts, *Aayyoo Oromia! Aayyoo*, proud daughter of Africa! *Aayyoo*, precious mother! Oh, the flesh of your flesh and the blood of your blood is yearning for you. The splinter of your bone is craving for reunion, *Aayyolee*. Like when I was a child, I'm hungering for the caresses of your hands and thirsting for the whispers of your love. I long for you like one in darkness longs for day-light. I crave you like a starved body craves food. I long for the sight of you like a thirsty person in the Sahara longs for the sight of an oasis. I reach out for you but this cold winter grips me harshly. And my heart bleeds. Yes, my heart bleeds, *Aayyolee too!* Why should this ugly hateful curtain of mist drop between us? Why should this eternal-looking darkness swallow us? When will this enveloping and choking night dissolve away? When will we rejoice in that magical togetherness and be lost in our familiar bliss once again?

Sitting here, thousands of kilometres away, on a day that went dark with a blizzard of a severe Canadian winter, struck with a sudden pang of nostalgia, longing and yearning for the warmth of your heart, I feel helpless and crippled to do anything but scribble and scribble away, believing that hearts can reach where bodies cannot, and wishing this letter, soaked wet with my tears, would carry my heartfelt tight hugs across vast bodies of oceans, across immense stretches of dry land, and find you as I see you now, clear and resplendent in the eyes of my mind: sitting there proud on your Oromo stool under the shade of the great and abundant *Odaa* tree. I can see the rays of that tropical sun filtering through the thick canopies of that marvelous African *Odaa* and catching your beautiful black face. How I want to run away and escape the cold heart and the cold weather of Canada! How I miss the burning heat of that tropical sun on my skin! How I want to flee the hypocrisy here and be myself with you once again! Oh, how desperately I want to see you with these eyes of my flesh! *Aayyolee too!* But you are so far away in the strained eyes of my stressed-out mind. Why does every inch of the distance between us stretch itself endlessly and why does the road have a limitless length when I need you? Why do the hours multiply infinitely when I'm anxious? I wish I could, somehow, by some magic, roll up the time, fold up the distance, and be there with you now, right now!

I dragged my utterly exhausted and morally depleted self up and went to the window of my flat. Beneath me Toronto was alive, even in the blinding snowstorm. Lucky people who could feel at home seemed to go about doing their business regardless. It seemed that I was the only one locked up there, cold and desolate. I stared out as if seeing you from such a distance was remotely possible. I turned to the east and looked towards where you are. But my sight was hampered by the snow whose magical fall fixed me into a trance. You've never seen something like this, *Aayyolee.* As many other things here do, this too looks elusively beautiful. Could I be captivated by this illusion and stay here for the rest of my life? *Aayyolee too*, but this can never be home.

Home is with you, *Aayyolee.* How can I stay away from home forever? Am I not the cut of your flesh? Am I not the spill of your blood? Am I not the splinter of your bone? You produced me out of your womb. You brought me into this world. You moulded and shaped me. You cut my eyes open. You made me see the world the way you saw it.

*Aayyolee*, you are the pupils of my eyes — the only apertures through which the lights of this outer world could enter to give me an inner sight. You are that sight. You made me what I am and you helped me grow into who I am.

The fertile soil which helped germinate the seed — me,
The river that fed it,
The breeze and the sunshine that helped produce food
for it,
The people, the plants and the animals that related to
it in many different ways,
Every small twig that scratched and pricked me as I
stepped on it,
Every slope that I slipped and slid on,
Every tuft of grass that caught me as I passed and
every one that I crushed under my feet,
Every spring and river that bathed me,
Every substance that nurtured me body and soul,
Every patch of cloud that drifted in the sky above,
Everything that I acted on and that in turn acted on
me,
Every pull and every push . . .

Even the way the stars aligned themselves at that point in time when you gave me the first breath of life, and looking at them, the name the Oromo astrologers gave me, pointed to me as a tiny little part of you, yet unique in itself, independent and different from you. Separate but in unity, *Aayyolee too*. Just like the forces between the stars and planets, forces of perfect repulsion balancing with forces of perfect attraction, our physical and spiritual forces also keep us separated but unified in the whole. I, a tiny little part of you; you, a tiny little part of the greater whole; and that greater whole, a tiny little part of the still greater whole of the universe.

Everything mattered, *Aayyolee*, everything counted, and everything bore witness. For there was no one but myself who was born there of you and by you in that particular space and time. I did not create the situation. I did not choose it. It just happened. It was just natural, and I just belonged in the natural and to the natural. And in confirmation of this grand naturality, the Oromo women flocked in ululating and performed those mesmerizing ritualistic dances for my reception.

But *Aayyolee!* Everything turned upside down. As you would say, instead of fingers, toes began to scratch the head. And what was natural became unnatural. Abyssinians set their feet in the heart of our ancestral home. They claimed and they owned it and they owned us. All our values vanished. They renamed our country, they named and renamed our towns, they named and renamed our big and small villages, they renamed our abundant rivers, they renamed our beautiful mountains and valleys, they named and renamed us, all after themselves. Suddenly we vanished from the pages of history, *Aayyolee*. A proud heroic people in the Horn of Africa disappeared overnight! History became the making of a few people. And its books refused to acknowledge our existence. They refused to respond to our cries. They stole our moral values and gave them to the writers of their pages. It seemed that the order of the universe was reversed. Being of you and from you became a crime punishable by death. What was lawful became unlawful. We were tormented for being lawful in the natural. For being who we are. For the "crime" Creation committed. In our own perfect niche, they made us appear curious misfits. We seemed to be strangers in a strange land where we did not belong. Abyssinians came out of thin air and helped themselves to the comfort of our home. Our own home entertained all intruder aliens but not us.

Ironic, isn't it? What an incredible reversal, *Aayyolee too!* They steal your history and accuse you of stealing. Whatever is theirs is defined as right and whatever is yours is branded wrong. Why is it wrong to be natural and to belong to the natural? Why is it a crime to be born there? To be your child? To bear your marks? To bear your name? To be called the Oromo of Africa? By whose law is it declared a crime? By whose law are strangers allowed to force themselves upon us and make us strangers in our own homes and refugees in our own land? By whose law are we doomed to toil and slave for them? By whose law are we forced to abide? Did we make those laws? Were we consulted? Do we not have lawmakers of our own? God knows we have the most capable *Abbaa Heeraa*, *Abbaa Seeraa* and *Abbaa Alangee*, those competent Oromo legislators. Tell me what went wrong, *Aayyoo*.

What was the universal truth you were telling me? What was the natural? What were your thoughts for my future when you held me in your hands for the first time? When you looked into the newborn face of your firstborn child? What were your dreams for me when you kissed my forehead gently? What were the dreams of those women who ululated? And what was the ululation? Was it an affirmation of the naturality? Or was it a wail of negation? What was behind the wrinkled faces of those elderly Oromo women; what was in their minds when they untied the *Sabbataa* sashes from around their waists with shaky hands, took the few coins they had in the world and put them in the palms of my hands, wishing they could give me more but making up for it with the tears of their eyes? Why did they bless me to go in peace and pursue my studies? What did my education mean to them? Do tell me please, *Aayyolee*. What was the natural then? How has it changed? What is it now?

How long does it take, *Aayyolee*, for the unnatural to appear natural? Oh, *Aayyoo too* the *Ayyaantuu* must have been crippled the day the natural was reversed. The stars that aligned themselves in a unique way to make our *Ayyaanaa* must have tripped and fallen into the bottomless pit of the universe. The moon, as it waxed and waned through its phases, must have shed bloody tears. The sun must have lost control and let her fire go wild. The rivers and the oceans must have perspired blood. The earth must have unwound itself out of its orbit. Somewhere, some lawmakers must have gone crazy. For there is no sense in this.

They raped you, *Aayyolee.* Yes they did! They raped you body and soul! They raped you before my eyes. To satisfy that insatiable Abyssinian greed, they raped your virgin lands. To stay on their thorny thrones, they sacrificed the precious fruits of your womb. They dragged your children out of your house and slaughtered them and left them for hyenas to feast on. They drove your able men to strange lands and made them food for the birds of the desert. Vultures and other scavengers consumed them. But your tearful, unbelieving eyes kept stubbornly looking yonder for those who would never come home. They tore out unborn babies from your womb, and as they slaughtered them, they vowed: "Baby serpents should never grow to be adult serpents." They fed your little ones to prison cells. They pitted your children against each other. They turned you against us and us against you. We became cold strangers to one another. In the middle of our utter confusion, they sent their roots father down into the heart of your rich soil. They entrenched and established themselves as the land of our ancestors became a slaughterhouse. Our people were killed in tens of thousands. Precious lives flickered out one after another. Their blood flowed and flowed until *Dachii Oromiyaa* was soaked to the bone, until the thirsty soil gulped it down, until the red blood flowed to the rivers mingling with the waters and reddening the seas. *Baaroo* and *Awaash*, *Abbayyaa* and *Muger*, *Raammis* and *Dhidheessaa*, *Soor* and *Waabee*, *Gabbaa* and *Gannaalee*, your great rivers all ran red in silence as pages and pages of history skipped them.

They set our villages afire, and in minutes, everything,
living and non-living, was ablaze,
The flames jumped up and down and danced as their
broad turbulent tongues licked the land
ungraciously,
The dry savannah caught quickly and spread the
fire,
Village after village burned down to ashes,
Men, women and children along with them.
Babies at their mothers' breasts,
The elderly as they reclined in repose,
Children as they gathered around to play,
Mothers as they performed their endless duties,
Men as they worked in the fields . . .

They all vanished as they screamed helplessly for help. Cattle in the pastures, grains in the granaries and crops in the fields were not spared. The smell of roasting human flesh mingled with other smells of the burn and filled the air. Oh, *Aayyolee too!* It's still in my nose and I can smell it now. I too was consumed by that flaring Abyssinian fire and was left for dead. But some miraculous hands rescued me, *Aayyoo Too.* My wounds are still soft under the thin scar tissue. They still ooze blood when hurt. Sometimes it gets beyond my endurance and the excruciating pain makes me scream. But here many people don't understand my suffering, *Aayyolee.* Many have not lived what I lived. They look at me but what they see is only the scar cover on top and not the wound underneath. They think I scream without any reason, and they want to shut me up. They say they want silence, perfect silence, over here. Their peace is not to be disturbed as ours was. I don't yet know if this is a conspiracy, *Aayyolee too.*

How can I suffer this in silence? How can I not scream? Isn't that what I am here for? To shout? To scream? Is this not the land where there is freedom to scream when you are in pain? Why can I not cry out for justice? Can I not tell people of my suffering? Can I not let others know? I could have stayed there with you, to suffer your pain and to die your death, *Aayyolee too.* But that did not seem a solution to me. I wanted to shout! I wanted to scream! I wanted to tell the world about the unbelievable enormity of the injustice. So that it will be stopped. I wanted to go to the land where freedom and justice reign high. Where the human being is dignified for being human and for being of the natural and in the natural. I came in pursuit of freedom and justice. To tell your tragic story. So I left you, *Aayyolee too.* But that does not mean I deserted you. God knows I did not and I cannot. How can I when I am a part of you? How can a part desert the whole and exist without the whole? Yes, I am a part of you, very much a part of you. But the part had to part, the branch had to break off, the twig had to detach itself, the leaf had to fall off . . .

I could hear you calling after me, *Aayyoo.*

"*Maaaaaaaaloo Kottuu Gali! Maaaaaaaaloo Kottuu Gali!*" I could hear you say, "Pleeeeeeeease come back! Pleeeeeeeease come back!" I could hear your voice echoing through the jungle as I plugged both my ears with my index fingers and ran away. I can hear you calling now. That same wailing call in that same tone of voice is haunting me. It is echoing through my troubled mind. I can hear it ebb and slowly die away, overcome and drowned, partly by my stubborn refusal to come back and partly by the shrieking noises of your Abyssinian tormentors. I know I have failed you, and I can never forgive myself for that. But I had no choice, *Aayyoo*, I ran away in search of justice, in search of *Heeraa*. I ran away in search of freedom. Yes *Aayyolee*, in search of freedom, in search of precious *Bilisummaa*. I thought I smelled it from afar. It was in the air, I thought I saw a glimpse of it. And I ran and ran after it, gasping for breath. Just to get a hold of it. I thought I did for a split second. But it slipped through my fingers. There is no freedom in the whole wide world, *Aayyolee*. There is no *bilisummaa*, not in one little corner of the world. There is only a shadow of it, I tell you. And all my race has become a shadow chase. Yes, a shadow chase, *Aayyoo*. I might have run away, but I have not escaped. *Aayyoo too*. The monster is everywhere.

I have now come to the peak of my search. I have come to the country whose democracy, freedom and justice are exemplary. I have come to the summit of the idealistic mountain I was plodding and trudging to climb. I can now see the whole scene right before my eyes. The contours, the swells and the basins of the reality beneath. The mountains and the valleys of it. The ugliness and the wonder of it all. I have finished my search, *Aayyolee*. There is no *heeraa*. There is no *bilisummaa*. And there is no point in shouting. Nobody listens to your screams of pain. There are none so deaf as those who would not listen. *Aayyolee*. And none so blind as those who would not see. Yours is a very marginal scream for them. Very trivial.

So I am not telling your story, *Aayyoo too*. I have no voice. My tongue has stuck dry to my palate. Neither am I writing it. My ink has dried. My pen has fallen. I have no story to tell, *Aayyolee*. Everything has fallen through. Dreams have shattered. The sky has caved in. The natural seems to have gone for good, and I want to come back. Yes, I am beaten, but I am not running away from the challenge. I am coming to begin from the beginning. To start cutting it from the root. Severing branches seems to do little good.

Do take me home, *Aayyolee*. Receive me with those wide-open arms as you used to do. From such a spiritual grief and from such a distance in space and time, I still seek your refuge like I did when I was a child. I desperately want to run back home to you. Protect me, *Aayyolee*. Shield me from the monster. Cover me with your *Wandaboo* skirt. Impart your strength, and let's go at it together. Let us make a new history. Rescue me *Aayyoo Oromiyaa!* Send me *Risaa*, send me the Oromo eagle. Or send me *Joobiraa*, send me that African bird of great wings. Fly me home, *Aayyolee.* This is not my place; I belong there.

# Jane Tapsubei Creider

## *The Woman in the Pit and Elephant's Trunk*

*Here are two folktales of the Nandi of Kenya. Nandi parents and grandparents tell stories to children and children tell stories to each other on sleep-overs.*

Red sprinkled with orange, green sprinkled with yellow, blue, indigo and a touch of violet — a rainbow across the sky — the colours Tiny Little Reed liked. Chesaina stepped out of the house and faced west, her eyes following the sunset. The sun's rays stood erect like tall, slender crystals growing behind Sang'alo Hill. The brilliant orange canvas horizon was capped by churning grey clouds moving back and forth above it.

A raindrop fell on Tiny Little Reed's cheek. Lightning struck across the sky followed by a raw clap of thunder. She turned around. "Oh, dear me!" she looked up behind her as she exclaimed. The mountains seemed to be reaching into infinity as they joined with the dark clouds. "Mother! I'm going to Tabarbuch Kap Boit's."

"I don't think you should go when it is thundering," said Taplongoi, Chesaina's grandmother. She thought Chesaina's mother was slow to react, and in the meantime Chesaina was getting away with murder.

"Tabarbuch will be cross if I don't, Grandma. She said a person who misses a sleep-over night should not come again — it ruins her sleep."

"Run then, Tiny Little Reed!" said Taplongoi. She called Chesaina by her nickname. She was small and thin like a reed, and people had nicknamed her "Tiny Little Reed".

"Good night *Gogo*. Good night *Eeyo*." Chesaina bid her grandmother and mother good night and rushed off to Tabarbuch's. Tabarbuch was a woman in the neighbourhood who had her own teenagers. Like all the Nandi families, she and her teenaged daughters lived in the family's main house. Her husband, Arap Boit, had a little house of his own a distance away beside the cattle kraal. The teenagers in the neighbourhood liked coming to Tabarbuch's and travelled far to reach there to be with other girls. When they were together, they sang, played games and told stories.

Tiny Little Reed joined the girls sitting in a subdued mood around the fire. They stared at their shadows on the wall. Tabarbuch sat on a bed made of clay raised above the fireplace. She had wrapped herself in a patchwork quilt of sheepskin and was watching the lightning's reflection coming through the woven vine door. Outside, the thunder was roaring like a lion.

The narrow opening between Mt. Tabolwa and Kaplemur had poured the storm down onto the face of the Nandi Escarpment. The trees tossed in the vigorously whipping wind. The house shook. The chickens were in frantic disarray in the *injor*, the adjoining room where the sheep, calves, chickens and goats slept. They flew aimlessly about when it felt as though the wind was about to pluck the grass-thatched house off the ground. Tabarbuch laid a log on the fire for more light to enable them to see they were still in the house.

"You girls had better use this roaring fire to make up your beds before it dies down again," she said.

The girls moved rapidly to take out their cow-skin bedding. Tiny Little Reed laid her bedding down, crawled into her calfskin quilt, and covered her face.

"Tiny Little Reed, it is your day to tell. Remember?" asked Tabarbuch.

Chesaina slid deeper into the calfskin and did not answer. The ground was shaking from the roar of the thunder as the rain lessened.

"*Ne? Kalya? Ingesis.* What's the matter? You are so quiet!" questioned Tabarbuch.

"Mother, I can tell one," Chelagat, Tabarbuch's youngest daughter, inserted deftly.

"Please, no scary stories tonight. I can't take more frightening after this rainstorm," requested Chepchirchir, Tabarbuch's oldest daughter.

"Tiny Little Reed has some stories which are not scary," said Tabarbuch.

"Only one," replied Chesaina.

"I bet I know which one you mean. As a matter of fact, you told it the other night," Chelagat, who liked going out of turn, stated, and followed her remark with a little sniff. "Ha!"

But everyone else said, "Yes, Chesaina! We like that. Tell us please, tell us!"

"All right," said Chesaina.

"There once was a woman named Chemanin with three co-wives. She was quiet, timid and not very original. She did everything the way she had first been taught. If someone told her to stand on her head for three days, she would do so without once trying to see what would happen if she stood right side up. Soon it became obvious to the husband and the co-wives that she was a little slow, and they left her alone. Her husband visited her once a month and rarely stayed for dinner — Chemanin was a bad cook.

"She lived in a dinky, dirty little house her husband built after her co-wives complained that she was too dirty and they were tired of telling her how to do things. She shared the house with her sheep, goats and calves. She gave the animals names and talked to them like people. Chemongur was the mother and grandmother of all the goats Chemanin owned. Chebomoi was likewise the mother and grandmother of all the sheep. Kipkigu was an orphan ram. After his mother died, Chemanin's co-wives talked, 'Poor little lamb! He will die like his mother! Chemanin won't know how to care for him.' But Chemanin was nursing him with warm cow's milk when the co-wives arrived at the house to rescue the lamb. She had acted quickly, cutting a small piece of cow-skin into an equilateral triangle, folding it over and sewing it into a nipple to fit over the mouth of a gourd for Kipkigu to suck.

"'Oh, she is as smart as barbecued cow's lungs that burn on the outside while they remain raw inside,' Chemanin's co-wives went back saying to each other. Kipkigu followed Chemanin around until he was weaned.

"Chemanin became sick when she was pregnant, and lonesome. Her co-wives sent their children to let her livestock out in the morning and bring back in the evening. The women in the neighbourhood stood aside and watched to see if any of the co-wives would help her. None of them did. Soon they took pity on Chemanin and stepped in. 'You're not being cared for here. Get away! Go back to your mother's; she will take better care of you.' Chemanin left, obeying as usual, and came back on her own when her baby was six months old.

"On the way along the path to her house, a mother snatched a child who was peeping at the doorway back inside and closed the door. An old woman popped out of a dense thicket of *irogonik* bushes growing along the path. She stood in front of Chemanin. 'I wish you hadn't come back to this place,' she said. Chemanin looked blankly at her. 'Go now to your house and don't pick up any object on the path, no matter how good it looks,' she said. 'The family who used to live over there — she pointed out a house in front of her — picked up a baby they found abandoned on the door stoop. They are never going to see another sunrise again. A family who lives near them are never going to breathe the same air as we breathe again. A strange sheep followed their sheep home and they took it in.'

"The country was in a state of terror when she returned. A troll, capable of assuming any form it wished — it could become a fly, a baby, small ants, a sheep — had arrived who ate both people and cattle. His appetite was so ravenous that he had already eaten many of the inhabitants. Her husband did not appear to welcome her and the baby home. There was no smoke coming out of the houses of the co-wives, and no cattle grazing in the homestead. Everything looked dead as Chemanin stood in front of her dinky house. She saw that the few people in the neighbourhood who were still surviving had barricaded themselves in their houses, but every morning another house had no sign of life — no smoke coming out of the chimney. A new family had vanished.

"Chemanin settled in her house, ate the small bit of food she had brought from her home, and went out very little. Not many days passed before she realized she was alone in the neighbourhood. She dug a pit under the cattle dung out in the cattle kraal and crawled into it with her baby boy. The baby was raised in the pit, his mother chewing millet grain to feed him. Chemanin named him Talamwa, Grasshopper, hoping that if he ever crawled out of the pit, he would appear insignificant, like a grasshopper, to the troll. When he was old enough to understand, she told him the story of the troll, and warned him not to go far from the pit. Before he went out, she smeared him with cow dung so the wind wouldn't carry his smell to the troll.

"When he was older, Talamwa made a bow and some arrows. During the day his mother took a nap and Talamwa sneaked out to shoot rats, mice and birds which he brought back to the pit for the two of them. Chemanin relished a change from eating the grubs which lived inside the cow dung and dropped into the pit when the sun was hot. The small amount of millet flour she had brought with her when she had moved into the pit was about to finish. Sometimes she smeared herself with cow dung and sneaked out to search for more millet in the houses in the vicinity. At first, when the millet was still plentiful in nearby houses, they had eaten a palmful every two days, but now that it was diminishing, they had to make a palmfull last five days.

"When Talamwa came with the game, Chemanin was happy, even though she feared for his life. She skinned the small animals, took grass to wrap around them, and put them under her grass bed. She sleep on them to cook them with the heat from her body for the following day's meal. Talamwa, however, was curious to know what kind of animals he had shot, and on each occasion he returned from hunting, he asked his mother whether he had killed the troll. Chemanin would say, 'No, you have killed rats, mice and birds, but please, you must never mention the troll's name again!'

"Talamwa continued to ask questions of his mother. One day when he came home from shooting and breathing the air outside, he asked her what it had been like living outside the pit. Chemanin told him it had been wonderful — they had lived in a house made of grass and plasted with clay. They had cooked from a fireplace and had drunk milk from a cow. 'Our clothing also was not woven from grass. We wore animal skins then and we took baths instead of smearing ourselves with dung.' She told him everything they had had outside of the pit. Then Talamwa became frustrated — he wanted to know how to get these things back. Chemanin told him how to make a fire by spinning a pointed stick in a dry log with some tinder, but said that the rest would wait until he was older.

"For the next few days, Talamwa stopped hunting when he went out and only spun the *pionit* the way Chemanin had told him to. Finally he succeeded. He lit a large fire and put some stones containing iron ore in it to burn until they were red. The troll smelled the fire from the forest and came out. He saw the smoke from far away and said to himself, 'How is this? I thought I had eaten all of the "flat-footed" ones, yet a fire has been lit. There must be some living over there yonder.' He went to investigate.

"On his arrival, Talamwa reached for his bow and arrows, but a voice came to him out of the air. It said,

'Don't reach for your arrows! Feed him. Let him eat these stones.' A shadow of a tall man wearing a Colobus monkey fur cape stood between Talamwa and the troll. It handed Talamwa a pair of blacksmith's tongs and said in a slow, drawn-out voice, 'Here, use these to feed it the stones.' The shadow pointed to the fireplace.

"Talamwa awoke as though from a trance with the strength of a grown man. He said to the troll, 'Ah! You have come to eat us. Wait! I will give you the food I am cooking.' He then took the stones out of the fire and told the troll to open its mouth. The troll swallowed the stones and then said, 'Oh! Let me go lie down a bit, my stomach is hurting.' Then the voice of the shadow came out of the troll's mouth. 'Go take a reed and peel it. Cut off my little finger with this reed and your cattle will be given back to you. Cut off my thumb and you will get back your people.' Talamwa did as he was told, and all the people and the cattle that the troll had eaten were restored to life.

"Talamwa looked for the shadow after the troll died. He didn't see it, but he heard a voice from a distance saying, 'Go back and bring your mother to rejoice now. She is waiting for you.'

"Although he was still a child, Talamwa was given a say in the house of the elders, and Chemanin was showered with love and included in the discussions of all the women in the community, so that today a person who appears awkward or simple is considered to have special gifts."

"Hmph," sniffed Chelagat. "I know why Tiny Little Reed is hooked on that story. It's because of that reed the shadow tells Talamwa to use. Chesaina thinks she was part of it."

"Here is a short one. It has nothing to do with my name," said Tiny Little Reed. "A long, long time ago, all things on this planet were related. People, animals, the stars, lightning — all lived on the earth neighbouring one another. Once in a while, Ms Kipkoiyo, God, who lived in the heavens, came to earth to check that everything was in order. Before she returned to heaven, Lightning went to Elephant.

"'What kind of creature is our friend?' he asked Elephant.

"'He is a man,' Elephant replied.

"'I know he is a man, but he is very different from us. I think he is dangerous. Have you watched when he is asleep? If he wishes to turn over from one side to the other, he is able to do so. I can't turn over even if I want to. I have tried it. I have to get up first.'*

"'It is the same for me. I have to stand up before I can turn over on my other side,' said Elephant.

"'I'm afraid of Man. I'm going up to heaven with Ms Kipkoiyo. The stars are coming along with us, Elephant,' said Lightning.

"Elephant laughed. 'Why should I run away from such a small creature as this man? I'm not going to leave all this grass and all these trees on the land for him.'

"'But Man is bad. Not only can he turn over when he is asleep, he kills other creatures for food. He does not

* *The Nandi identified lightning with the rooster because of the latter's bright red comb.*

touch anything and leave it alive. You eat grass and leave it to grow again. When he cuts trees to build his house, the tree trunks that he leaves behind die. He cuts the grass to thatch his house, and he digs the ground to make clay for the house. I can't remain on earth," said *Ilet.* I'm going to heaven with Ms Kipkoiyo, and I'm taking with me the wish she let me hold for the creature of the earth.'

"Ms Kipkoiyo had seen that the creatures of the earth looked sad when other creatures died. She thought she should sacrifice something of her own to undo this grief, but what could it be? Not the sun because there must be day. Not the stars — humans need the stars to guide them. And not the rain — the foundation of life on earth. Maybe the moon. It is not warm and it is not cold. The creatures of the earth could live without it. She told Lightning to wish the creature of the earth this: when the moon dies, it will die for good. When the creatures of the earth die, they will come back like the moon, on the fourth day.

"Man was pleased. 'Now I will rule the Earth. Every creature has to obey my commands because Lightning, the one I fear, is gone,' he told Elephant.

"'Why does a small creature like you want to rule the Earth?' asked Elephant. 'I can blow you away in a single puff.'

"'There is only one thing I need to do to become the greatest in all the world,' Man said and ran into his house. He dipped an arrow into a poison pot. With the bow and arrow, he returned to the kraal and shot Elephant. 'Blow me away now,' he ordered.

"Elephant cried out loudly as the poison ran through his body. 'Oh, Ilet!' He curled his trunk up to heaven. 'Please help me! Take me to heaven,' he wept.

"'I hear you, Elephant, but I can't. Everyone is given one chance, and I did ask you to come with me,' said Lightning.

"'I beg you! Take me!' Elephant cried again.

"'Repeat after me, my friend,' replied Lightning. 'Ms Kipkoiyo says when Moon dies let him be resurrected.' Lightning reversed Ms Kipkoiyo's wish. 'Let Man's life be shorter. When he dies, let him die for good.'

"Elephant repeated the words, and as the saying ended, he closed his eyes and died peacefully with his trunk curled up. And the elephant's trunk has remained curled until today and he lives twice as long as man," said Tiny Little Reed.

"That was too short! Can you tell another?" begged Tabarbuch's youngest daughter, Chelagat.

"No, I have to sleep. I'm getting up at dawn to go help my grandmother milk," said Tiny Little Reed.

"We all have to be up early to weed the millet. Thank you, Tiny Little Reed. Good night everybody," said Tabarbuch. The storm had subsided, the chickens were quiet, the fire had died down, and the girls felt happy and secure.

# Yvonne Vera

## *A Woman Is a Child*

*I wish she had rotted in my womb.*

She has spoken more than the mouth is allowed to speak. She has spoken what cannot be carried in the mouth with wisdom. She has taken his words from him, for she has challenged him with that which he cannot speak of without madness. Even one possessed by an evil spirit cannot do the thing she has done. The departed have raised their arms to the sun. A father cannot speak to his kin, without shame, of a daughter's nakedness.

There is no language to contain this deed. Only what she has destroyed is known. Only the things which existed before can be talked about. They are talked about now only to be unknown, to be unremembered, to be unspoken. She has dug his tongue from his mouth and pulled it out like a wild and poisonous root. What has she spoken, standing naked, in front of her father? She has shown him her naked body. A challenge, a taboo.

Tariro does not fear what she has claimed as her own, neither dreams nor loneliness, not even life, though she has been told that is certainly to be feared, and not to be thought about too much, or too closely. But she is always close to what she has claimed, and she has claimed life. She lives in intimate lunacy with herself. She has killed Father, blinded him with the sight of her naked breasts, her arrogant hips, her exposed navel. A bold gesture of defiance, of her own growing wisdom. She has killed Father. She remembers his astonished face, his teeth falling to the ground. That was how she killed him.

Bark peels like an unkind memory. The snow lies along branches of a jagged birch.

She thinks of rain, wet things which cannot breathe. A silence claims her, and she lives in its disguises.

Here, in this new land, there is nothing. Surely, one has not lived. Could one be so silent, so alone, and have lived? Tariro has not seen her shadow for half the twenty years she has spent here. She harbours those spent years like a secret which she has disguised into a memory.

Tariro looks through the glass at gestures draped in

flamboyant designs, the hands stiff, the legs stiff, handbags cast across silent arms, fingers pointing at nothing at all. Who would like to be so absurd — eyes glassy and blind? Eyes without memory. To be absurd and then to die, that will be brief scorning freedom. Laughter touches her with shaking fingers. She has lived. How could one doubt that when one stood so different, so apart, and when one was so filled with unfinished desires?

That time long ago, surrounded by shadows, she had been almost whole. Her shadow follows her, growing from herself, preparing a path into the future. The shadow moves with the sun, circling her, turning her into day. When she sees her shadow grow from her feet she knows that she has lived, proclaimed her presence on the earth. Here, she has abandoned hope. She remembers his commands, his voice falling from a great height. She remembers Mother.

> Take his word and let him watch you place it under your armpit. He must not see you refuse his word, my child. Life is a courtship of gestures.

The darkness lies at her feet, slides cold down the window, shakes the branches, scatters the snow.

Tariro sees death not as a forgetting but as a fulfillment of longing and a return to beginnings. But she had not begun here. She trembles to lie under such sodden ground. Already, she feels herself clogged with wet clay. In her dying, she must be filled with the sun.

> I have married a barren woman, who cannot bear male children.

Father mutters commands that make her fearful of the world. When she sleeps, eyes follow her, and punish her with cruel hands. She sleeps with her hands between her thighs. His words follow her into sleep.

> Who shall carry my name? Shall my kind forever depart from this earth? The children of a daughter are the blood of others. A daughter is an interim of immortality.

She does not want to carry anything for him, not even a name. He must find a son to carry such things for him, for she would never do it, even if she could. She picks up a spear that father keeps against the wall and raises it to the sky, stabbing the air. She opens her eyes: the earth is beneath her feet.

He threatens mother with bare fists.

> Do not sit on a stool like a man. What man shall marry a woman such as this who sits with parted legs? A woman must sit on a goatskin with feet curled under her weight. The air passing through the fields must not find its way into the darkness between your legs. A woman who sits like a man will never find the attention of a suitor.

A girl is born. His words become stones.

> Kneel on the ground when your greet a man. A man is not a thing for a woman to greet with her feet firmly planted on the ground. A good woman claps her cupped hands offering echoes which celebrate a man's presence on earth. Kneel on the ground to give praise to a man. A man will not carry into his home a woman whose body is as unbending as a pestle. Do not bring shame into your father's household by standing and casting shadow on a man.
>
> The voice of a woman must be like the sound of her cupped hands. A woman must not raise her voice to a man. A woman is a child.

She seeks a defiant act that will stand against his words. She stands against him with her body. Her body is stronger than his threats and his taboos, greater than the shrine he carries in his mouth. She remembers his anger and dismay. His lips tremble. His arms dangle beneath limp and tired shoulders. He crumples to the ground, seeking wisdom from the departed.

She bears the spear in her hand. She is naked as the spear.

She has claimed her body like a shield. He is silenced. He cannot speak of the thing she has done, for there is none to whom he can speak it and survive. He can only speak this indignity to himself, without words to accompany his speaking. His words have been finished.

> What the eye has swallowed cannot be taken away from it. It is so with my daughter. I have swallowed parts of her body which a father does not know a daughter possesses, which a father forgets in his daughter. My daughter has made me see her mother in her. This is not a thing to be talked about. My daughter has put my manhood in a basket. My daughter has turned my mouth into a hole in the earth. My mouth is filled with ants. My mouth is full of forgetting. She has covered my mouth with dung. My daughter died yesterday.

His eyes are silent and dead. His eyes have lost their wisdom.

The morning finds her freed. She has triumphed over his words, and now she can begin a reconciliation with her body. She departs from her ancestral ground in search of a memory that will heal her.

In her new land she conjures dreams to protect her secret triumph.

Words are not for forgetting. She has learned a new language with which she tries to forget her loss, words that would free her. She has claimed her body. She has become separate from him. They have parted in a ritual of disbelief.

Here, there is nothing, only the damp ground and the cold wind. There are many words to describe the things of here but none to describe the things of silence, the things of yesterday, the things Tariro remembers.

> I have moved from one silence into another. I have seen the sun setting beneath water.

In the distance, the horizon is filled with water.

> The language of my body is a stranger here. Skin without kin, I am surrounded by resistant tongues. Yesterday I spoke. Nothing will protect me here. To be silent, to be still, invokes death.

But she had died yesterday.

# Jan Carew

## *Canopus*

Canopus on the Nile
and the temple to Serapis
where young initiates
dark, and lithe as reeds
serve wine
to priests murmuring
orisons
to the indifferent tides.
Royal messengers from Alexandria arrive
panting to announce, the Pharaoh!
The priests scatter like birds
to recite incantations of welcome
with a monotonous zeal
under the eye of High Priestesses
from Isis.

# *Nocturne for Roots*

My mother left me rocking in a cradle
under tall amarata trees
snakes and lean jaguars guarded me.
My mother went to the fields searching for roots
I lay in spangled bowers
where leaves and shadows
clapped hands in the wind.
Afternoon sunlight
was the only intruder.
Morpho butterflies and firebirds
hung like lanterns.
My mother returned
with a laughing heart.
Legba, Master of the Crossroads,
Lisping like a snake,
led her to green and golden fields,
she plucked roots fragrant with earth-smells:
cassava, yams, tanyas, wild eddoes
that turn a seaweed amber
with boiling.
My mother carried me on her back
my ear close to drums of her heartbeat.
She sang forgotten lullabies
accompanied by a fugue of rainfrogs
and nocturnes of six o'clock bees.
Her breath was soft as the rustle
of a hummingbird's wings
Darkness overwhelmed us,
At day-clean the search for roots began again.

# *Africa — Guyana!*

Labadi, on the Ghana coast
where palm fronds hiss like snakes
and moonlight cheats the dark
of its suzerainty;
palm-wine drunkards lean on moonbeams
listening to surf
roaring in their blood;
the beaches reel
before lips of rising tide edged with spume;
roots are white fangs
bared at the eroding wind and sea;
fishermen in long canoes
part high reefs of foam,
combing the manes of white horses with tridents;
a Fanti dance in a limbo of lagoons;
the stench of mud and crabs in the oleous breeze,
dancers swaying like kites
and Ewe drums talking.
High tide erases my footprints
from Labadi to the Angola coast
and north to El Jadida.
The middle-passage,
the reaches of Sargasso,
Atlantis of the legend,
are tombs for my ancestral bones.

Memories of two motherlands —
Africa — Guyana —
scrawled carelessly with broken spears,
and shattered gourds from which I once drank
buried their tribal secrets in the sand
before my parting.

Africa — Guyana!
Drunk as Boshongo Lords,
palm-wine drunkards chant,
"It was the same mangrove,
the same beaches with wreaths of amber foam,
the same sky, dyed a Berber-blue,
the same white clouds passing before the sun
like processions of marabouts."

What language shall I speak to the lisping tides?
White worshipers of Kali
have long since tightened silken scarves
around ancestral throats.
Labadi is a name to conjure with.
Palm-wind drunkards sit in magic circles
incanting.
I hear the murmur of my beginnings,
talk to night winds, and tides,
fishermen,
dancing out of a bellows of sea and sky,
hear me speak.

"ABRUNI-MAN! And yet he has my cousin's face,"
they reply.
Our gourds are brimming over.

"I am your cousin's face three centuries away!"
"Where do you hail from again, my brother?"
palm-wine drinkards chorus drunkenly.
"GUYANA! AFRICA — GUYANA, THREE CENTURIES AWAY!"
Surf, lisping tides,
palm-wine drinkards,
and moonlight casting hard, communal shadows
on white sand
listen indifferently.

# Rudolph Allen

## *My Grandfather and I*

The summer had come. College had ended. It was now my sixteenth birthday, when my father called me into the living room. "Tony," he said, "you'll be spending two weeks with your grandfather in the country. He asked explicitly for you."

A thousand thoughts went through my mind. The last time I had seen him was when I was twelve. It was my birthday. I was glad that I was going because it brought back great memories of our first encounter at twelve ... *I see you flutter and fly ... You butterfly of my heart.*

My mother came into my room and stood above me. She was considered taller than my father. "It's good that you're going. Besides," she said, looking down on me, "it'll be a bit of a break for you to spend some time with your grandfather. How many boys know their grandfather?" I could not think of any because my school friends did not speak of their grandfathers. I said, "I don't know?"

I remember when I first saw the house where he lived in the country. It was a grey house, with a broken-down veranda. An aged man sitting in a large chair. And his attention was interrupted by his dog, who had suddenly rushed forward with a volley of shrill barks at his intruders. The man on the veranda slowly rose and his head seemed to touch the ceiling. He was dressed in a white suit, with tall black boots, and came down the stairs two at a time. His feet seemed not to touch the ground, as if dancing some intricate steps. He advanced with great rapidity and stood before us. He was simply a giant of a man. He embraced my father, then my mother. "And who is this?" he said in a musical voice that seemed to ring out over the mountains and hills.

I glanced up at him. His skin shone like copper — it had a golden tone. There were wrinkles around his neck. He kissed me on both cheeks. His skin was soft. The dog came jumping up to me and craved for affection. "Down, Charlie, be good boy," he said, and he immediately obeyed. I looked at my grandfather and then at my father to see if there were any resemblances. But I could not find any.

On Friday, Dad gave me the present that I had to give Popsi. I remember the first time that I had heard that name, Popsi as he was called.

That Sunday morning I waited patiently for my parents to come to the car. I had already placed my suitcase into the trunk and had taken my place in the back seat. I looked through the window and saw my parents coming through the garden to the front gate. They held hands. They always did. He waved a hand airily. "So you're ready. Good!"

With a galvanic, less voluntary movement, the car went into motion. We were on our way. We passed quickly through the city, Kingston, and went westward. I had seldom passed through this way. The car lumbered laboriously, as it was a small car, an Austin, a British product, as my father had great faith in all British products.

Slowly, we journeyed north, through mountains and hills, green and lush with their vegetation. There were plantations after plantations with rows and rows of banana trees and coconuts. I could remember where Popsi had lived and wondered if he had painted the house as he had promised me. Suddenly, the car jerked to an abrupt halt. The front window was covered with steam. My father got out of the car. The top of the radiator was blown off. Steam was pouring out of the radiator with hot water. "We'll have to get water!" I heard my father say to my mother. He went to the back of the trunk and retrieved a canister. "Tony," he said, "there's a stream down there."

I followed where he had pointed. I could see a small river in the ravine. "Go down there and get us some water," he said. I took the canister and went on my way. It was not difficult. I was very agile and scampered down the ravine where I retrieved the water int he can. But, it was difficult on my way back. I came up slowly. My father watched my progress from the edge of the cliff. "Well done!" he said, as I gave him the can. He quickly poured the water into the radiator, but at intermittent intervals. I watched him as he did this. We waited for an hour until the radiator had cooled down. Then I had to go to the front of the card and crank the engine.

The car sputtered and then came to life. I resumed my seat in the back. The surrounding environment was beautiful. I had never seen such green vegetation in the countryside before. The vegetation was lush and there was never any brown, only green. I felt that I was in a different country altogether. The roads were meandering and narrow and each hill or knoll seemed to rush up at you. There was seldom any traffic on the road. Occasionally a bus loaded down with bags of bananas and plantains protruding as they pass us by. It was the evening before we had reached our destination.

I remember the first time that I had travelled to see my grandfather, when my father explained to me that he lived in the parish of St. Mary. It was another parish altogether. "That's Richmond," he said as he pointed to another hill. I then looked and all I saw was empty space. No one in sight. In fact, I saw few persons on the road. "It won't be long now!" he said. I had expected to reach our destination in a few minutes, but I was disappointed.

It took over half an hour before we reached it. This trip was no different.

We stopped at the base of a hill and Dad pointed up the hill. I tried to see what was on top, but my vision was blocked by dense vegetation and hills. I retrieved my suitcase as my father and mother led the way. We passed over a small stream with a small bridge that spanned the water. The stream was rapid. We went quickly along a narrow path as the clearing in the grass indicated. To the right and left of me were fruit trees: mango, grapefruit, orange, tangerine, guava and breadfruit. It looks to me like the Garden of Eden. No one welcomed us.

My parents walked quickly before me, and I struggled with the weight in my hands. Soon I saw a clearing and a small cottage at the base of the hill. It was not there before. A tall person in shorts came over to us. I recognized my uncle Alfred. He was the black sheep of the family. Dad always spoke of him in a disparaging manner. "He was lazy," my father said. A good education but he refused to work. He was an architect by profession, but Dad said, "He only works for six months and then he takes off the rest of the year." My father did not approve of his lifestyle. He thought that life was for working not leisure. The two of them never seemed to agree on anything.

"Let us come along," my uncle replied, and he took my suitcase from my hands. I was very thankful. It was very heavy. I tried to smile at him. He was very tall as he stood above both my parents. "How're you? I've not seen you in such a long time," he said, smiling down at me. I always like him as he was kind to me. He seemed to ignore my father as he took my hand in his. We walked up the winding hill and I could not see a dwelling or a single person on that hill. Then it occurred to me that the hill was covered in clouds.

The house stood out against the landscape. It was white. Charlie came bouncing down the steps, barking and wagging his tail. He bounced on me with both his paws against my legs. I patted his head. Then Popsi came out of the front house, bouncing down the steps with an alacrity that denied his age.

My uncle Alfred and grandfather were of the same height, and their nose and mouth were similar. On the other hand, my father was short and obese with a large stomach. We went inside. I was not prepared to find my present surroundings. The living room was large and sparsely furnished. But I was surprised to see coffee beans in one huge heap in the corner. it must have showed on my face. For he said, "I just began to use this side of the house for storage, Tony." He turned to me as he said this.

"Come along," said my father," and see the rest of the house you'll be living in for the remainder of two weeks." There were no electricity of running water in the house and I asked my father about this. "All the water has to come from the river over the hill," my grandfather said, "and I like it that way!" The dining room was also large, with a table that could seat twelve persons. To one side was a large basin with water. "I guess you would all like to wash up and have something to eat," said my grandfather. He moved quickly to the side.

My father was the first to use the basin and wiped his hands on the white towel. Then my mother followed the ritual. Finally, it was my turn. Charlie had by now taken a fancy to me, as he advanced with great rapidity and stood in my path, looking up and down and barking hard, whereupon, without hesitation, I stood my ground. My grandfather came over quickly and caught him by his collar, and spoke to him gently and led him outside. I was relieved, and continued the ritual of washing my hands.

The meal was sumptuous and simple. It was my favourite: ackee and codfish. My grandfather offered me port. I had never had wine before. A first I hesitated, but my father smiled at me when my grandfather offered it. As we clinked glasses, my grandfather asked how the trip had been.

"You should come to the city more often," my father said.

"I've no inclination to do so!" responded "Peeps. "I've been away for too long. The only person I would like to see more often is my grandson." He looked at me and smiled. I noticed that no one spoke to my uncle Alfred. I wanted to include him. "How is your project getting along?" I said. At this he felt reassured and began to speak at great length on his project. He said, "It'll take a year to complete!" I could see that my father was elated at this news. "Well, I guess you'll have to stay to see it through then," he said. The conversation then turned to politics which was a favourite topic of my father; outside of business this was his life.

"I suppose," he said to my father, "that Britain will have to eventually give this island its independence. We're self-governing now! What of the future?"He turned to Peeps as he said this. At first I caught some hesitancy in my grandfather's expression. Then he shrugged his shoulders.

"Eventually it'll happen. It came to Cuba, but then we had to fight for it against Spain. I would not like to relive those days again. It was so long ago it does not seem so real ... only the killings!"

The pain in his eyes told me that he had not wanted to talk about it. He had grey eyes like those of a cat. They seemed always to be smiling, but for now they were quite serious. I excused myself from the table and began to explore the house on my own. I noticed that there was an additional room, but when I entered, I saw it also had fruit provisions. The rooms in the house were large, and there were two bedrooms. One was exquisitely furnished while the other was sparse.

I concluded that the sparse room was my grandfather's. My father said, "You'll sleep with Popsi for tonight. I went into the room and undressed and put on my pyjamas. Popsi, I noticed, slept in his ling johns. He kissed me good night on both cheeks, and his whiskers felt hard against my skin. I gave a startled jump and my grandfather started laughing. I felt at ease immediately and slept at the far end of the bed which was large enough to hold three persons. It was the largest bed that I have ever seen.

The next morning after breakfast I decided to explore the estate. I saw paths that led nowhere spreading over the hilly and empty land, through tall grass, through thickets, down and up stony hills ablaze with the heat of the sun. The solitude of the surroundings revealed nature in all its splendour.

I stood at the edge of this wonderous garden with its tall grass and trees, as seen for the first time why Popsi was reluctant to depart from this place he called Home. The living trees that were low in the growth were lashed together by creepers, and the bush in the undergrowth was dark green. They blended with the grass on the ground that gave an impression of continuous green vegetation.

It was a quiet day, and I spent the day with myself. It was not until the evening that my parents left. Popsie and I waved goodbye to them as they drove off along the narrow and winding road.

That night around the table with the lamp between us, my grandfather told me his adventures in Cuba. The light cast a shadow upon half his face as he spoke.

"I was born in Spain and grew up in Madrid. Then I went to Cuba as a young man to farm. I always wanted to be a farmer. But then the revolution came; I took the side of the Cubans against my countrymen. I never regretted that decision!" he said. "Besides, I always believed in a people's revolution. It can never fail. That history, always be on the side of history." His grey eyes flickered and bore into me. Charlie lazed quietly at his feet.

"At first it was difficult to get arms, we had machetes and knives, but that was not good enough for the task at hand."

His face took on an animated glow as he told me he had led a group of twenty-five men at night dressed up like Spanish soldiers and walked into the garrison outside Havana and gained access to three thousand rifles. This he said was the high point of the campaign. He did not dwell on the raids where he had to take lives — for I'm sure he did.

We both sipped the hot milk with honey that he had provided. Then he switched to lively stories of ghosts because, I suspect, it was near bedtime.

"Once," he said, "there was a rich old woman who had died, but before she passed into the world of the dead, she consulted a voodoo priestess, to protect her wealth that was to be buried with her. The guardian was rolling-calf that breathed fire.

"Well," he said with a mischievous look in his grey eyes, "Bra-a-nancy, the spider, decided to raid the grave and take this wealth. But he had not bargained for what happened next. The rolling-calf started to chase him breathing fire! And this is why when one places a fire to a spider, it runs in all directions!"

That simple story had always remained with me. Whenever I hear a similar story, i remember my grandfather.

I had looked at him then and for the first time saw a soldier. I knew this deep down even before he had told me his story. It was the way he walked erect, with a carriage of his shoulders straight and upright. His speech was musical, but masculine in its tone. Then, and always, I remembered his words and they always had a "sh" sound to them. It was his Spanish sound that hungered to be used. He spoke reluctantly of his campaigns and what he had to do in order to survive. I did not ask him many questions in that area. If he had wanted, he would have told me. I felt a sense of unease.

But I discovered that he had always a sense of humour. He told me of a wedding he had to attend and the speech he had had to give. He said, "A recently married couple just got back from their honeymoon and began to settle into their domestic life," he paused as he said this to see if I was attentive.

"The husband," he continued, "immediately invited his male friends over to his home. Upon their arrival, he showed them his home. "He said, 'All that you survey is mine. I'm the master of all that you see!' He showed them the living room, the kitchen, the bedroom — the complete house — and repeated that he was master of all this."

My grandfather had paused for a great effect and I hung onto every word. He continued, "His friends were surprised and said, 'You mean your wife does not mind?' Upon their questions he said, 'I'm the master of this household.' His wife at this time had heard this and said nothing. It was getting late. By then his wife came into the kitchen where they were all gathered. She took out the food, the drinks and the wine from the refrigerator and said, 'You can all continue to eat and drink — there's sufficient food and drink for all.' Taking the husband's hand she said, 'But the master of the house is coming to bed!'"

We had grown close, my grandfather and I. As I made my farewell to him that Sunday morning, I saw him standing erect, and with one hand he bade me farewell. To me he never died, but as a soldier only faded away in memory, and only his gentle nature resurfaces in me whenever I remember him. Standing alone on that narrow road, with the sun at his back and his white hair silhouetted by the rays of the sun, I saw myself in him, a poet, a soldier and a farmer.

# John Hearne

## *Living Out the Winter*

In Guyana, the East Indians and the Africans between them were tearing the place to pieces. They were doing small, dreadful, useless things to each other all along the coast from the Pomeroon to the Courentyne. The blood of children soaked the pink laterite of the roads, making pungent mud pies in the dust beside the broken shells of school buses tossed onto their sides. Old men and their wives drained the last of busy, open lives into the hidden, grey-green waters of the back-dams and canal heads; scarlet jets rushed from severed arteries in arcs as pure as rainbows, turned black against the sun, and sprayed the tall blades of sugar cane and the delicate, lizard-tongue shoots of young rice. The melancholy stench, the grunting and the sobbing of gang rape, rose from the ground under the kookorit palms on the horizon at night, rode widely on the wind and made the whole colony drunk with nostalgia for old, exalted cruelties.

It was time for me to go. I had been in Guyana too long this time and there was nothing left for me to do except stay and add my sadness to friends who were sad enough already. There was nothing more to add to what I had already written except more statistics; and the Guyanese were not a people who deserved such a reduction. Over the years, from one visit to another, I had been given more kindness, affection and commodious hospitality here than any traveller had a right to expect. Their manners, their sense of honourable obligation to a stranger, their sweet and courteous exchanges did not belong, it seemed to me, to the age around us but to some fine, archaic inspiration of chivalry. Now, they still took time out from killing each other by inches to press with gentle insistence gifts of food, attention and their selves on me. As a visitor travelling those violent roads alone between the villages, I was a guest, and my only danger was that in the small, stilt-raised houses I would be forced gradually to drink and eat more than my health could stand.

One afternoon I flew out to Trinidad. The day I left, the Africans decided that single assassinations from the bushes, isolated rape by night and scattered burnings were slow, stingy ways to fight a war. They took out a little township up the Demerara River, opposite the bauxite works at Mackenzie. It was a beautifully planned operation, executed with drastic efficiency. They came in from the forest on three sides just before dawn, burning all East Indian houses from the outskirts towards the river. There was some killing, of course, but more raping because they understood how completely destructive rape is to the East Indian sense of honour. So if I had stayed in Guyana, I would have had a new story full of fresh insights to file.

From Port of Spain I sent a cable, a night letter, to my wife in London, asking if I could come home now, and two days later she cabled back to say, Well, not now but some time. This was less than I had hoped for, but it was a great deal better than I had any right to expect.

"Don't sit there as if I didn't tell you," Margaret Cipriani said. "You men all think you can play ass when you have a mind and then just go back as if you have a right. I warned you something like this was bound to happen. Three months ago at this same table, I told you she was going to light a fire under your tail. I know that woman."

All the strength, grace and beauty of our territory rest in the faces of our women, in what they have salvaged and refashioned from the clumsy shipwreck of our past. Their faces are our only certain works of art, and it is to them that we turn for reference and reconciliation.

"Well," she said now, but she smiled as she said it, "what are we going to do with you?"

"I think I'll stay in Trinidad," I told her. "I don't think I want to go to Jamaica just now, and going back to England wouldn't be a very good idea at the moment. I'll stay here."

"You'll stay with us?"

"No," I said. "It looks as if I'm going to be here for a while. I'll find a place of my own before my company begins to wear thin."

"Now you playing ass again," her husband Louis said. "You think I could go to work every day knowing you was staying by a stranger's house and I have an empty room and a place at my table?"

Margaret Cipriani! Louis Cipriani! You hammer such fine shapes out of a man. Between the fire and the anvil of your strong loves one comes sensuously into possession of his special temper.

But all the same, it was time for me to leave the Ciprianis. His poetry was beginning to appear in all the good places, and two writers should not share the same house with one woman for too long. I began to search that day for the sort of place I could call my own until it was all right for me to go home.

In the Press Club one afternoon, Cappie Reckord, a boy who worked for Radio Trinidad, put me on to what sounded like the place I was looking for.

"It will suit you fine, man," he told me. "Feller used to work at Barclays Bank did stay there. Him and me had shares in a horse, you see, and I pick him up sometimes when we was going out to the track. That's how I know it.

It's really a nice place. Your own veranda screened off and quiet, and a big room lead off it so you don't have to use their entrance. My friend transfer to San Fernando last month, but maybe they don't let the room yet. It's a man and wife set up. Name of Ramesar. Indian people. At least, him is all Indian, but she have enough black in her to give the leg shape and make the breasts stand out strong. Why you don't give them a ring tonight? Both of them work, so you'll have to call them at the house."

He paused and winked, with an odd little ducking gesture of his head. All the lewd and cynical disenchantment of Trinidad were in that inimitable wink and nod. If you live in Trinidad for three days you must learn to resist constant invitations to join an urbane and heartless conspiracy. A frivolous and expert malice is inherited by every Trinidadian like some honorary but unsupported title.

"Maybe it's more than board and lodging you get," Cappie Reckord said. "The woman *stack* — and that little dry-foot coolie she marry to don't look as if him can begin to give her the vitamin C. I see her a few time when I call by there. Jesus! What a poum-poum going to waste! God never in this life build another race of woman like the real *douglah*. When my friend was there, him tell me that she was always coming into the room to ask him if the maid change the sheets, or if him need a clean shirt for the morning. That sort of thing. Wearing one of them wrap-around housecoat so short that you can't tell whether it's pussy or black panty showing under it when she sit down. My friend tell me that if him wasn't fixed up already and getting all him want, him would have try a shot — but this little Chinese gal him was going with at the time would have take the strength out of the Jolly Green Giant, so he just leave well alone. Man! If you get that place and play it right, life could be beautiful."

"All I want is a cheap, quiet place where I can work," I told him. "The beautiful life is a complication I can do without."

"Eh-eh! Listen to the man, though. You live in England so long corruption setting in. It's a good thing you decide to take a cure down here before the English brainwash you past redemption."

Because of what Cappie Reckord had suggested about the Ramesar woman, I nearly did not telephone them that evening. A disappointed, indiscriminate wife, an anxious, perhaps angry, husband, both under the same roof with me, represented the last situation I wanted just then; the first one with which I would be unable to cope. I was near enough to a straitjacket as it was, but I had enough left to know what would make a certainty out of a possibility.

Then it occurred to me that cynics like Cappie are, at best, gamblers. They bet on the worst always coming up and half the time they are right. But only half the time. And their bets are only blind plunges: not based on really careful consideration of form. That evening after dinner at the Ciprianis', I telephoned the Ramesars.

The house up in St. Clair was everything that Cappie Reckord had promised: a high-ceilinged, turn-of-the-century, Port of Spain fantasy with deep, encircling verandas and dark wooden floors. It had a preposterous, ramshackle charm; some festive, slightly askew imagination had conceived it; and half-hidden behind the luxuriant mango and poui trees, it looked more like a big, crazy tent than a sober frame of wood and stucco. My room was at the back, opening off the end of the eastern veranda. Two walls of stout lattice work, painted green, enclosed my end of the veranda and separated it from the rest, giving me what was really another room. There was a little door cut into the lattice work facing the yard above the steps; and sometimes at night when the winds spilled down from the northeast, the green, cool fragrance they rifled from the huge lime tree across the driveway made my head spin.

The Ramesars had accepted me as their paying guest with a flattering enthusiasm.

"Not the *writer*?" Victor Ramesar had asked me over the telephone after I had given him my name.

"Yes," I said. In those days, I still inflated slightly when a stranger had heard of me and got excited about contact.

"Well, well, what do you think of that, eh. You been writing some great books, man. Just what we need in the West Indies. Our own people writing from the inside about *us*. I saw in the paper where you was visiting, but I didn't know you were going to stay."

"I won't be staying all that long. About three months, I should think. Perhaps that won't be convenient for you. Letting for so short a time, I mean."

"No, man. Don't give that a thought. If you like the place and want it for three months, we'd be proud to let you have it."

And Mrs. Ramesar, Elaine, said much the same thing later, after I had seen what they were offering and told them how much I liked it.

We sat in the big drawing room and sealed our agreement over a drink.

"I only got rum, man," Victor Ramesar said, with a touching shy apology, as if he felt he were causing *me* embarrassment by his inability to offer something expensive. "I know you can lose the taste for it after you live in England."

"Rum is fine," I told him. "At English prices, I haven't been able to acquire a taste for anything except beer and wine."

"Whisky high in England, eh?"

"Wickedly high. Rum too. Sometimes in the winter I break down and treat myself to half a bottle, but it's only when I come back to the West Indies that I don't feel sinful about taking a drink."

He brought my glass over, the dark Fernandez rum looking oily and potent around the ice, and I held it while he splashed a little soda into the liquor. Then he went back to the side table and mixed two more drinks and brought them back to where we sat. He handed his wife one and raised his glass.

"Here's to a happy association," he said. "Well, well! I never thought we'd have a famous writer staying under our roof. I read all your books, man. And Elaine here, too."

"Thank you," I said, and raised my glass also. "But I'm not a famous writer. I'm just one of a lot of writers trying to get famous. I'm sure I'm going to enjoy it here. You've got a beautiful house. They knew how to build in those days. The bungalows they're putting up now are just boxes to sleep in."

"If I tell you what this house cost me to keep up, man. It was all right for the old-time people when you could get a girl to clean and polish floor for a couple dollar a week, but now a place like this is just a damn white elephant. Me daddy did take it 'bout ten year ago for a bad debt, and when him die, him leave it to me. If I could get a price for it, I'd sell it tomorrow and buy one of them bungalow you was talking 'bout."

Looking around as he told me this, I could believe him. Their furniture — vaguely and synonymously Scandinavian, not quite comfortable, slightly depressing with its standardized gaiety and self-conscious modernism — was solid enough; but it was not big enough, and there was not nearly enough of it for the space. No juggling could have made it adequate, and Elaine Ramesar had done the sensible thing and arranged the pieces in only one section of the big room.

I could understand, also, why they needed to let a room to a congenial boarder, although they were both working and there were no children. The house had not been painted for a long time, and some of it was not used at all; but those floors had to be kept polished and the shingles replaced if he hoped to sell it at a good price to government for offices, or even to some speculator looking for a site, who would pull it down to build a high rise with air-conditioned apartments. And the rates on the half acre of dankly prolific Trinidadian soil on which the house stood would be a lot more than he would want to meet every year. To keep the jungle from the steps and the house from erosion, he was probably paying out in part-time wages enough to buy food for twenty men, women and children in Port of Spain each week. My contribution, small as it was, would be a relief.

With the move to the Ramesars', my life seemed to acquire, if not serenity, at least an order that had been missing from it for too long. In the mornings after they had gone to work, I would have breakfast on my end of the veranda, and then I'd sit down to the book that had been a troubling — no, frightening — tenant inside me for nearly two years: a surly, demanding invalid for whom I had performed innumerable small and exhausting services every waking hour, who frequently and petulantly called me from sleep, and who resented even those visitors who whispered and walked on tiptoe. Now, and suddenly, it was still a demanding guest, but vigorous and competitive, challenging me to use all the things I had learned, exhilarated by company. At lunchtime, I would stop where I knew that I could have written another sentence, maybe even a whole paragraph, which would have satisfied me next day, and drive round the Savannah in the beat-up secondhand Minx I had acquired, down to Frederick Street to Luciano's to eat a great deal of oysters and brown bread and drink cold Guinness. The swamp oyster of Trinidad is about the size of a man's thumbnail and its flavour stands in the same relationship to that of any other oyster in the world as the taste of the strawberry does to that of any other fruit: doubtless, I mean, God could have done better in both cases, but doubtless, God never did.

After lunch, three or four times a week, I would go to one of the cinemas for a preview. Writing a film column for the Sunday paper was one of the freelance jobs I had landed. The other was a twice-weekly commentary on the international news for Radio Trinidad; and the afternoons I didn't go to the cinema, I would record at the studio. Both jobs paid only what such jobs do in the West Indies, but they gave me the rent and my basic food, and I tried to write them as closely and well as if I had been doing them for the *Times* and the BBC. Nobody as far as I could gather, except for friends like the Ciprianis, read what I thought about new trends in film; but a number of people would tell me how much they had been impressed by the things I said about de Gaulle and Castro and Kennedy (the one who was still a year away from the underpass in Dallas) and the Middle East.

In the evenings, I usually went back to the Ramesars for dinner; eating with them if they were in; having the maid bring it out to me on a tray if they had eaten already or been invited out. Sometimes, if dark caught me still in town, I would go out to the Ciprianis in Petit Valley and take potluck with them, or go to a little Chinese restaurant where you could get a pepper steak and a beer for a dollar.

The nights that I did not talk out with Louis Cipriani, until two or three in the morning, our attempts to rescue a few enduring metaphors from our starved, appalling past, there were parties; loud, loose, accidental Trinidadian parties to which everybody comes like a casual Columbus, ready for treasure, astonishment and new delights of the senses.

Most nights I was home early and would read until very late, and go to bed with the scent from the lime tree coming through the lattice across the veranda and into the bedroom through the old-fashioned double doors which I never closed. One afternoon there was even a letter from my wife waiting for me: a dispassionate and sometimes sardonic missive, to be sure, but there were seven pages of it, and reading between the lines I could sense friendliness; yes, friendliness definitely kept breaking in. It was not enough, yet, for me to push my luck by going home, but things were looking up.

So why did I then allow the Ramesars to intrude on what had begun to come to me more by good luck than any sensible management on my part? Because they both made the house such a good place to live and work in, treating me not like a friend, which would have involved me in all sorts of tedious obligations, nor as a financially expedient stranger, but as a member of the family: a distant undefined cousin by marriage who was temporarily claiming his share of living space and paying his way? Well, partly because of that, I suppose. You won't really understand us in the West Indies until you understand our habit of adopting into some sort of kin relationship with whoever sleeps under your roof for more than a couple of nights. The sociologists call it the "principle of the extended family", I believe — but it stems, simply, from the fact that to be a West Indian is a damned lonely business and that we are always looking for ways to alleviate our loneliness.

But it wasn't only this that accounted for my growing and often painful involvement with the Ramesars. I had begun to like them; and what was obviously happening to their marriage was what had nearly happened to mine. And with that fatuous, light-headed gratitude of one who has been rescued from a long, dark fall into sadness I wanted to make some sort of return — to somebody. I felt I owed the world a service.

When I say what was happening to their marriage was what had nearly happened to mine, I don't mean, of course, that the details were the same. They never are. The brute weapons with which a man and a woman try to destroy each other haven't changed since we first started recording the business for the guidance of our children; and the strategic aim has always been the same, too, I guess. Total annihilation. Even the few tactics we have evolved are so old as to be by now almost ritual. But the terrain is always different, as are the uses made of it, and the occasion that causes the war. All of which has been very good for the writing trade.

With the Ramesars, the occasion was so conventional as to be almost trite: Victor Ramesar was perhaps the least ambitious, most uncompetitive man I had ever met. Most men dream of taking a little revenge on the world for cheating them at birth, but Victor was grateful for the modest gifts with which he had been started in life: gentle, fine-drawn good looks, a mind competent enough to take him into the administrative ranks of the civil service before he was forty (to a position from which he would never rise, nor even try to rise); a spirit that not only enjoyed the superior achievements of others but was consoled by them; a mild but utterly pervasive conviction that every person was a potential friend to be nourished; an equally mild, equally pervasive conviction that to demand more or to strive for it would be greedy and might involve him in cruelty. With a better mind or with a good fire in his liver, he could have been a holy man — at the least, one of those histrionic idealists who want nothing except a platform and an audience to join them in their exhilarating journeys into new thought. As it was, he was simply the sort of husband who, after fifteen years, filled a woman like Elaine Ramesar with daily sensations of boredom, contempt and the furious, unforgiving disappointment of the wife who knows she has only herself to blame for not choosing better in the first place.

It was not that she was one of those shallow, insecure women who feels safe only in a marriage of accumulating possessions and the reflected glow of a high-status husband. But she was not the product of a vigorous and aggressive breed. Her father had started cutting sugar cane on the Caroni estates east of Port of Spain at twelve: just another lean-shanked East Indian child without enough protein in his diet to sustain a field mouse, and who, under the molten suns, livid skies and the stooped, unremitting labour of those brutal fields, would have shrivelled into old age by forty. Instead, at eighteen, he had broken caste and race and invested himself in marriage with Elaine's mother, a Negro, the only child of a local mechanic: one of those self-taught, inspired tinkerers, really, who seem able to follow the course energy must take through any piece of machinery in the way a bloodhound can follow a single scent through a forest.

In those days, when the East Indians were still only a generation or so away from their importation as indentured labour, still unsure of themselves, more than a little frightened by the harsh, individualistic Creole society, still *coolies*, there were several such marriages. At least among the East Indian males strong-minded enough to risk the anathema of the Brahmins and to court the Negro women who had come to recognize that in an Indian husband they were pretty sure of getting a permanent partner; one who would leave a wife only if she were unfaithful, and who would take his responsibilities as father and provider with great seriousness.

From these unions came the *douglahs*: big, heavy-boned hybrids with skins the texture and colour of the icing on a chocolate cake, vivid, troubling faces, and coarse, straight hair like the manes of black horses.

Two years after Elaine Ramesar's father married, his father-in-law got drunk at a picnic down at Mayaro beach, swam out too far, and the last they saw of him was his head being carried like a coconut on the swift brown Atlantic stream, out and away towards Africa. This could have been a financial disaster for the daughter and the son-in-law he had left, since all the real capital of the little workshop and garage he had run had lain in the intuitive skill of his big, shapely hands. But the combination of an East Indian husband willing to be advised by a wife with all the traditions and techniques that the West Indian peasant woman has had to learn over three centuries of keeping the family together is not a partnership to be taken lightly. Elaine's mother sold a junior share in the repair side to another Negro man, managed the spare parts section and did the accounts herself; and with what she had got from the part sale of the workshop paid down on a used Bedford truck. In this, her husband began hauling dry goods — cheap cloth, pots and pans, zinc sheets for roofing, nails, salt, even secondhand sewing machines — to the small villages that had begun to grow throughout the Caroni district and beyond as more and more East Indians began to acquire confidence in their new society, to increase and to leave the estate barracks.

By getting up at four on three hundred and fifty mornings a year, returning home at nine on three hundred and fifty nights, and by almost prophetic instinct for those occasions when a dollar's credit given today was going to mean two dollars' extra cash purchase tomorrow, he was soon making more for the family than the repair shop. When Elaine was born, twelve years later, they were living in Port of Spain, and her four brothers were wearing the uniform of the island's most expensive, most rigorous preparatory school.

In the course of that winter in Trinidad, I was to meet all the brothers: full-fleshed, genial predators who had staked out crucial commanding heights in commerce and the professions between them. One was a dentist, another was in real estate, a third was a solicitor, the eldest, Lloyd, managed what had grown from the secondhand Bedford truck and the little mechanic's shop — that is, the third-largest removal business in Trinidad and the Volkswagen agency.

They were, in fact, close in kind and attitude to their in-laws, the Ramesars. Old Budhram Ramesar, Victor's father, had come to Trinidad with the advantage of being able to speak, read and write English, and had never got nearer to the cane fields than the eastern suburbs of Port of Spain. What Victor had told me about his acquiring the house in St. Clair as payment for a "bad debt" more or less summed up a happy career as an independent speculator working on the fringes of the law until the day he dropped dead of a heart attack while trying to promote a Caribbean trade fair which, had he lived to see it through, would probably have made him several times a millionaire. When his estate was probated, his three sons found themselves with $375,000 owing on bank loans and the house in St. Clair. Victor Ramesar had not been quite accurate when he told me that his father had "left" him the house. It had been given to him as his share of the inheritance by his two brothers who had realized just how much solid return could be wrested from $375,000 of outstanding loans by two legatees for whose continuing good health the managers of four banks offered daily prayers.

I met these two brothers, also, during the course of that winter. They would "flash by" occasionally, as they both called it — one in a cream Mercedes, the other in a green air-conditioned Buick — to spend an hour or so. Half listening to the conversations as words drifted down to my end of the veranda, I began to form the suspicion that their visits were prompted not so much by family feeling as by the fact that Victor, the civil servant, could give them gossip about his colleagues.

Nothing about confidential government matters, of course, but simple, casual information as to who was doing what to whom. The paths of an import permit or a building licence can be made much smoother if one knows which official to play off against the other. They both shared with Victor fine-boned, small-featured good looks; but where his face was soft and contemplative, theirs had the hard, alert rapacity of hawks.

Sometimes when one or the other of them was there, Victor would come to my end of the veranda and suggest through the lattice that I might like to join them for a drink. There was always whisky then — Johnnie Walker, Black Label, Chivas Regal, Dimple, Haig — brought by whichever of the brothers was paying the visit.

It was with such a father and father-in-law, such brothers and brothers-in-law, that Victor Ramesar had to live out a daily comparison. Elaine had come from a family of doing and disturbing men. And from a family of equally turbulent males, she had picked the one who would never make any new impression on the earth whether he tried to do so or not.

All of this is what I am able to organize now. While I was at the Ramesars, I registered hardly anything more than that something was wrong and that I was sorry for them both.

I was sorry for him because she humiliated him in my presence and he accepted it: sorry for her because she humiliated him in my presence and was allowed to get away with it.

Some of these humiliations were overtly sexual — as Cappie Reckord had suggested. But I would have been a fool had I read them as signals of readiness. The visits to my room in the short housecoat, the attention I was given when we took meals together, the suggestive banter that excluded him were not for me, really. They were against him. Sooner or later, I was certain, a lover would be brought into the situation, but it would not be me.

I suppose if there had been any money to spare from among the family enterprises, she would have persuaded one of the brothers or brothers-in-law to give it to her to use to make something of him — as her mother had done for her father. But all the brothers and brothers-in-law had sired enormous broods, tribes almost, and there was not enough left over to risk on Victor. His capacity for ruthlessness was too limited. So he continued to initial files at the Ministry of Development, and she to make out invoices and bills for the brother who held the Volkswagen agency.

It would be useless and tedious to recite all the other ways in which Victor was reminded, daily, of his inadequacy. An embittered woman looking for some excuse for not loving the decent man with whom she lives can only hope to provoke him into doing something that will confirm how right she has been all the time. And if the man will not be provoked and she is herself also a basically decent creature, what else is there to do but keep repeating the dozen or so cruel yet trivial attacks on his confidence, his integrity, until she comes to believe them.

For Victor accepted her recriminations, her unpredictable gusts of shrill anger, her retreats into wordless sulks, even her obvious use of me, with a solemn meekness, a bewilderment that was infuriating. He had never learned what his brothers, and hers, were probably born knowing: that a woman will forgive her man almost anything except a too humble evaluation of himself.

One early evening after one of the brothers had flashed by — I cannot remember whether it was the white Mercedes or the air-conditioned one — there was a particularly distressing quarrel. No, not quarrel, which implies some sort of heated exchange. You could not call it even a *scene*. It was just the ugly, corrosive sound of a woman trying to find grievances to justify her rage. She must have been cooking this outburst a long time on a low fire because she did not raise her voice. It was only low-pitched phrases that occasionally ricocheted through the lattice like shell fragments falling on the margins of a battlefield: "Fifteen years an' we right where we started . . . Never do a damn thing but go out to work an' come back to this damn morgue . . . Furthest we ever go is two weeks in Barbados . . . Everybody else have something to remember . . . Not even a damn child into the house . . ." And so on. The banality of our most profound despairs! We so seldom have even the bitter sustenance of real tragedy, of dramatic catastrophe, to console us.

A little later, I looked up from the letter I was writing to my wife and saw him mooching forlornly under the pomerac trees on the front lawn, across the drive. It was only a few days to Christmas and the pomerac was in full flower; against the showy Trinidadian sunset — all hard lemon and furnace red — the pink blossoms were of a not quite credible delicacy; and when they floated to the grass in unexpected showers, they stained the air under the trees with a soft blush and powdered the ground like improbable, rosy snow. I wondered if it was snowing in London, and if my wife and the man to whom I had forced her to turn were walking in it. But even thinking this, I found I was feeling sorrier for Victor Ramesar hang-heading it under the pomerac than I was for myself.

On impulse I rose and went to him under the trees. Casually, so as to conceal that I had heard anything — or rather, so as to offer him the courtesy of the lie that I had heard nothing — I asked if he and Elaine would come to the cinema with me that night, as my guests on my press pass. He hesitated, and the big, lustrous, dumb eyes searched me with what in another man might have been suspicion, but which with Victor were only confusion and a sort of appeal. Then he went into the house and a few minutes later came out again to say that Elaine had said yes and thank you.

The evening was not a success. Elaine was still sulking, and Victor was still picking his way through the rubble of guilt or unvoiced protest or perhaps just tired sadness — whatever it was with which one of Elaine's assaults left him. When we went up to one of the little nightclubs in St. James after the show, they both kept talking at me: he with what, to my embarrassment, I felt was gratitude simply for having rescued him from an evening alone with her at home; she with a bitter eagerness to hear about my life in London, the people I knew, the world of success, variety, glamour. She made so much of the dingy, anxious round that is most of a young writer's life, invested my most careful and dispassionate replies with such brightness, that I began to feel phoney. All the small triumphs and exhilarations — being able to make your own hours, subsidized travel, parties where the names of half the guests were sufficient, on introduction, for you to know what they had done, your own name being known by some of those people because it was attached to something you had done — all of this became, in the light of Elaine's need to be vicariously excited, something false and tawdry. She was using me again to prove to herself and to Victor how he had allowed life to pass them by. But this time, I was party to the act of humiliating comparison. That I tried to turn the talk in other directions was not enough; by consenting, however reluctantly, to being drawn, I allowed myself to become the co-respondent in a dismal kind of adultery.

After this evening, the Ramesars and I often went out together. It had been near Christmas when we first became companions of the night. Christmas and Shrove Tuesday, Trinidad gives itself over to pleasure with the exquisite, nervous concentration of a racehorse in the gate. The Christmas and New Year festivities are a warm-up, really, for the serious business of Carnival. All over the island, but particularly in Port of Spain, the preparations begin to accumulate on the morning after Twelfth Night. A tenth of a year's wages will go into the making of a Roman legionnaire's uniform, a Papuan warrior's head-dress, a medieval king's coronation robes, each accurate down to the last sandal strap, the last bird of paradise feather, the last tippet of ermine. The public library sets aside a room entirely stocked with volumes on costume through the ages, and prodigious exercises in historical research are undertaken by the bandleaders — men whose schooling may have stopped at sixteen — and are submitted to the Carnival office in ten-cent notebooks for registration. In the working-class districts, fantastic efflorescences are conjured out of dressmakers' scraps, coloured tissue, tinfoil and cardboard and added to war-surplus American navy uniforms bought for a dollar apiece. On the Tuesday morning before Ash Wednesday, ten or fifteen thousand of these King Sailors turn Frederick Street into a garden bed. The champion calypsonians anxiously tighten the sprung rhythms and file the barbs of the satires they will offer in the tents during the fortnight before Carnival to the most acute and demanding popular audience in the West Indies, maybe in the world. At nights, the drone of the steel bands, practising in a hundred yards, beats like an enormous pulse under the skin of the city, just beneath the level of conscious listening.

It is a time of parties: planned parties; informal gatherings that become parties by chance; parties that begin in one house and move across the city to another, coalescing with and dissolving from yet others on the way. And as Carnival drew nearer, the Ramesars and I were increasingly invited out as a sort of family group. After New Year, I had asked the Ciprianis if I could bring them to a big Sunday picnic across the mountains on the beach at Blanchisseuse; and since then it had been more or less assumed that they were with me. In the West Indies, people never like to miss an opportunity for exercising their right to be hospitable, since, for so long, it had been about the only right they could exercise spontaneously. Things are changing now, I suppose, with independence and all, but the habit seems to remain.

And with these invitations among new people, or among people they had known only to nod to, the Ramesars began to end their marriage. They, or at least she, would have ended it anyway, but getting to know the Ciprianis and others was too much for what was left of it.

It was not, I must stress again, simply a matter of her wanting vulgar success. Few of us had much money. Not in the way her brothers and brothers-in-law had money. And only one or two of us would have done anything that we did not enjoy doing to get it. But most of the men among whom she was now moving were doing things that not many others could do half as well. You could hear it, as you always can, in the conversation: much of each man's talk being about his trade, and the other men listening because there is always so much to learn about your own craft from somebody else who practises his adventurously. And you could sense it in the attitude of the women: each of them sometimes proud, sometimes exasperated, always proprietorial about having to put up with a man to whom work was not simply so many paid hours to be got through but a way of life.

But I did not realize what our company was doing to Elaine Ramesar at the time. Indeed, I had begun to feel hopeful, a little proprietorial myself, about the marriage. She ceased, almost, to find fault, and when she did it was casually, with more rough teasing than sullen accusation. The brooding sulks lightened, and sometimes the exchanges that came to me in my corner were almost affable, couched in the intimate shorthand of a long-standing partnership.

Thus, the suddenly emptied house in which I found Victor standing dazedly when I came in one afternoon overwhelmed me almost as much as it had him.

She had taken everything. All that was left was my bed, the table with my books and manuscripts, and the long Berbice chair in which I read at night. She had even had the stove uncoupled from the gas pipe and taken that too. My soiled clothes had been freshly laundered and packed with the others in the two suitcases out of which I had been living for nearly half a year. Victor's fresh linen, suits, shirts, ties, everything, lay on the floor of the bedroom as she must have tossed them before the removal men took the wardrobe away. In the little washroom beside the kitchen we found his stale clothing piled in the concrete sink. The maidservant, a big, good-natured slut from Grenada, had been paid off; at any rate she was not there.

A note had been left for me on top of the shirts in one of my suitcases. It apologized for any inconvenience I might be caused, but explained nothing. I didn't want to look at Victor, but there was nothing else to look at in the big house that now echoed like a looted sepulchre.

He said, "She can't do this to me." And I waited for what I was certain he would say next, "How could she do this to me?"

There was no way I could tell him, with kindness, that if he had to ask the question, he already knew the answer. And it seemed to me he had had enough cruelty for one day.

There was a numb panic in his eyes as he looked about the house she had stripped. A lot of a man is the sum of his possessions; and now, except for the chair and the bed she had left me, he did not have even a place to rest what remained of him.

He sat on the edge of the bed carefully, on the extreme edge, as though he were apologizing for taking this liberty. There was a little rum left in the bottle I kept for going to bed when I finished reading and I poured him all of it into the plastic tooth-mug on the little glass shelf above the washbasin and ran a splash of water into it. There was no ice because there was no refrigerator. I was trying to find something to say as I gave him the drink but just about everything that came to mind seemed empty or patronizing.

"I'm going to kill her," Victor said, holding the drink but not tasting it. "I'm going to find her and kill her."

It carried less conviction than any threat I had ever heard uttered.

"I'm going to sue her," he said next. "She going give me back what she take or she going find her ass in jail. She can't do this and get away with it." He looked up at me hopefully.

"Yes she can, Victor," I said with regret. "She's allowed to take everything under your roof if you're not here to stop her."

But he knew that. He was simply stumbling from threat to threat for the consolation I could not give him.

Then he looked away, down into the drink I had given him, and his weak sweet-victim's face blurred and crumpled and he began to weep.

"She could have had every damn thing," he said. "She could have had the house and everything. But why she had to do this to me? After all the years I love her, how she could do this to me. Like this!"

And with that, the Ramesars began to pass out of my life. I went back to the Ciprianis' and stayed on since I had got a letter asking me when I was coming home and then I knew that I was not going to be in Trinidad much longer. One afternoon at a wedding, I met a girl, a barrister, who had read one of my books and who wanted to know me well for a while but who had no illusions about what knowing me would become. From time to time, I would go to the big, hollow house in St. Clair in which Victor was beginning to reassemble a life. But there was very little to talk about except Elaine. She was now lodged in the tribal embrace of a brother's family and they treated with affable, condescending neutrality all of Victor's attempts to see her. It was not that they had anything against him, but they didn't have anything for him either. He was a loser. And in their world, losers were a nuisance — bad luck.

I saw her once after she had left him. She was lunching at Luciano's with a big Norwegian who flew a crop-dusting service. I had a drink with them but Victor's name did not come up; and when I next saw him there seemed little reason to say anything about the matter.

Carnival was now nearly upon us, beginning to toss the island between its paws. At nights, the sound of steel bands thudded in the bloodstream while in her flat on St. Vincent Street, six stories above the city, my girl and I wrapped ourselves around each other like the tails of two kites. In the days when she was in court, I wrote steadily at her Formica-topped kitchen table. Just before Carnival I got a letter from my wife telling me that I was missed, and another wanting to know whether I would accept three thousand pounds for doctoring a screenplay as soon as I returned to London. Both letters came on the same day.

With all I had going for me then, it was hard to remember or to do much about the tears of an unconsidered man.

# Gérard Étienne

## *La pacotille*

*Translated by Keith Louis Walker*

The unending constriction of the prison cell. New metamorphosis. A force radiates from deep within me. I hold on to the hope of being able to record in my memory every slightest gesture of the beast.

Yves Barbot had sketched a portrait of him one afternoon when we were at Saint Pierre High School. The beast had just stirred up the entire Caribbean with outrageous words concerning white Americans. The young people allowed themselves to be taken in.

Finally, a distinguished black man was going after the great American boogeyman. An authentic son of the people who is not going to allow his toes to be stepped on. His rhetoric was gone over with a fine-tooth comb. One recognized the most fashionable of the Marxist-Leninist clichés. "Onward the Revolution" screamed the headlines in the *Haiti Journal.* Euphoria in the public school classrooms. The knight in shining armour, people were saying, was going to give a new dimension to history.

Big mistake, Yves Barbot was saying to me. The monster is making himself the lap dog, the beggar, for a few bundles of dollars. He was changing hats, the liar, as soon as he received the manna from the star-spangled republic. He got into step. Conforming to the rules of the game as spelled out by the Pentagon.

And so began the tribulations of the readers of Lenin. The dim-witted ones whose heads were turned by the words of the beast. The clever doctor changes with the rising of the tide. A black man with paid hit men, with street assassins, with intellectuals who harbour the deepest hatreds for mulattoes because mulattoes wash three times a day, because they don't do their business in front of everybody, because they accept the poetry of the fields even when it turns their stomach. A mulatto with the officers of his palace honour guard recruited because of their effectiveness in whitewashing the sins of the daughters of the King. Oh yes. He changes skin, the little demon. Dispenser of justice when he addresses the populace. Great Superintendent of Finances negotiating the slavery of his zombies with the barons of the blood banks.

Record the gestures of the beast in my memory. The features of the face of the beast in my head . . .

A weight on the chest . . . I breathe deeply so as not to lose my guardian angel. I should have known that this would happen to me one day, that there exist men who are born precisely to pay for the wickedness of others.

In my childhood neighbourhood, I was always the first suspect when my pals destroyed a shack. Nothing could save me, even when I was sound asleep snoring on my little reed pallet. The same problems in boarding school: a chamber pot of urine overturned onto the bed of the chief monitor Jeudi, a little lizard in the soup bowl of a snitch, a few good whacks with a stick on the dog of schoolmaster Castor, an escapade at the Magloire school compound — every naughty deed bore my fingerprints.

I should have known that this would happen to me, already on record at the police station. Ringleader of rebellious youth. In spite of everything, I search for an opening in this enclosure that the capitol has become.

Shadows in giant silhouettes cover the Church of the Sacred Heart. During more than half an hour a half-dead sun tries to make a tiny hole through a big cloud that, moving very slowly, manages to invade the manor of one of the mistresses of a general of the beast, known for her excesses during dark ceremonies at the palace.

The rivulets in the city streets are multiplying day by day. One has the feeling of wallowing in puddles of yellowish water where germs produced in laboratories for the annihilation of a race of beggars carry it off on the backs of earthworms.

I walk in harmony with a storm, calmly, consciously, with determination to remain steadfast until the assassination of the President. I feel free of all attachments with the good-for-nothings. With the religion of the leaders. Free to know why there must be so many crimes in order to sign one's name on a worthless piece of paper. Strange sensation when one feels oneself torn from the pull of the earth's gravity, when an angel takes you by the arm in order to guide you, in complete peace, to the middle of an oasis in the middle of a desert that had been invented by our ancestors, a species of blacks, alas, disappeared from the face of the earth because of their royal blood, their cleanliness, their faith in thunder and lightning.

I can still hear the cries. I jump with a start. Lose my way. Could it be the voice of Jacques, the Black-Sun, who follows me everywhere, who unstintingly offers me at every moment of weakness some counsel to keep me from slipping into madness. Yes. I can hear Jacques' voice. Charles' also. I walk along the street of Champ de Mars Square to the Bicentennial seafront promenade. A flirt — the sea. Thud of the waves. I see a woman dashing up above the hills that overlook the capitol.

Oh no. Death would be afraid of my guardian angel. It pulls away from me, abortionist of tropical tombs as I slip into my catatonic state, as the gaping wounds on the body take in the flies. I await it yet in spite of my fear, this prophetic death, similar to the Black One that gave birth to me in a pile of shit, beautiful, majestic with gloves of pineapple leaves. I want it for myself. In a dream embroidered with apocalyptic visions. Far from the gaze of a military prelate. Right in the middle of a cornfield forbidden to the bush priests whose missals contain infallible recipes capable of soothing devils with rattlesnake tails.

There was blood everywhere. In the colourlessness of the landscape which rose towards the seeming curvature of the sky, the days brought death into every family of a captured rebel. Crime was felt everywhere. Murder. Everywhere the traces of the beast left on the tongue the taste of ashes. Never will time have been so heavy in the voices of people, nor as shadowy in the look of people one crossed in the street, people that one loved. A relative, a friend, a comrade. The mad hours of July slipped away in laments.

In Jérémie, the monster's brigades cut down mulatto families . . . Villedouin. Bajeux. Sansaric. In Cap Haitien the wipeout was pursued against the high school students who had rebelled against the barbarism of a local magistrate.

Nothing could stop the machines of the monster. They roared through everywhere. Even in the churches. At Saint Anne's, two members of the opposition were slaughtered as communion was being celebrated. In the cathedral the faithful were eviscerated with bayonets. At the Church of the Sacred Heart of Turgeau a young man was cut down as he distributed the parish news bulletin to the faithful. Nobody, not anyone, was safe from the fury of the monster, the madness of the monster, not even his own doctor who he made crawl on his knees in his office and lick the dust from his carpet, and yelp in the presence of ministers who were pissing in their pants, not even the brother-in-law of his wife was safe, that Lucien Daumec whom he stabbed himself while, from the other side of the palace torture chamber the head of Félix Magloire was ripped off, not even the handsome palace officer, his quartermaster, whose legs were mutilated because he dragged his girlfriends into the bordellos of the capitol. It smelled bad. It stank. Wherever one was after an outing of one of the President's brigades.

Of all the people known no one could live with the traces of the monster on his face. The shame. The weakness. The impotence that makes you paralysed. It was necessary to strike in order to avoid a collective suicide. We were at ground zero.

The day promises to be bloody. The sun is rising with more difficulty. In front of the gate of the high school, I await the word from the Organization.

The night was long. I was moaning and groaning late into the night from stomach pains. There was something within me that was making me increasingly tense, a kind of voice that makes you aware of the imminence of danger. Of the proximity of a precipice. Fear gripped me to such an extent that morning that one would have said that I had just fallen from a cloud.

And for good reason. We had left each other last night. Harassed. Worn out. We were wringing our hands in despair. Gérard Michel had lost his life-of-the-party attitude the same as Lucien Rateau. We thought we had glimpsed a suspicious silhouette in front of the house of the coordinator of the movement. To the point that the contacts have been interrupted. Yet an emergency meeting was necessary in order to take stock of the situation. We had failed in our attempt to attack the monster.

Twenty cases of Molotov cocktails distributed to the militants, from the four corners of the capitol. In Gérard Michel's little truck which transported the precious gift. The comrades were crazy with joy. They were saying, yes, yes, the end of the monster is approaching. Fire would break out first in the popular zones. Thousands of hovels would be levelled by the flames. Thousands of zombies forced to take to the streets. Machine guns would be unable to stop the flow of the homeless. At the same time the Turgeau neighbourhood would go up in flames where two kilometres from the house of the son-in-law of the monster, Pierre Déjean would settle accounts with the palace chief of staff, Monsieur Jean-Baptiste, as well as with one of the most corrupt of dishonorable soldiers, Colonel Jacques Laroche. It would be almost impossible to counter the attack by the Organization. The monster's brigades have impounded the water trucks of the city.

Gérard Michel's little truck was on the move until very late into the night. Surprise attack at the appointed hour. Alas. The fatality of destiny was accompanying us. Not one single device exploded. In the gas stations, on the rooftops of schools, the shacks of Bel-Air, Saint-Martin. In the guardhouse of the entrance to Saint-Joseph, of the entrance to Léogane, to Carrefour. Under the benches of the police headquarters, even in the guard hall of the National Palace.

Well, it's true. One must tip one's hat to the power of public rumour. The monster, volatile, inaccessible, invincible. The monster, a heart of bronze, a head of bullets. In his bunker. Nothing escapes the mediums. It smells of conspiracy, whichever way one shuffles it. Four invasions, an attempted kidnapping of his bastard, eight armed confrontations with his valets, explosion of a few bombs in the Vallières market, blockade of the capital, without counting the clandestine radio broadcast, *Vonvon*, which harasses him, hunts him, which makes his life difficult by giving a detailed report of his activities, even his trips to the bathroom, of his daughter's orgies with handsome young men. Nothing can make him bend. It can smell everything, the spies of the monster, from the confidential report of a member of the American Congress to meetings of the opposition in the basement of an apartment in New York City. The worst is the boldness of the monster.

Once the storm passes, he recovers the facts concerning the weapons of his demons. The fly buzzing around the pig in a military uniform that swallows him up. A military hat that hides his owl face. He harangues the populace, unleashes his savage hordes which reduce the capitol to pulp.

Jacquelin Métellus foresaw our defeat. The awaited arms were not delivered. Already we were provoking the monster by occupying the runway of the army air force. Four long hours in the thick of the night. A few metres away from a guard. Holding our breath. Bodies exposed to mosquito bites.

Towards six in the morning, an airplane actually landed. The weapons, the pilot told us, would be in a small boat in the port of Saint-Marc. It would push off before eight in the morning. We were continuing to provoke the monster by doubling his police on a rut-filled road, by outwitting the vigilance of the brigades who were setting up barriers at the entrance of every village.

There we were at the rendezvous point. Ahead of time. Under the inquisitorial eye of a corporal. I took my courage in both hands. No, said the corporal. No vessel had dropped anchor. The gods were against us. They had set us up. The accursed bastards. The Miami spies who had, however, placed at the disposal of our militants a landing strip, who had introduced them at the White House to the great enemy of the monster, who had even brought into the plan a mafioso arms dealer. The entire structure was crumbling. After months of consultations. Of negotiations. Of recruitment. We had ended up founding the National Union. To hell with the twilights, the black nationalists, the Africanists. On the liberal right, Biamby, Villedouin, Michel. On the left, Ben, Alfred, Métellus, Guilène. We shall overcome the monster. We shall pursue these outlaws. We shall return afterwards to our original positions, even if it means putting all of our ideas into the same hat for the profitability of the pigsty. Defeat. We must begin again.

First, the spies. If not the precipice. Then some negotiations accompanied by ruses, tensions. We were not far from the end of the world.

The watchword did not come. I was clinging to the portal of the high school. Beside myself. In another world. Anxious to know where the remaining bit of energy can still lead us after two consecutive defeats. Where can this foolhardiness to confront the monster lead us without assuring ourselves of the solidity of our sword of justice. I was about to go inside the high school when Thimo Innocent got out of a taxi. Poundings of the heart. Devastating news. Discovered, the stash of Justin Léon. Also Colonel Villedouin is in the clutches of the monster. The resistance of Captain André Chanoine cost him a bullet in the heart. Luc Métayer dead in the jeep that he was driving to the National Palace. The neck crushed under the boots of two savages. Time is flying by. Every man for himself.

Oh no. We will not go to hell before putting him in a secure place. We have sworn it. The embassy promised it to us.

Too late. A truckload of policemen, a jeep of gunners, a 57-millimetre cannon in front of Guilène Roy's house. Cordoned off the entire neighbourhood. Searched from top to bottom all houses. Kept in custody, passersby. An actual battalion of soldiers launches an assault on the camp of an opposing garrison. Yes, a garrison. A twenty-two-year-old lady, our liaison officer, the heart of the Organization, who had gotten two revolvers for us after a foray into the chateau of a bandit, who every day traversed the capital, distributing the watchword, inspecting our information cells, spying on the monster's flunkies for firsthand information. Yes, a garrison. This young lady who went and deposited a pile of tracts on the desk of the watchman at the National Palace, who threw everything to the wind, high school, family, friends, in the name of the revolution, of this boiling rage she felt so deeply when she learned of the prostitution of her former classmates, young girls of fine families bled through the mouth by old barons of the regime, bled through the vagina by pigs who can do it to them for hours because of their filthy concoctions, harassed by the beasts who pluck them up from the streets in order to spirit them off in full sight of high-spirited young men. When she decided to identify with the people, to be the people, to speak in their name because she had lived the misery of the huts, eaten therein, shit on the floor, while not so far away was her grandfather's villa, because she was of the line of seasoned mulattoes who think black.

My heart was not beating. The first time that I saw her. Gérard Michel, however, had prepared the scene. The indispensability of a good clash of ideas which would be the prelude to a good collaboration. We emptied a few glasses of cola. I used to love the fresh bread from the bakery of Gérard's father. We scarcely looked at each other.

I really felt uncomfortable in the company of a mulatto woman who had almost the identical physical characteristics of Gladys, the girl who had turned my head at Camp Perrain, for whom I had written some romantic verses. In her pigpen, the little nigger boy. Thus, Gladys' father had decided as well as the monster's wife. Sleeping Beauty will live out her old days better in the company of the private secretary of Monsieur le Président. Guilène squarely breaks the ice.

"A disgrace for the country, for the Caribbean, these dirty blacks in power. Yes. I, indeed, say dirty blacks. I could also have said pigs, thieves, murderers, demons. I could have said blacks without honour who bring grist for the mill of white racists. The worst is that they continue to lie. The mulattoes. Always the mulattoes. Two massacres in the history of our country, isn't it enough, no."

I do not respond. Fist pressed to my lips. If she were a girl of my social group, perhaps I could understand this outing against the death squadrons. I realize in an instant the wrong done to us in attributing to Guilène's caste the responsibility for our accursed condition. That at least was the position of the monster when I had met him during his election campaign. Of all the young people present that afternoon in the living room of the manipulator candidate for the presidency, only Gérard Innocent seemed to disassociate himself from a form of racism directed towards mulattoes. Fortunately Alexis came. New light thrown upon the question. The country would free itself from its yoke only when one eliminated from the scene those characters who hid themselves behind black sentimentalism in order to perpetuate the hell on earth for blacks. I am trying to recall the first verses of "Melody of Stupidity." It goes like this:

"You are all standing there waiting for a miracle that will save you from the storm, ready to bargain a possible collaboration with the opposition. One should, it appears, pay you for the distribution of a tract. The truth is that you are the spitting image of the monster. You would do the same vile things in his place. Rather than getting a move on, you would prefer to remain the slaves of a swine. It costs nothing to steal the belongings of a mulatto. Go for it!"

Harsh words which my pride prevents me from swallowing. Of course, mulattoes are not responsible for the filth of the pigsty. Put in power the most capable, they had suggested. Of course one does not move in front of the time bomb. We cry. We console each other. Only the boys of my generation are scarcely twenty-three years old. Left to themselves. Without leaders. Without a political framework. It's already enough that they can recognize enemies. I am leaving.

Gérard Michel signals me to stop. It's at that moment that I look Guilène in the eyes. My God . . . what a beauty in a state of rage. She sends a friendly smile my way, just to let me know that she had just conquered me, that unless I was in the pay of the monster, I shall never abandon the Organization. Caught.

We separated at Dalles Avenue with the intention of meeting the next day. In Washington, where she was studying, she learned of the heartbreaks of her family. Jules, exiled to Canada. Frank, arrested for nothing. Albert, shot for nothing. With all of that, the nightmarish blow, the assassination of her grandfather, Claude Roy, liberal politician, the owner of an opposition newspaper. Under the saddle, the monster. Just barely in power. Too blatant, the deception right under the nose of the world. A racist general must have favoured the coming of the beast to power after he employed the sickest of practices, the murders of partisans of different political positions, the torching of opposing parties, massacre, on a night in June, of thirty thousand people who were taking the road towards Fort-Dimanche, where, they believed, a popular leader was incarcerated.

The fiery journalist was supposed to give the signal for the fight in spite of the first victims of his caste, in spite of the vandalizing of the presses where publications were coming out which were condemning the crimes of the regime. Claude Roy was not living, he had been harassed from all sides. Machine guns at night blew out the windowpanes of his house. Someone slit the throat of his dog, his houseboy, his housekeeper. Someone demolished his car.

Nothing could reduce him to silence. He attacked the monster on the very ground of the pet subject of his intellectuals, the question of colour prejudice, publishing dossiers which revealed the preparation of the genocide of the young people attracted by the Cuban Revolution. The entire city was begging the journalist to clear out of the pigsty, less from fear than from a lack of munitions. Of volunteer soldiers. Nothing could make him listen to reason.

Guilène decides to avenge two birds with one stone. The people, her grandfather. She joins the resistance. The opposition accumulates defeat after defeat. No way of agreeing on a platform of action. The old petty quarrels start up again. The different camps rip each other apart. People turn over to the monster adversaries they feel are becoming too powerful. The solution was inescapable. Return to the country. Track down the monster until the explosive uprising of the country.

The days went by. One evening she came upon a friend of the family. Gérard Michel, at the Paramount cinema. A vile spectacle awaited them as they exited. A soldier pistol-whipped the young Elie Lafontant whose uncle was rotting away in a dungeon at Fort-Dimanche. Not one shout of protest. The beast was devouring his prey in full sight of a crowd of zombies. It was brewing up inside Guilène: the revolt against the barbarism inside the paddywagon that took her back to Pétion-Ville. Yes. No Organization to do the clean-up that needed to be done. Quite the contrary, replied Gérard. In action for several months a group of patriotic soldiers surrounded by civilians from all tendencies, from all social categories. Grounded solidly in the capitol, the MLN represented the most formidable force in a position to conquer the monster. They will strike soon. Guilène launched into the revolution without any further ado.

We had not left each other's side for quite some time. The atmosphere was becoming more and more tense. Opponents were dropping like flies. Raymond Jean François to whom I had promised munitions even if we were working in different groups was undergoing electric shock torture in the office of Jean Tassy. Serge Alfred who used to visit me regularly was shot scarcely one hour after his arrest in Pétion-Ville at the same time as Antonio Vieux. The noose was tightening around all of the individuals, groups, cultural movements suspected of fighting in the opposition.

It almost seemed that the beast was sniffing out his adversaries from afar. Twice, in the course of the one week, the car of Lieutenant Edouard Guillot stopped in front of the high school. The man stared at me in an impertinent manner. *La pacotille* seemed a man marked for the monster's brigades. One should not be caught without cover in the capitol. Dangerous also were our rides in taxis. It would have taken very little for a captain in the pay of the monster to put the grabs on me in a little transportation van. It is suspicious for a black man to be in the company of an eighteen-carat-gold mulatto woman. A black man casually dressed. He was looking at us with contempt, as a way of signalling his disapproval to Guilène. In this pigsty of savages, mulatto women like Guilène have it made living in the posh villas of the black men in power. Have yourself covered by a comrade in the movement, such was the instruction of our group.

The more frequently I saw Guilène, the more her personality aroused in me burning questions. Go for the beauty of the revolutionary, her sharpness of mind, her ability to find sensible answers to the most complex questions of strategy. Go for her total freedom in a country where the conquest of young ladies is done at a distance, through third-party pimps. So many reasons for admiration. Even veneration.

Only, I was angry with myself for playing around Guilène a role that took me back to a time when young ladies made fun of me because of my sandals with holes in them, my socks with holes, when despite my performance in high school, I was the servant of an illiterate woman, during the time when families hid their virgin daughters so as not to expose them to the seductive magic of a *pacotille.*

Yes. My relationships with the young ladies of all categories convey a series of failures, deceptions, and repulsions against the prejudices of a pigsty which uses murder, blackmail, the degradation of a young man condemned to masturbation when he has empty pockets, because he bears a family name not approved of by the lords of the pigsty.

I reproached myself for being the lapdog of Guilène, the one who was receiving orders, without grumbling. Who was listening while drooling, was acquiescing to the slightest argument, even if he recognized its weaknesses, even if the words to contradict her roared within his mind. I strained myself so as not to say anything, in order to do nothing that might express a point of view contrary to hers. I was therefore Guilène's little creature. The little nigger who would eat his inferiority in front of the mulatto woman, the exact portrait of the spirit deep in one's guts that one must marry before placing a ring on the finger of a black woman. I was Guilène's *pacotille.* The one she tortured by using the weapon of purest camaraderie.

And so a void dwelled between us. No, an anguish. Something unseizable. Inexplicable. This kind of feeling that causes you to go from happiness to misery, from the joy of walking with someone in the rain to the sadness of not measuring up to the dreams of the person, from paradise to hell, from light to shadows. This kind of religiosity within that pushes you towards a wide-eyed admiration of the other, towards the deification of the other, to the point of losing your identity on the other side of your soul, to the point of leading you to a revulsion against yourself, against the environment that has produced you.

I used to envy Guilène. I ate, slept and drank her from the moment the sun rose until the sun set. I gave her shapes, all the forms of an inaccessible virgin, an object of a tyrannical love, of a destructive passion. I utterly consumed her, my saintly friend, my comrade for all times, with a joy always tinged with sadness. With this flame that burns you, that prepares your fall. At certain moments, I wondered if the struggle implied the total submission to the values of Guilène, to the metaphysics of Guilène, if it were necessary to bend oneself to the beatings of the heart when a gaze sought to penetrate my mysteries, my silences, my itchings, the fear of not measuring up to a personality that is fascinating. Yes. From Guilène to other fairies, the borders were widening. She smiled there when others were moping throughout the day, there where some refused a second birth through the acceptance of a common voice in tune with one's country. From Guilène to the others, the differences were growing, so much so that the slightest deviation from the behaviours that the mysterious forces dictated were upsetting me.

And so there began to stir within me a fierce struggle. Painful. Which led reason up against its contradictions. Which raised up the displeasure of an existence with infinite questions to which no one could respond. Which revealed the tragic male rather than the comrade-in-arms whose most banal gesture was to be tempered by cold logic.

Of course, the monster must be killed. The monster's lackeys. The monster's accomplices. We must destroy, yes, destroy a major part of the monster's pigsty so as to eliminate forever the cells which have produced the monster. With that, I feel free. With this theme, I feel authorized to go forward. To act, to question revolutionary ethics. I also have the right, in the area of fights, to envy Guilène, to force myself each time she drags me behind her, that I walk in her footsteps, that I implore her not to go too fast because of the ponderousness of my steps.

Just as the hand that threw two Molotov cocktails last night onto Osner Apollon's car had no gender, in the same manner Guilène evolves in the landscape of the individuals who are making history. There my desires stop short. There ends my freedom. Yes, obey the sharpest feelings for the mandate that the people have given me. The mandate to destroy in their name. Because no one has shown them any signs from heaven, because they are torpedoed, because everything is stolen from them, even the water from a well which has just barely been dug with money from the Canadians. Yes, the mandate of the people. A duty. A choice. The gratitude of recognizing oneself in the excrements in which he moves, of carrying their wounds to the limits of a dream of liberation.

Guilène in all of that. I did not receive from her any mandate to pursue her. To seduce her. To take her on the beaches of her country house. A mandate. A mandate which would make me drool in front of her body, indeed, to desire her. The delicate matter of the little black man's hang-ups. Ah, no. A matter of political ethics. No. To live freed from the disgust of having responded to the call of the demon for a pleasure pushed aside because of emotions too strong. Freed from remorse. Freed from the remorse of having asked for it because an affective void within me can find nothing else in order to be fulfilled. That is life. The real life that leads to the adoration of others because others can be gods in their own way.

I was realizing the bruises of an aborted desire. No, it is I who had created this desire the first time that I saw Guilène. It is I who had nourished it by nurturing the most outrageous dreams. And so, it's my own personal desire, not Guilène's, much less that of my comrades. I could of course deny it through other more violent desires. I could also calm it by masturbating in front of Guilène's photo, by envisioning her as the virgin who regularly used to play with my penis when I was in boarding school, when I used to play with Charles-Pierre Antoine. I could also kill it, resurrect it each time that I need Guilène as a surrogate mother, as a compensatory force after my God.

My desire brushed against Guilène's body, smelled her body. Rosy down spread on the bed. Eyes blue, still bluer when the evening was falling. Frail legs which obeyed the movement of the waves. Silken hair in which my eyes travelled in search of a porcelain cranium. A cranium which established our limits outside of politics. The obstacles of a bloody history made by beasts.

I consumed Guilène in this uninterrupted desire. I possessed her in this desire at times savage, at times refined. I held her so tightly in my exhilarated states that she let herself go on the couch under the curious gaze of her grandmother. Yes, I had changed. Happy under the pressure of the desire to take a woman. Happy that it did not erupt at the moment when I held her frail fingers in my hands. Happy, oh yes, that the flame be consumed by a return to the passion of Ruth, the Moabite, that the lust be transformed into contempt for oneself.

Satan was laughing at me. The macho types of my peer group would scold me. I held fast. It was absolutely necessary to sully the memory of the other one. It was absolutely necessary to listen to her voice every time I was confronted with my passions, that I confronted a burning desire. The other one lost somewhere on the neighbouring island. My mother. Thrown violently to the ground. In my presence. A fourteen-year-old boy. The brute dropped his pants. The room creaked. Birds took flight. Mother did not cry out. The neighbourhood was sleeping deeply. The heavy breathing of the brute burst my eardrums. My mother, however, regularly gave him food to eat. She used to wash his clothes. Sew his trousers. One evening, even, mother took him in her arms to help him drink a cup of tea. A malarial fever was ravaging him. A boy moulded by the teachings of the Scriptures. Who used to go wandering in the woods with his mother. The brute, the grandson of a highly respected pastor from town. Later on, when I started to play with the girls from church, I swore to Mother that I would not be the brute she had known.

The brute gave way to the angel in my relations with Guilène. She was doubled over with stomach pain. Her legs would no longer carry her along the road which led to her residence. Already during the meeting at Biamby's house, her face showed unusual signs. In the clouds, the comrade who made eyes at me whenever my hotheadedness excited the spirit of the fighters. The scalding critic of our strategies had asked not one question of the militants charged with the surveillance of the movements of one of the President's lackeys.

The drained face of the grandmother at the door. Not reassuring news. A suspicious presence reported Grandmother Cecilia was prowling around the house all afternoon. Too late to spend the night away from home given the state Guilène was in. She continued to twist in pain. She was moaning. Her teeth were clattering. Hot, high fever.

I was afraid. Just when I was about to leave, Guilène held me back, begging me to lie down next to her. And so I undressed Guilène. The middle-class lady. The mulatto woman. She shuddered under the touch of my trembling fingers just like the virgin on the bed of her handsome knight. And then I could feel rising in me the heat of the beast I had fought against so hard through my prayers, the memory of the rape of my mother, the sufferings of my sister Ruth. I was drooling at the sight of a body that I had not even hoped to touch in my life, a body I was devouring, that I was finally going to possess. Yes, possess a creature that I was touching, that I used to approach only in dreams, in thoughts that led to sweet sleep when I had arrived in the capitol, when I used to observe Guilène's world moving according to the rhythm of an unfinished poem. I was going to have all to myself the feverish body of a virgin, not the virgin from on high. The great unknown one. The unnameable. No. A virgin who has my blood, my pains, my chains. Because the colonel was violating her, was spitting on her modesty. Because the colonel was whipping her for the slightest sullenness. For she had no identity on a plantation where she saw lynched the black man with whom she would have loved to dance, to wander, to enjoy the poetry of the wilds. My turn to be the only master of Guilène.

I was going to take her. Yes, really take her. Leave nothing for the mulattoes of her caste. What a victory over a society that had thrown my mother into the filth. I would shout this victory from the rooftops of the four corners of the capitol. I would invite my friends to savour it with me. François Latour, Max Toussaint, Alexandre Abélard, Edouard McGuffie. Yes, what a triumph. It will also be a victory for the people. Dirty negroes segregated by dirty mulattoes. Who make it known to the civilized world that a negro cannot straddle the belly of a mulatto woman. I have done it. So the panties, in the back pocket of my pants. For an entire month if necessary. As proof of my prowess, of my heroism, of the exploit of a lone little negro man who has succeeded in eating the ass of a mulatto woman.

Something just was not happening. I could not separate my desire from morality. I was expecting from Guilène at least some violent gestures, some kicks, a fierce resistance to the urge to jump on her in order to satisfy my madness. My filthiness. I expected from her an anger that would lead her to address me with the insults used constantly by the illiterate mulattoes of her caste. From dirty nigger to opportunist, from opportunist to son of a whore. And then I would fall upon her with the same violence as the brute upon the belly of my mother. With the same violence as the beasts upon the bellies of the young girls taken off in broad daylight in the streets of the capitol. With the same cynicism of those black men who ravage the black woman every time she falls under their claws.

Of course. If she had even looked at me with contempt, if there had been on her face the slightest sign that would have proven her feeling of superiority over a negro, I would have found a justification for my madness. For my aggression. No. Guilène's smile. The mysterious smile of Guilène. Perhaps the solemn request for pity. No. Too proud to ask for pardon. Too courageous to bend to the languages of a desire that she had not ordered. She would have preferred death to submission.

Such confidence. Absolute confidence. The kind that speaks to the angel, not to the beast, which makes you hear the voice of your God in all of its splendour. The kind that places the Organization above all else, which gives you the hope of finding again one day some part of your beloved outside of the circuits of a destructive passion. The obedience of a child. And then, it started to flow, to flow, with such an intensity that I was trembling with fear. Blood.

Which freed me immediately from the weight on my conscience. A kind of repulsion inherited from the anger of my uncle when the daughters of his mistresses were in the room bent over in menstrual pain, when they were washing their blood stained linens in the bucket in which water was transported. Guilène was shaking her head, ran her frail hands across her face. Relieved. Happy to have relived with me the mystery of which only her mother had been a witness. The blood that was going. The blood that was coming. Where I was reading the power of Guilène. The fertility. The engendering of new lives. God be praised. I would have conjured away my revolutionary morality if I had sullied Guilène's body. A body which first of all belonged to her people. In all that it contained of fervor, of courage, of electricity. That was it. She was going to love me. For real. More than a comrade in arms, I was becoming her double. Her accomplice.

# Paul Tiyambe Zeleza

## *Foggy Seasons*

The fog was so thick that one could almost touch it, squeeze it, and break it. Shanisa drove slowly and carefully, for it was also snowing and the road was slippery. As she exited from the highway she suddenly saw the taillights of a car in front of her. Her foot hit the brake, and as the car swerved towards the ramp, her clammy and cold hands tightly gripped the steering wheel. Then the car started spinning and she almost lost control. She froze with terror.

It felt like the time she was eight on the plane from Kenya. The plane soared into the blue skies like a giant bird, and for a while it glided smoothly and effortlessly until it stumbled into the thick, swirling clouds, which bounced it up and down, like a yo-yo. Her heart leaped and sank and everyone cried and screamed from their sick stomachs, so that nobody could make out what the captain was trying to say. Shanisa clutched tightly to her doll and her father put his big, wet hands around her, muttering something to himself. But the plane did cut through the thundering clouds and after what seemed like an eternity they arrived in Toronto. It was a hot, humid day, in fact, hotter than any day she could ever remember back home. She was confused: where was the snow? Where was that cold that could pierce the skin and crack the bones and freeze the heart? Where were all those people wrapped in thick, furry Eskimo coats, hurrying from the cold and from each other? Instead, there they were, scantily dressed in shorts and T-shirts, relaxed, milling around and talking loudly. Her elder brother Mamba said this was summer; the cold she had heard about would come in winter. Yes, it was truly cold, colder than their July when they wore woollen sweaters and huddled around the electric heater in the evening instead of going outside to play in the moonlight.

When the car came to a halt, Shanisa leaned forward and her shaking arms hugged the steering wheel. Lifting her head, she looked around and sighed, relieved that she had escaped so narrowly. She drove home even more slowly than before and when she arrived she got out of the car in a state of agitated nervousness. Foggy seasons scared her. That's when all the terrible things seemed to happen.

This was supposed to be a happy evening: she had planned to treat herself to some wine beside a warm fire, while listening to her favourite singers, Lionel Ritchie and Anita Baker, celebrating her success in closing two housing deals on the same day. This was a remarkable achievement by any standard, especially given the depressed state of the housing market. But now all she wanted to do was to go to bed and forget her close shave with fate.

Walking up the stairs, she saw something protruding out of the mounds of snow covering the flower bed. Upon closer inspection it looked like Jessica's doll, Sheba. She must have fallen from Jessica's window. Her smooth, plump face was smothered by snow and crushed petals and her weathered body was pierced by the thorns of the rose-bushes. Lifting the doll up, Shanisa looked up to Jessica's window and rocked Sheba gently.

Hardly had Shanisa opened the door when Jessica and Peter rushed down the stairs to welcome her.

"Mummy! Mummy!" they cried, jumping up and down.

"Careful now, careful," she smiled as she put down her briefcase and the bottle of wine she was carrying. She hugged and kissed them.

"Jessica, here is Sheba. I found her by the flowers." Jessica flinched momentarily and almost grabbed Sheba from her mother before running upstairs to her room. Shanisa stared at her, shaking her head slightly.

"And you," she turned to Peter, fondling his hair — "how was your day in school?"

"Fine," he replied.

"How come it is always fine? Is that all you can say? What's that scratch on your face?"

"Nothing."

"You didn't get into a fight again at school, did you?"

"No, Mum, I fell." He made for the stairs, afraid of the stern look on his mother's face.

"Have you done your homework?"

"Yes, Mum," he mumbled.

"Yes, he did his homework." Lauren, the babysitter, came to Peter's rescue.

"Thanks, Lauren," Shanisa said as she hung up her coat. "You don't have to come tomorrow, for I'll be home early. So see you on Friday. Please drive carefully. I almost had an accident."

"Oh, no! What happened? Are you all right?" Shanisa found Lauren's concern touching and smiled. She was a fine, trustworthy kid, despite coming from such a troubled family; her father was an alcoholic and she lived with her mother in a home for battered women. She planned to go to community college to study nursing.

"I'm fine. It was no big deal," Shanisa said as she took Lauren's coat from the closet.

After supper she got the children ready for bed. Then she cleaned the dinner dishes and put the dirty laundry into the washer. On her way up to her room she found Sheba again, crumpled at the bottom of the stairs by the shoe rack. Sighing with irritation, she picked her up and made for Jessica's room, but then decided against it. What was wrong with Jessica?

At that moment she felt like pouring herself a stiff drink, to forget the worries about her children, her loneliness, and the accident that evening. What would have happened to the children? The thought of George taking over their upbringing so terrified her that the idea of having a drink quickly petered out. Well, there would be other days to drink, to celebrate, and maybe someone to celebrate with. Perhaps she could celebrate the day her divorce from George became final. Yes, that would be something worth celebrating, for it would be a moment to put behind her all that pain, the lies, the fears, the memories, the waiting, and change her life and reinvent herself. Lord, who could believe that there were only two weeks to go!

It had started so well. They were so much in love that they ignored the objections of some of their friends and relations. Shanisa and George met at university. He read law while she studied sociology. They were introduced through a mutual friend, a student from Nigeria. George liked hanging around with foreign students and going to the African and Caribbean parties on campus. He was intelligent, easygoing, humorous and fun to be with. Shanisa liked him but did not take him too seriously until the night he kissed her as they came from a dance. One thing led to another, and before either of them had time to catch their breath and think of the implications of their relationship, they were going steady.

They got engaged when they were in their final year. Shanisa's mother wished her happiness and only asked her to be sure that she loved him and that he also loved her. But Mamba hit the roof. What, marry a white boy, couldn't she get herself some decent brother? It was George, not a "brother," who had asked her, she had replied, and lest he forgot, his own grandfather on their father's side was a *mzungu*, white, like George.

It was a lovely little wedding. They moved to George's hometown, and in fact lived with his parents for a while. It was a handsome little city, set amidst meandering rivers and small lakes and an undulating landscape, and immensely proud of its quaint Victorian architecture, narrow streets and sleepy tranquillity. The old families jealously guarded their ancient intimacies and pretensions and resented the intrusions of new neighbourhoods, residents and highways. When she first arrived with her husband the older people would stare at them as if they were an exotic display at the city zoo and little children would look in eternal wonderment. But nobody ever said anything offensive to them within earshot, except the odd car driver screaming an obscenity or two before disappearing from sight. It was all so polite, so cold, this silence that greeted their visibility.

Shanisa found George's family complicated to deal with. His father seemed to like her, but she wasn't quite sure of his mother. She was friendly all right, but never too intimate, always keeping a discreet distance, and she could be a little bit patronizing. Shanisa liked cooking and tried to be useful around the house, but her mother-in-law would usually find something to complain about. Ever so gently she would say, "Dear, don't you think the food is a little too spicy for our unseasoned palates," or, "Dear, don't you think that your dress reveals a little too much of your wonderful legs." Before Shanisa could reply she would walk off, calling her husband or George.

Shanisa told George about this but he said she was misreading his mother. "She doesn't mean any harm. She has always been picky. In fact, I think she kind of likes you."

"Kind of likes me? Really?"

"Don't get sarcastic now. Yes she does, I know her. She never liked any of my previous girlfriends. If you have anybody to complain about, it should be my father. He is a pain in the you know where."

"I am your wife, not your girlfriend, so she needs to show me more respect. As for your father, I have nothing to complain about him. He has always been nice to me."

When she became pregnant she insisted on moving out. George reluctantly agreed, but his mother was not too amused.

"Are you going to let her run your life?" she berated him. "I thought you were more intelligent than that. Do you know what she does with the money you give her? She sends it to her people in Africa. I saw her do it. You ought to be careful."

"Mother, it's my wife you are talking about. She is not like that."

"What makes you so sure?" At that moment Shanisa entered the room, but she pretended not to have heard anything. George and his mother smiled nervously, commenting on how big she looked and joked that she was probably carrying twins.

They moved to a nice small bungalow. For a while, things seemed to return to the good old university days. She slowly got used to the city, and like a creeper it grew on her, enveloping her in its shallowness. When Peter was born she was always amused by the women in the shopping malls who would stoop to the baby in the stroller and comment on how cute he was. Some would even try to touch him, feel his swarthy skin and soft curly hair. Through Peter and later Jessica she came to know some of her neighbours, and when they started school she met more people. Occasionally the children would bring friends from school to sleep over, but George never allowed them to sleep out.

However, she had nobody she could regard as an intimate friend, and George gradually became engrossed in his career, especially after he left his father's firm following a bitter dispute. He joined a rival firm and started working longer hours, so that she and the children hardly saw him, even on weekends. When the children started school, she found it hard staying home alone, for George did not want her to work. He wanted the children brought up properly, he said. It was so difficult to get good child care, he insisted. In any case, children should be brought up by their mother as he had. Besides, he made enough money for both of them.

This worked for a while. Shanisa was the dutiful wife,

who diligently looked after the children and did housework during the day, prepared elaborate dishes for supper, and warmed the bed for the increasingly infrequent nights of passion. George tried hard to fulfil his role as a good provider and bought whatever she or the children asked for. It was easy to ask for the big things, but not for the small personal items. And the car, a BMW, was also out of bounds. So Shanisa hardly went anywhere, except when he took her out, for she didn't like taking the city buses.

The strain became intolerable and she insisted on getting a job. Whenever she raised the subject he would scream that he was breaking his ass so that she and the children could have a proper comfortable life. When she reminded him that she had never intended becoming a permanent housewife, he would storm out and sulk at her for the next few days. So tense did the situation in the house become that the children were afraid of saying anything to either of them that might be upsetting and provide them with an excuse to fly into one another.

One day, she warned him that if he did not mend his ways, she would leave. He dared her to. She herself didn't think she could actually do it. She had neither money nor friends to turn to. She hadn't kept in touch with her friends in Toronto, and she couldn't go to Mamba and give him the satisfaction of saying "I told you so." She was advised by one of her friends, Lauren's mother, whose marriage had just broken down, to join her at the shelter for battered and homeless women. She went there and filed for divorce. George was shocked and tried all he could to win her back. But she refused.

She applied for every job she could find. But she was either too qualified or not qualified enough, or lacked the required work experience. After many months of fruitless searching she decided to enrol in a real estate agent's course at the local community college. After she finished she joined a real estate firm. It took several weeks before she sold her first home.

It was now two years since she had left George. The divorce proceedings had taken longer than she had originally anticipated. But they tried to be cordial to each other when he came to collect the kids every second weekend. She heard from the children that he lived with another woman. She herself had gone out with several men, but she found none of them sufficiently interesting for a serious relationship. The really good ones seemed to be either married or gay.

"Mum! Mum! Aren't you coming to read us a story?" she heard the children shouting for her. She rose from the stairs, looking at her watch and rubbing her eyes.

"Were you sleeping?" Jessica asked.

"No, I'm a little tired, that's all." she said, trying hard to suppress a yawn.

"You don't have to read a story for me," Peter said sympathetically. "I can do it myself."

"You don't know how to read properly," Jessica said mockingly.

"Yes, I do too!"

"No, you don't!" They started throwing pillows at each other.

"Stop it!" Shanisa screamed. She felt like grabbing and giving each one of them a good smacking. Peter ran to his bedroom, leaving behind a frightened and crying Jessica.

"Stop your crying or I'll give you something to really cry for." Jessica could see her mother was not joking, so she quietened down and covered her face with the blanket.

"Pull off the blanket from you face," she demanded. Then lowering her voice as she sat on the edge of the bed, she said, "Which story do you want read?"

"'Hanzel and Gretel', from the part where the children meet the old witch in the forest."

"Why that's not the way to read a story."

"That's the part I like," Jessica insisted.

"You can't read only the part you like and leave the rest. It's one story, the exciting part and the boring parts."

But she relented. Shanisa always watched with fascination the concentration on Jessica's face when she read her one of her favourite stories, how her dreamy eyes moved and disappeared to the strange and enchanting worlds of the imagination. But when she finished Jessica did not smile as she normally did.

"What's the matter?"

"Nothing, I want to go to sleep now."

"There is something wrong, isn't there? Why did you throw Sheba away, first out of the window, then this evening you left her beside the shoe rack downstairs?"

"I didn't do it," she said defensively.

"You know that doll means a lot to me? My father bought it for me when I was almost your age, and I gave it to you because I love you." Jessica cringed when she saw her mother raise her arms, but Shanisa simply wanted to hug her.

"It's all right, you can tell me. What's the matter? Did you take her to school today as the teacher asked you to?" She felt Jessica's body tremble for a moment, and then she started whimpering as if she were about to cry. Shanisa held her in her arms and stroked her back until she fell asleep.

When she returned to her bedroom, Shanisa no longer felt sleepy. She tried to read a book, but she lacked concentration. The TV was no better; there didn't seem to be much to choose among the glib newscasts, tired sitcom repeats, mindless games, trashy dramas, violent films, sleazy talk shows, and World Vision infomercials about starving people in the Third World. So she just lay on her back, staring at the shadows of the bedside lamp projected onto the ceiling, wondering about the clients she would meet the following day. They usually fell into three categories. There were the anxious older couples whose children had grown up who wanted to sell their big houses to move into smaller dwellings. Then there were the hard-nosed middle-aged couples seeking to move from smaller to bigger homes. The last group consisted of the overly excited first-time home buyers. All her clients always seemed surprised when they met her for the first time. Some were of course more adept at hiding their surprise than others. But almost everyone asked her where she came from. When she told them that she had grown up in

Toronto they wanted to know her country of origin. And they also sometimes wanted to know what had attracted her to come and live in such a small city.

Once she was pleasantly surprised to see her father-in-law at the office premises.

"George never told me you worked here, otherwise I would have hired you as my real estate agent," he chuckled.

"You're not selling the house, I hope," she said jocularly.

"Oh, no, you know Gretchen would never forgive me for that," he winked conspiratorially. "We need bigger premises for my firm." Then he became serious and asked about the children. He was obviously fond of them. Despite their differences, which both of them tended to exaggerate, Shanisa found George and his father were also very much alike, especially when it came to their wives. George's father worked and his wife had always stayed at home.

That was the last time Shanisa talked to her father-in-lay, for he died a few weeks later of a heart attack. At the funeral she saw George with his new wife and baby. His mother, with whom she exchanged a polite conversation, seemed to have aged several years since Shanisa last saw her a year before. She was clearly devastated by her husband's death. They had migrated as newlyweds from Germany during the Second World War. They hardly talked to their children about why they left. In that, they were like Shanisa's parents who never fully explained to the children why they left their home country.

All Shanisa could remember is that one night, when

she was a little girl, someone came to pick them up in a truck and they drove until the next day when they found themselves in another country where the people spoke a strange language. Their father simply said that they had to leave because their lives were in danger. Shanisa cried for the clothes she had left behind, her friends, and the spacious house with its large backyard full of mango, pawpaw, guava and peach trees, and the sandbox and the swing set where the neighbourhood children gathered to play.

Several months later they took a plane bound for Canada. Before they left their parents told them that Canada was very far away, and it was a cold country full of *wazungu*. There were indeed *wazungu* everywhere, in the buses, the streets, the shops, and in the apartment building in which they lived. But there were also a lot of people from Africa, Asia and the Caribbean. Shanisa heard of countries she had never heard of before. It looked like the whole world was there, every shade of colour, every religion, every accent imaginable.

The children stayed in all day. They only went out when their mother went to the shops. They would stand by the window for hours watching other kids play on the grounds below. After a while they got to know a few people in the building. In the meantime, their father continued looking for a job. He first tried gas service stations, for back home he used to own several, but to no avail. The fruitless search for a job began taking its toll on his spirits. He became more distant, looked older, and one day even talked of returning home.

"Don't be silly. How can you even contemplate going back after what they did to us?" his wife said. The walls were so thin that the children could hear everything, as well as the squeaking beds and the groans and the screams and the music and the laughter of cheap television jokes from the neighbouring apartments.

"But there is not future for us here," he protested. "There is not future for these children."

"Is there a future for you back home? Didn't they say they were taking over your businesses because you were a colonialist who had built his business by exploiting the local people and that you mother was a prostitute?"

"Stop it! Please, that's enough, stop it. The children will hear you."

"It seems you need to be reminded of why we left in the first place. You seem to have forgotten what I went through. You may have lost your businesses, but I lost something far more personal, my dignity."

"Let's sleep. I am tired," he said, sounding very much like a broken man.

The next day Shanisa and Mamba acted as if they hadn't heard anything, and their parents acted as if they hadn't had a fight.

A few days later, on a bright, crisp morning, Shanisa and Mamba started school. They were so excited, so apprehensive. They were dressed in their best Sunday clothes. At home they used to wear school uniforms. It did not look like the school at home, for it was enclosed like a barn and the classrooms, the library, the teacher's offices and the gym were all located inside. There was a small playground outside with swings, slides, monkey bars and a sandbox.

"Work hard. Don't let anybody intimidate you," their father said as they went to the principal's office.

"If there is any trouble, don't hesitate to call me," their mother added. Shanisa clung to her skirt and begged her mother to stay with her.

"Now, behave yourself. You're not a baby," she said sternly, and hugged her. "You'll be all right."

The principal was an elderly and large woman, with a freckled face, red hair, and watery blue eyes. Her voice was gruff like a man's. She bent down and held Shanisa's hand, asking what her name was. Shanisa mumbled.

"Could you speak just a little louder?" The principal tenderly patted her on the head. Shanisa looked down and sucked her thumb.

"Shanisa," she said.

"That's a nice name," the principal smiled. Shanisa liked her instantly.

But she hated the rest of the day. The teacher of her class was much younger than the principal. She was probably Shanisa's mother's age. Her name was Mrs. Henderson. She read out the attendance. When she came to Shanisa's name she had difficulty pronouncing it.

"Sha . . . Sha . . . Sha what?" she stammered. The other kids giggled and some made faces at Shanisa as Mrs. Henderson walked towards her. Shanisa's eyes started to water. She briefly looked up to the teacher. Mrs. Henderson had long dark hair down to her shoulders and a face that had the shape and paleness of a peeled half-ripe pawpaw. She stood beside a shivering Shanisa.

"Look at me when I am talking to you," the teacher said. Shanisa's body stiffened and she slowly lifted her head.

"How do you pronounce your name?"

Shanisa looked down.

"Do you speak English?" Everybody laughed. "Be quiet class!"

"Please, can you pronounce your name." Mrs. Henderson repeated irritably.

"Shanisa," she whispered.

"Sha what? You had better speak up," Mrs. Henderson scowled.

"Sha . . . Sha . . . ni . . . sa!"

"Would you mind if I called you Shany?" she said as she tried to smile. But she didn't wait for Shanisa's bewildered response. And so she became "Shany" to Mrs. Henderson, which some naughty kids soon converted to "Shiny." Shanisa hated that name. For this reason she later adopted the name Shelly, which she used until she went to university.

At recess she told Mamba that she wanted to go home. He, too, hated this school.

"What language are you people speaking?" some kids asked them, scornfully.

"None of your business," Mamba said.

"Blackie, blackie, blackie," they chanted. And one whispered loudly, "niggers!"

"Leave us alone!" Shanisa cried, and hugged her brother. Mamba felt like kicking them.

"Just ignore them," a girl named Christine said. "Would you like to come and play on the monkey bars with me?" Shanisa looked at her, then at her brother, who nodded. Smiling faintly she said, "All right."

"You like them? You are disgusting," one of the kids who had been teasing Shanisa and Mamba said to Christine.

"Oh, be quiet, you mindless, mean twits," Christine said as she ran to the playground, pulling Shanisa behind her.

When their parents came to pick them up Shanisa and Mamba were both deeply distressed. They didn't want to come back to this school, they said. Why had they left Kenya, their old school and their friends?

"What is a nigger?" Shanisa asked her mother later that evening.

"It's a term of abuse against people like us," she explained.

"Is it like coloured, half-caste, or point five? That's what they used to call Daddy at home."

"No, it's different. Here your father is black, like me," her mother said, touching her braids. "Don't you ever use that word. If anybody calls you that report it to the teacher, do you hear?"

Shanisa hated the school, indeed, she hated everything about her new surroundings, including herself. She hated being called black, for she was brown. Back home they used to say she was brown. And it made no sense to her why the *wazungu* called themselves white when they were pinkish. Back home they were simply called *wazungu* or Europeans. She would stand in front of the mirror, close her eyes, praying that when she opened them she would be lighter, with a more pointed nose, more like her father's. Why had he married her mother? Why had his father married his mother? If none of them had made that mistake then she would have been all right, the kids in school would not be teasing her, she would not be wearing those dumb braids, which made her look ugly, ugly and damned. Didn't her first mid-term school report say she was a slow learner? At home people used to say she was clever.

Each day she had to be forced to go to school. They poked fun at her accent, so she was afraid to speak. And she and Mamba were always being asked foolish questions: Is it true people in Africa walk naked or wear grass skirts? How come they didn't have tribal marks on their faces and bones in their noses? How did people sleep in trees? Why did they eat each other? Could they show them a tribal dance? One day Mamba got into a fight with a boy who told him, "Nigger go home." He was called to the principal's office.

"In this school and in this country we don't settle disputes through violence," he was reprimanded. The other boy was told not to use such words again.

When his father learned of the fight he was furious with Mamba. "I don't want to hear that you have been involved in fights again. Is that clear?"

"It is not my fault. I am always being provoked," Mamba insisted.

"It doesn't matter. Violence doesn't solve anything, it never has and it never will. Just ignore them. They forget that their parents or forebears were once immigrants, too just like us."

It was not until almost a year after their arrival that their father found a job. He was so excited. He was going to be a security guard. His wife didn't look too impressed, but she tried hard not to spoil the mood,so she said little. She made a special dinner that evening and it all felt like they were back home.

Their father had so many plans. Getting a job seemed to have restored his self-confidence, given him a new zest for life. He told them that he would continue looking for a better job, until he saved enough to start his own business. Their mother was soon caught up in the excitement and she announced that she would go back to college and get a new teaching certificate in order to resume her teaching career. It felt like a party. Mamba put on rumba music, and his father asked his mother for a dance. She acted bashful for a moment.

"Come on, Mother!" the children cheered. Their father stood in front of her and bowed.

"Lady, may I have this dance?"

"Yes, you may." She rose, laughing her prolonged, hearty laughter, which they hadn't heard in a long time. They clapped and applauded as their parents danced. Their father was whistling as if he were playing a flute.

"Join us, come on," he beckoned them. They did and danced like they were dancing in the moonlight back home.

That was the last time they were so happy together. Their father died a moth later. It was a foggy night. He left home at three for a four-to-midnight shift. Nobody ever found out exactly how he died, except that his body was found in a pool of blood by the gate of the premises he guarded, his head bludgeoned almost beyond recognition. The premises had been broken into. The next day his gruesome picture appeared on the inside pages of the papers as an inconsequential statistic of Toronto's homicide rate.

Beside his body, the police had found a packet containing a doll. That morning he had promised Shanisa a doll. He was getting his first paycheque.

It was the most distressful time for the family. They hardly knew anybody, but to their pleasant surprise some of their neighbours and the people from the church offered help. It was a respectable funeral.

Shanisa didn't like her new doll, so she hid it in the closet, preferring to play with Melissa, the doll she had brought from Kenya, which since her arrival in Canada had gradually acquired a new significance, representing the person she prayed of becoming to the Almighty Creator every night before going to bed: a little girl with big blue eyes, a straight little nose, long blonde hair and a tiny waist, who would be loved by everyone.

"Why don't you play with Sheba, the doll your father bought for you?"

"I hate it!" Shanisa said.

"How can you say that? It looks like you."

"I don't want it to look like me," she cried. Her mother didn't insist. But one day Melissa disappeared. She suspected her mother and never forgave her for that.

It was not until she was much older and her father receded into a faint memory that she brought Sheba out of the closet. She would pick her up whenever she felt low, caress and rock her like a baby, kissing the smile radiating on her plump, dark face, gently squeezing her dimpled cheeks and searching her big, soft brown eyes for the face of her father, as she whispered how she loved him dearly and missed him terribly.

In the years that followed her father's death things were difficult, but they gradually rebuilt their lives. Shanisa's mother abandoned plans to go to a teachers' college and found a job as a salesperson in a shopping mall. They moved to a larger apartment. Mamba finished his Grade thirteen and found a job as a construction worker. Things turned sour when Shanisa's mother got herself a boyfriend called Rick at her workplace. The children did not like him. For one thing, he was much younger than she was, and divorced, too. Matters got really bad when she mentioned the possibility of marriage. To her shock, one day she found Rick trying to make a pass at Shanisa. She broke off the relationship, but she and her daughter gradually drifted apart. When Shanisa entered university, her mother decided to return home, saying there was nothing more for her to do here, that she didn't want to end up in some miserable old people's home when she got old.

It was past midnight when Shanisa was woken up by the smell of something burning and the cries of the children. Before long, the fire alarm went off and she ran to the children's rooms. None of them was there. She ran downstairs. The kitchen was quickly filling up with a dense cloud of smoke and the children were choking and crying.

"Let's get out of here." She grabbed both of them to the sitting room. She returned to the kitchen and opened the oven. And as she had suspected, there was Sheba, shrivelled and charred beyond recognition. She threw the remains into the sink, turned on the fan by the stove and opened the windows. As she stared at the doll sizzling in the water, it all came back, all those memories, the bewilderment, the anger and the infinite sadness she felt when her father died. Now what would she remember him by? And why did she think that Jessica, her little sweet Jessica, was beyond the same incomprehension, the same rage she felt when she first came to live in this frozen land of many solitudes? She had ignored all the signs, preferring to see Jessica as a mirror of her future, and not her past as well.

The children were too scared to sleep by themselves so she tucked them into her bed.

"I didn't mean to do it, Mummy," Jessica sobbed. "I'm sorry, Mummy."

"It's all right. I know you didn't mean to, it's all right.

We'll discuss it tomorrow." She rubbed Jessica's back until she stopped crying and fell asleep. Then she went downstairs to pack Sheba's remains. She put them in a box and wrapped it with a white cloth. By the time she finished, dawn was beginning to break.

# Courtnay McFarlane

## *Catharsis/ One*

Craig
was jumping/in Tracks/
capital T/D/C/Washington
carryin' on/makin' noise/being
loud
in black and white/polka-dot-
ted pantyhouse
tight white tank top/ matching
canvas Keds/the slip-on
kind

He is/was drag/fierce drag
not just disco drag/but drag-
queen drag/suburban b-boy
drag
radical drag/Afrocentic

drag/Lola Falana at Caesar's Palace drag
Angela Davis in the Panthers drag/even upwardly
  mobile/credit to his race
Black business man drag of:
Wall street blue/pin-striped suits
pale coloured shirts/rep-striped ties
Any costume/clothing
was drag

On his slight/brown frame
Craig strutted/worked his drag
not a comouflage
but for visibility/high
Wore his id/intellect/identity
like he wore two-piece suits
silk chiffon scarves
and boyfriends
A sign/A shield
that protected/yet distanced
him from brother who couldn't deal with out/outra-
  geousness
'Cause it wasn't enough to be Black and Gay
Black and Gay/and fierce/you had to have politics
politics/and a high vq/visibility quotient

Fierce BGM with high vq
was seeking same/seeking same
Craig knew power
was in voice
visibility
drag
Craig.

David
hugged me tight/against his belly
kissed wet/called me darlin'
that last labour day/
Eastern Parkway/Brooklyn
Showed me photos of his trip to Toronto
To-ran-toe/To-ran-toe/he pronounced it

No CNTowers/Caribana revellers/CastleLoma
in his snapshots
But dicks/long/short/dark/pale/black/white
Told tales of each man
reduced to penis Polaroids
for the sake of anonimity

Do you know him hon'/David would ask
thrusting a photo of a black man
long/uncircumsised/wiry pubic hair
No I didn't/wouldn't
and he would recount details
of personal history;
Oh this chile' lived in the suburbs
good god-fearing Jamaican parents
very bougie
Sexual idiosyncrasies:
he like to do it doggie style/made a lot of noise
Other details:
dark/dark eyes/almost purple black
the colour of Kalamata olives
the odd curve of the man's mouth

Remembered details
like the good journalist he is/was
from his penis Polaroids
David.

# Sylvia Hamilton

## *Listen to the Language*

They were out on the streets
"a herd," someone said.
"They've ruined it now for the
  Black C-o-m-m-u-n-i-t-y"
Another, "they were out there
  too, swinging clubs,
calling names."
"They," our boys in blue.
"They threw someone through
  a window."
And who did you say was
  arrested?

## *Shoes*

When I finally
got her attention
"Size seven and a half, please"
as I reached for the shoe.

Contempt, veiled
as laughter:
"You can't afford those!"

At that moment
I resolved to try on
every size seven and a half
in the store.

Not that I would ever buy —
only that I would try.

She needed to know
I had the right,
if I chose to
try and buy whatever
she had to show.

Very politely, "The grey pumps, please."
"The Almalfi in green."
(I hate green)
Canvas deck, why not.

When she was finally
surrounded by boxes,
her face truly red,
I left shoeless.
Only Ilmelda would not be pleased.

# Stefan Collins

## Why

On May 18, 1993, I will be celebrating my eleventh year of living with HIV. I stopped eating red meat. I stopped all my addictions of hard drugs and alcohol. I take no antiviral medications because I strongly believe that if there is to be a cure, it will come from the earth. I try to live healthily and positively. I should be ecstatic at being a long-term survivor. But why do I feel that isn't enough?

When I was first diagnosed with HIV, my doctor told me the results over the phone and said that I had three years to live. From that moment on I took control of my life. I became political. I started off from a system that was not organized, a system that did not include black gay men of black people period in the process of decision making. Yes, I have to give credit to the white gay men who fought and took it upon themselves to take control of the situation. Why have they left me out of the race. Why, eleven years later, do they continue to do so. Mind, I have seen progress that specific ethnocultural AIDS organization have taken it upon themselves to address the issues of AIDS within their own communities. I salute you, my brothers and sisters, for you have lifted my burden of no longer feeling isolated within this AIDS movement.

I chose to be visible. I chose to put a face to AIDS because, for me, silence is not a means of safety. It is death — a price too high to pay. You know there will be costs when you choose to be visible. But why do I still feel alone? After all these years of paying prices, why has it been only the sisters who have laid my head on their bosoms and comforted me. They have rocked me to sleep, wiped my tears and held me tight until I couldn't feel any more pain. They have held me through nights when I felt out of control because I didn't know what opportunistic infection might strike next. It has been the sisters who have put themselves on the front line to make my voice and the voices of those in silence heard. As well, they have jeopardized their own safety just to let me know they care and are willing to take on this struggle of crying for their own. Some of these sisters were worse off than me and had more to lose because of the dilemma society has put upon them just because they are women. Why? Is it because history tells us if it weren't for the backbone of our black sisters, the black man would not be where he is today. Talk about privilege. How come the brothers are not moving fast enough to take care of their own. Why is it they're leaving it up to the sisters to take on the role of provider. I do not see the brothers on those front lines. I keep hearing the excuses as to how racist the system is. How AIDS is a ploy that the white man is genocidally trying to wipe out of the black race. Please! Shit, you can theorize all you want, my brothers. But the point is, what the fuck are you going to do about it? And still they give me silence. They complain that there are no services that target black gay men and that somebody shuld start some up. They say, "Stefan, shit, you're out there, so why don't you do it. It's needed now."

So I start a support group for black HIV-positive men. But the reality is that no on attends meetings regularly, and when I confront them on the issue they give me every excuse imaginable why they can't attend. "Shit, I don't want to be seen or have it known I got AIDS. I got no time. This shit is just too damn political. I want something more sociable. Why then do I see these same men in the bars, cruising parks, working the steam baths, cruising washrooms, and even selling their asses. You know how it is: "I've seen you, but you haven't seen me, but I've seen you" kind of thing. These black gay men are supposed to be men who are politically astute, men you know the information of AIDS transmission. They constantly say they don't want to know of their HIV status and yet they would rather hear about someone else's 911 in detail yet. "Stefan, you work in AIDS. I hear Richard got AIDS, is it true?"

Yeah, they'd rather know about someone else's problems than deal with their own dirty laundry. I love it when they ask me about that because I usually turn it around by asking them: "Why is it that you so-called politically astute black gay men are all slowly become infected with the HIV virus?"

I don't get a response, but only silence. "Exactly what I though you would say," I tell them.

Let's face it — these men are not out! They only come out when it's convenient for them. So when do they break down these silences? Whey does AIDS become their issue — at what point do they decide it justifiable to give someone dying of AIDS their love and respect and support? Does it become easier if we are all innocent victims? Damn it, you don't need a degree to give someone some love and respect. So when do they start caring, when AIDS knocks on their doors and walks into their lives/ Well, hello, homeboys, it is already too fuckin late!

Their silences are painfully intense. My brothers, if you cannot give me any love and respect, then there is not room for you in my life. We have to break down these silences, my black gay brothers. I need you, my brothers. I need to hear your fears, your pain, your joyous. I need you to her mine. I need to feel you strength, your love, your support. I do not need your sympathy, I do not need your pity. Nor do I need your insincere words because I don't have the time for what you consider the truth. It is not enough that a lot of my support comes from gay white men. This is not acceptable. I desperately need you, my brothers, because I cannot do this alone any more. We need each other.

Why is the silence much deeper with black heterosexual men. In all the years I have been positive, I have received very little support from black heterosexual men. They have to be confronted on this issue. You have to get past their fucking homophobia first. But what does this tell me and others who are suffering in silence? I am sick of hearing their conciliatory words I'm sick of hearing excuses as to why they refuse to be involved. Even when they're challenged about taking care of their own, you're guaranteed to hear their view on homophobia, racism, sexism and classism. They can be very adamant about it if they want to be. The strange thing, though, is that you see the same men in places where they shouldn't be: the parks, washrooms, steam baths, trucks, bars and even on the stroll. The ironic thing is that these same men even occasionally fuck other men — mind you they're the tops and do everything imaginable with other men except kiss them. And yet, they insist on not being identified as gay or bisexual. Shit, I had a close straight friend tell me the other day that he picked up this man — no, excuse me, a man picked him up — and they had hot, hot sex. When I asked him if he used a condom, his reply was, "Man I'm the top and I don't do this often, and besides, AIDS is for Faggots!" You figure it out.

Why, when I'm challenging community AIDS organizations on issues of the needs of people living with

HIV/AIDS, when I challenge them on the service delivery, do they give me nothing but silences? "Stefan, you are a healthy sick person. What needs could you possibly have. You look strong, vibrant, alive!"

Those smiling faces tell nothing but lies. Or do my words fall on deaf ears? I ask myself, Where the fuck is this coming from? Are they not listening, or do they not want to hear? Hello! Anybody home? Yes, it's all well and good that I volunteer my time to speak on behalf of your organization on issues about being an open black gay man living with AIDS. When you reward me with two bus tokens, I have to challenge you on that garbage. Why don't you understand when I tell you how I struggle to pay my rent, because I have to live on a fixed income of $631 per month. When I tell you that after I pay rent, bills and for complementary and alternative therapies, and when I tell you it leaves me with barely enough money to buy food, why don't you understand me? And when I tell you that I am forced to depend on AIDS organizations and family and friends to help me get by, how do you respond? When I tell you that feeling this way makes me feel I'm losing control of my life, where is your support? And when I tell you these things and much more, you still don't hear me. You choose to stay silent. When I talk about how AIDS organizations won't hire me because they say HIV-positive people get sick and die or that I'm too confrontational, or when I hear excuses — "Your body language says you don't want the job. You lack focus." — and still these people insist on wanting my experience, my knowledge and my time.

Where is the justice in all that? I'm not saying that I'll sell out. I still strongly believe that we have to share our resources and experiences. But give me my propers — give me some fucking respect! They have to be called up on that shit because if they're too stupid to figure out that if they have to wait until I'm on my deathbed before they recognize I have needs so that I can access their services, then of what use will they be to me? Well, then it is obvious that their systems/programs do not work. I guess they're waiting for a crisis to happen. But what does this tell me? What they have fallen into believing is that misconception that AIDS victims are associated with looking decrepit and decayed. What kind of fucking messages are they putting out. "Stefan, when you speak, you know how to push buttons . . ." I tell them, "You have to take care of me too!" I guess I threaten a lot of them by being visible. In Toronto I am the only black gay man who is visible in the media and who's putting a face to AIDS. Most people of colour who are out there stay silent!

Why do people make relationships harder to maintain? Let's face it abstinence is not realistic, especially in a society that sells sex for anything and everything. It's not easy to have to make one's own decision on how and who to tell. It's the reactions, negative or positive. You are never fucking sure. I don't know how to say it — do I tell them after the fact or do I tell them before? Either way I risk losing a friendship or possible relationship. It is rejection that I am most afraid of, but I have to tell them. Humour works for me. It makes it easier for them to deal with the situation. You come to realize who really likes you and who doesn't. People stop touching you: they don't want to hold you, don't want to kiss you. Some are quite supportive, closer. Others reject you. Sex changes.

How come the family thing didn't work out? I told the ones who I thought were close to me and to my dismay they weren't. They isolated me and said, "Stay out of my life." That was a harsh reality. They weren't close to me at all. I was in Nova Scotia working on a video called "Life After Diagnosis". While I was there I decided to confront the black organizations on why they weren't dealing with AIDS. They invited me to a community meeting with them. I wanted to know why the black community wasn't dealing with the issue of AIDS. "Let the white organization deal with it. Besides it's a white gay disease."

When I questioned them about the cocaine problem in the community, they said it was just a phase. And when I stated that of the first five people who died of AIDS, four were black men. The room became earily silent, except for the odd sucking of teeth and cussing. "Aren't you so and so's boy? Didn't I change your shitty ass?" The crowd started to get restless. They felt a connection, or should I say a déjà-vu. You see, when one dies in Nova Scotia you can guarantee that someone in Vancouver will know in less than five minutes.

Immediately I started to have visions. I know I was the next hot news item.

It took me seven years to tell my mother. I was in Montreal and I spent the day in anxiety trying to figure out a way to tell my mother. I tried to con my relatives into telling her. They already knew about my status before I got to Montreal. The news was that I was on my death-bed. Anyway, none of my relatives felt that it was their place to tell my mother. I finally got up the nerve but only after I smoked a joint. The best time to tell her anything is when she is doing dishes. I finally just blurted it out. The silence was profound and seemingly endless. Finally, when she did speak, her words caught me by surprise: "I knew it. I just wish you'd change your ways."

It's a bit late for that, I thought to myself. I reassured her that I was perfectly healthy and that she shouldn't worry. I also reassured her that if she felt that she needed to ask me anything, I'd be there for her or she could talk to her sister. "I see you still eat like a pig." My family calls me Jethro from the "Beverly Hillbillies" because I have a strong passion for food. Shit, good food is like good sex.

Why do I believe that some things are best left unsaid — I live with HIV. I don't want to deal with my family because they can't deal with what I have. That's not my issue, that's their issue. Now they do not talk about it. I need to hear their fears. I need to hear their pain. I need to hear their voices. But they stay silent. When I make choices regarding my health, I feel burdened by knowing that these choices affect their lives, and still they remain silent. And in their silence they suffer a pain that they themselves must endure. The reality is that their pain is something I cannot touch, just as they cannot touch mine. As they remain silent I ask myself, "Have they bought into that stereotypical response of considering me a healthy sick person? Do they see me as not having any needs — mentally, physically or spiritually?" Therefore, is my illness, my sexuality — my very being — not justified? Their silence is silencing me!

My children took it pretty easy. They are seventeen, thirteen and nine. They have been tested and they're not positive. They are very supportive. They're very aware. So how come my youngest son has to suffer, because he has to deal with one of his classmates whose dying of AIDS. When he's sees that, he sees me. Daddy's going to die and that's the way he chooses to deal with it. How come I have to accept this in silence, because his realities preclude a closeness that I very much need. It makes me feel powerless. I hope he will come around eventually, I must suffer peacefully in my silence, until then, knowing that my reconciliation must come from him.

How come more and more each day death becomes more of a reality. It used to be that I could distance myself from peoples' deaths, but now it is the people who I have to come to love and respect that are dying. I can't distance myself any more. I'm not afraid of dying. We do that anyway. There's no choice in the matter — so why dwell on it. But I'm afraid of being alone, of dying lonely with no one in my life to share my hopes, dreams and fears. I am afraid of that pain — a pain worse than death. Loneliness. I hope that I'll never be alone because of all that I have given of myself. No matter how much I'm surrounded by other people, when push comes to shove I alone am responsible for decisions affecting my life.

Why after having to experience or deal with all these harsh realities, do I still find life valuable? I feel I want to do something for other people. I feel like giving more and sharing. I feel wanted all over again. Life is more valuable, despite HIV. I'm lucky to be still here — to live and do the things I want. Having HIV is great! It has changed my life. I have no regrets! I am very lucky go have HIV! How come I feel it is a blessing. Why do I no longer feel alone?

# Richardo Keens-Douglas

## *Moonface*

It was a beastly hot July a long time ago and the sound of laughter came drifting across the cornfield on the little bit of breeze that was in the air. It was coming from Moonface Wellington and his friends. It was Moonfaces' thirteenth birthday and his parents had thrown him a party. And everyone was having the time of their lives, as they usually do whenever Moonface was around. They were playing hopscotch, rounders, hide-and-seek, Jacks. Some children were even playing doctor under the watchful eye of the older folk from a distance. Everybody loved this little boy named Moonface. His real name was Maurice, but he had the roundest face and the biggest and brightest eyes this side of the mountain. Just like a full moon. So affectionately they called him Moonface.

Now the following year just before his fourteenth birthday Moonface started to get sick. But no one really took it on, because he was a strong boy and he always bounced back in a couple of days. But this sickness didn't seem to want to leave him this time. They tried every remedy in the book, but nothing appeared to work. They took him to the local doctor, even that seemed futile.

Then one morning like magic he got up and was as well as well can be. The sickness had disappeared just like that, and he was back with his friends doing all the things he loved to do.

But about a month later, bam, the sickness returned. This time it came back with a vengeance. He got weak, he started to lose weight, his eyes dimmed. Some days he couldn't even move. He just wasn't the old Moonface everybody knew. Eventually they brought in a specialist who discovered he had a fatal disease that there was no cure for. It was a disease that was spreading throughout the world at a rapid pace, and somehow Moonface contracted it. Well, when people heard Moonface had this illness, everybody immediately became magicians and slowly started to disappear. His best friends stopped coming out to his farm to play because their parents wouldn't allow them.

Then curiosity got the cat. They all wanted to know how he got the disease. His parents said, "It's not important how he got it. The fact remains he has it and we have to deal with it." His parents told them over and over it's not an easy disease to catch. You cannot get it from touching, or from a glass, or from caring and showing some love. His mother told them all the ways the illness is spread. Gave them all the material necessary for educating. But that wasn't enough. The people of the town wanted Moonface out of the school, out of the playground, out of the gym, out of the pool. They picketed. They stopped buying corn from Moonface's father. Their faces changed. Moonface couldn't understand it. People that he loved and played with all his life, all of a sudden, didn't want to be around him.

Then strange little things began to happen. One day the family went into the town to do some shopping and when they came out of the store the tires from their car were slashed. One night they were coming home from a little night drive and as they were approaching their farm they saw a red sky. It was the toolshed. Someone had set it alight. Thank God it wasn't close to the house and the wind wasn't high that night. The three of them just stood there and watched. They didn't even make an effort to put out the fire. They just sat on the porch and watched the shed go up in smoke. "The human race is a strange race," the mother said. And they calmly went inside and had a cup of cocoa.

Moonface became weaker and lonelier as the months went by. His parents didn't know what to do. It was the saddest farmhouse this side of the mountain.

Then one night Moonface was lying in his bed, and the way he had positioned his bed, he could see right through the window all the way up to the moon and the stars. And you could tell the moon was keeping him company that night because the beams were shining right back onto his face, lighting up the room. That became one of his favourite pastimes. Painting pictures with the stars.

Then all of a sudden that night there was a quick darkness that flashed across the moon. He jumped up and ran to the window. And what he saw, was a ball of light speeding towards the earth. It looked like a million candles rolled into one. And it just kept falling and falling until it disappeared behind the little hill across from the cornfield. Well, right away Moonface got excitedly curious. He quickly bundled up himself, put on his hat, and out the house he crept trying his level best not to wake his parents. And across the field he trotted like a tired little pony.

When he got to the top of the hill he thought he was going to faint. It was the most energy he had used all week. His head started to spin. He had to sit down. Slowly he reached for the ground, and as his bottom touched the grass he noticed a figure coming up the other side of the hill towards him, shining a light. It was a strange looking light, filled with bright magnificent colours, similar to a rainbow. As the figure got closer and closer to him, Moonface noticed that it was just a little boy the same size as him, and the beautiful light was coming not from a flashlight but from the palm of his hand.

Well Moonface was so surprised to see a little boy coming up the hill with light beaming from the palm of his hands that he didn't have time to get frightened. And in the blinking of an eye, the little boy gently lifted his hand and shone the light right into Moonface's eyes, and the next thing Moonface knew they were both sitting on top of the hill chatting and laughing, and he never remembered anything about the light shining from the boy's hand. It was quite extraordinary. It was as if they had been friends from the day they were born.

Moonface asked him what he was doing out in the fields at this time of the night, and if he had seen a ball of fire falling from the sky. The little boy said he didn't see the ball of fire, and that he was a new neighbour. They sat on that hill and the little boy asked about a thousand questions and Moonface answered about a thousand and one. Time just seemed to stand still for a little while.

They planned to meet the next day at the same spot. The following morning after breakfast he was back on the hill. His parents couldn't understand the sudden strength Moonface had gotten. This went on for about two weeks. Every time he came back from playing with his new friend on the hill, he would come back stronger and happier than when he left.

Then one day he brought the little boy home to meet his parents. The parents were happy because the change in Moonface was because of his new friend. But they found it quite strange that every time they asked him where he lived, he would casually lift his fingers to the heavens and say, "Out there." So the parents thought that that was just some modern-day young people's slang for "Don't ask me my personal business." And so the case was closed.

Then one day Moonface and his friend decided to go into the town. Something Moonface had stopped doing since the day his father's car tires were slashed. Moonface was having a great time showing his friend around the sights. Then all of a sudden, he noticed people were staring at them. He heard a familiar voice say, "He must have the same disease as little Moonface. That's why they are friends." Moonface's heart just sank. Because he had never told his friend that he was sick. And sweat started to form above his lips. His friend noticed the change and asked, "What's the matter?" Moonface looked at him and, with all the honestly in his heart, said, "Once I used to have many friends. You see, I'm gong to die. I have an illness that there is no cure for as yet. And I was afraid if I told you . . ." And before he could finish saying what he had to say, the little boy put his hand up, smiled and said, "I know you are ill." Then he put his arm around Moonfaces' shoulder and they kept on walking through the town.

After they strolled in silence for a little while, Moonface asked, "how did you know?"

"Come to the hill tonight around midnight," the little boy said, "and I will tell you."

That night when Moonface got to the top of the hill, there his friend was waiting. His friend took him down the other side of the hill and they headed through a wooded area until they came to a clearing. Then the little boy looked at Moonface and said, "Remember that night you saw the ball of fire?"

"Yes," Moonface said.

"Well that was my ship. I'm from out there."

"I knew it," Moonface shouted. "I knew it."

"I knew you knew it," said the little boy. And they started to laugh.

"You can't see it, but it's over there, hovering above the clearing."

And all of a sudden the rainbow beam started to shine from the palm of the little boy's hand, and he aimed the beam towards the space above the clearing, and very slowly, very slowly, a ship started to appear, flooded with beautiful blue lights. Then at the top of the ship a huge door began to open, as if it had all the time in the world. And like magic, a silver-green ramp just floated out of the ship and came to rest upon the ground. All by itself.

The little boy stepped onto the ramp and he said, "I must go back to my home now. Come with me." And immediately Moonface started to remember the wonderful times he used to have before people became scared of him. The time he used to swim in the streams, fish with his friends, play tag, or simply pick the corn in the field. Moonface stepped onto the ramp and started to follow his friend. Then his friend stopped and without turning he said, "But you know one thing?"

"What's that?" Moonface asked.

And very slowly his friend turned and looked at him and said, "We will never come back this way again you know. If you come with me, you will never be able to return to earth. Because when I leave this galaxy I cannot return. I came here by accident."

And Moonface just kept walking towards him. It was as if he didn't understand or hear what his friend had said. Then all of a sudden Moonface stopped, and tears began to form in his eyes, and he turned and started to head back down the ramp.

"Come with me," the little boy said. "Where I'm going no one will scorn you. Where I'm going there's a cure for what ails you."

Moonface stopped, turned around and their eyes met. "No. I can't," he said.

"Why?" asked the little boy.

"Because I have to give them a chance."

"But they don't love you because you are sick, different."

"I know," said Moonface. "But one day they will. One day they will come to understand. And they won't be frightened any more. And I also believe we will find a cure."

And his friend looked at him and smiled and said, "Ah, my little earthling, you do have faith in the human race. I'm glad you are the one I met."

And all of a sudden the ramp started to float up to the sky, and slowly descended to the ship. And just before it disappeared, Moonface shouted out, "Stop!" And the ramp stopped. Moonface ran closer to the ship. The lights powdering his face with a blue tint. "What is your name?" he shouted. "We never exchanged names."

"Where I am from they call me Moonface," said his friend.

"That's my name too!" screamed Moonface with laughter.

"I know," said the little boy.

And the ramp continued down into the ship and the door closed. With a sudden spark the ship just shot up into the sky like a million candles rolled into one. Moonface stood there for the longest while just looking up into the starry darkness. And with a smile on his face he calmly turned and went back to his home.

# charles c. smith

## *atavism*

wind moves against ocean
gulls cry beach sand swirls
i thought i would be drowned
by the waves i never could swim
and have never lost fear
of the floor below green water
its shifts or sudden
disappearance

a paradigm of living
i do not like cannot take
without thought of those
who never come back
but find their place
among the seaweed and the
  shells
somewhere under in a watery
room  provided for burial
the lost body  making its way

without light  without comfort
of a blanket  to make the flesh dry

my brother  liked the ocean
so went under  to the houses
kept neat and hidden  in green dark
my father  named me after him
at times i have his yearnings
and when cool water  rushes
at my back  i feel a gentle
undertow  sucking, sucking

## *between destinies*

there are times  i wonder what it must have been like
for you  with me inside a full six months and kicking
and him outside  lying flat and still
in a casket open for two days in a funeral parlour

other times  i think of you spending your night
looking out the bedroom window  into a sky
full of dark promises  and small lights you hoped
he would pass by  so that you could see him
as he would always be  an angel fading into space

and when they lay him  like a boxed parcel
into the gaping  sun-dried earth
you must have felt  torn as no other

between destinies  with a small heart
at work in your womb  and the gentle brown
eyes of a young boy  closed forever

semblances of your pain  must have appeared to you
and i could see you  seeing yourself with
an arm cut off  the blood bursting into a pool
or standing in a field  of fading green
as the earth opened up  below your feet
to suck you in  like a vegetable

i was always told  it took six men
to drag you  from that burial
kicking and screaming  how badly you wanted
in  while the earth fell on him like a ton

later you told me  this was something
you would never recover from  and that
your heart beats  like a barking dog
each year  on the day of his death

then you swear  there are moments when
you see him again  through me
as if he had walked  out of circumstance
into my body  so that when i stand
in front of you  you see a part of him

the earth just could not swallow

# *daydreaming about my father*

a red patch of earth  comes out
of nowhere  leads
to nothing

at its centre  a tree
stranger to such open land
where only  sky
and cloud  convene

elsewhere  patches of daisies
crocus  lilies
yellow and white heads
answerable  to whatever rains

answerable to the slow
tight circle  of birds
that have returned
to their summer  homes

i imagine you  resting
in this  place
far from  the motions
of either  of our lives

you are not  like
yourself  you are
now a quiet man  and the rose

you wear like a medal
is the signal you give me

to enter this precious kingdom

and i do and you speak
and i hear within this silence
how you like a sad boy have grown
away from your past

the black filing cabinets endless
telephone calls and clients clients clients
dragging you down
into the grave you did
not regret

i imagine you now
as you would likely see me
a man with an open
wound the size of a fist
inexplicably held to a position
despite the cap and gown
of accumulated years of intelligence

the only difference is i move
out of the footprints you made
long ago more knowledgeable
of the place you now occupy

and this  you must realize
is my growth  through years
of understanding  you
who could never comprehend
the significance  of being called
nigger

# Dee September

## *Grief*

sorrow slithers through my fingers
grows dark and smooth damp
a snake in the undergrowth
and bears witness to my weeping

everything is on fire:
my thighs for your fingertips
my eyes with the burning of salt
from sad wandering goodbyes

it was a beautiful dream
until you left me with sirens
screaming inside my head
ghosts on a marathon run

i cradle and slow rock
your invisible crying voice
call you close to my side
into the throbbing sound of night

but you are gone from my kisses
fleeing the amber embrace of fire
i spread ashes upon a lonely grave
to stop rose petals from bleeding dry

## *Weight of War*

woman you are weighted down
by the experience of war
those childhood dreams of love
snuffed out by ringing bullets
when you close your dilapidated door
the arms of poverty embrace you

you measure your lost beauty
in rough calloused hands
hands that have tilled dry earth
to yield a crop of sorrow
for a hunger that never feeds

woman you are weighted down
by the experience of war
your woman's dreams of life
strengthened by a million singing voices
when you open your worldly door
the power of freedom welcomes you

## *In a Breath . . .*

i drift between sorrow and joy
taste my loneliness
in sockets of darkness and fear
suckle my ecstasy
in smooth curves of the sea

given the circumstances
of cruelty or tenderness
i know i will plunge
deep into jagged pain
or soar on wings of laughter

in a matter of breath intakes
i pass through miraculous beauty
or fall victim to brutish terror
my emotional time-saver
is the smallest gift of life

death is life's mournful time-server
passing into the green of existence
from the fossil to the embryo
between the bomb and the heartbeat
i drift amongst passengers in history and blood

# Leleti Tamu

## *Every Goodbye Ain't Gone*

memories race pulse and heart to you
taking time with me through shivers
then laughter
you catching my tongue licking wetness
fingers rolling inside
your breath slips down my neck opening me
like morning.
you're gone
music and mangoes can't reach this heat
where your swiftness caught me and holds
me still hurry back love
i'm waiting.

## *Town*

old town billowed whiteness
our paths swirl through it
down york street pass the castle
crossing the bridge
i've fried all that reminds me of
sun purpled waves a ripe plantain
a piece of saltfish
number 4 on the cd catches my mood.
this piece of heart that shallows breathing
sweats palms
as i wait for you with all i've saved since
2:30 i feel you on this road trace you
with the same amount of time it took to
know your face
in this you're tender after 5 days of
watching the stream from the window hiding
from the uncommon sight of 2 black women
out here, i haven't told you yet that each night
i can only sleep after i've screamed on your tongue
your fingers out here this colourless quiet cuts
silently here blonde heads walk prized pets not
knowing bush has bombed children and resistence
never knowing another boat didn't make it from haiti
that rodney isn't the only one out here sleep takes time
i wrap myself in 3 blankets 2 black women out here can
never leave the world our lovers our mothers
we must see in the dark long before the evening comes.

# Minister Faust

## *The Brown Moth*

I pumped into my pedals, gliding down 108th Street on my bike, past piles of grass and leaves, smelling the sweetness of the season's final barbecues. My lungs filled with fall air.

I don't know what it was that eventually bunched up inside of me and made me go to see him. Many things — guilt, grim curiosity, friendship? I don't know. But like many people who catch a whiff of that hospital antiseptic scent of death, I had recoiled.

I stood on my pedals to accelerate across 76th Avenue, dodging cars and pedestrians. Will's place was coming up soon. I had finally worked up the courage to see him, though at every intersection I considered other places I could go. I hadn't seem him since the spring, when he'd found out that he was ... that he was dying.

Will — even with his prognosis he'd finished out his semester and didn't skip a beat. Even made the dean's list. But no school for him this fall. Even though it would have been his last year.

I leaned deep into a turn onto 78th Avenue and scrappy leaves dragged themselves against asphalt in my breeze. And the beating of my heart and the rushing of my blood reminded me that I'm a young man, and somehow seeing one of my own so close to walking beyond the frail veil did something to my nerve. When I found out about Will, a guy just like me, suddenly so many impossibilities seemed much more real. Suffering. Death. Over. When you're young and you chase out between parked cars, or scale walls outside your apartment, or play with matches and lighting fluid, or you get old enough to drive and drive drunk like a maniac ... you think you're slick and smooth, but that aint why you do it. You do it cuz you don't even realize you're not immortal.

You're a gambler by default, thinking like everyone else that *you're* the one who can make it, you're the player, the mack, the one who's so fly he *can't* be touched. And then one day you get a call that Will is dying and you know it's all a lie and your coffee tastes just a little flatter and your sleep is just a little less sound.

I yanked on the handlebars of my ten-speed and bounced up over the curb in front of Will's apartment. A typical walk-up for Strathcona — brown brick face on a shady street. One walk-up after another after another, peaceful anonymity in a neighbourhood that maintained churches and convents and hospitals — even St. Joseph's terminal hospital. A neighbourhood made up of students and old folks, young people waiting to live, and old people and one young person, waiting ... I mentally slapped myself for my internal lapse into melodrama.

But I found that news of Will had done this to me, made me crazy like this. Things used to just mean themselves. A plate of food was a plate of food, a flat tire was a flat tire. But since springtime, I found myself finding meaning and significance in everything, searching for something ... why? Was it because Will was such a decent guy? I mean, that had to be part of it. Here was Will, selfless, kind, did well in school, had a good career in front of him, lived with his nice girlfriend in a nice apartment in a nice neighbourhood. Will had a way of making you say "nice" a lot. Great conversationalist — never let you get bored, always knew just enough about whatever interested you to keep your attention, always knew how to draw out your most interesting anecdotes, thus making *you* feel interesting. Had that rare kind of quite magnetism that built truly lasting loyalty.

Or so it seemed. I mean, how loyal had I been? Since spring I'd spoken with him maybe a dozen times. What the hell you supposed to say to a guy who's dying? Yeah, yeah, I *know* ... the same things you'd say to anyone else.

Convenient until you're sitting there across from him and completely on guard to make sure you don't blunder into the densest of *faux pas*. What could you possibly say that would have any meaning? What the hell good was I when people seeking consolation need the sincere statement "Yeah, I know" more than anything else?

Ten minutes. Ten minutes I'd been staring at the front door buzzer.

Had to go up.

Locked my bike against the railing, pushed the little white button. A shock ran the length of my hand's nerves. A small voice fluttered out from behind a greying metal grill.

"Yes?"

"Will, how ya doin? It's me."

"Come on up."

A small buzz and I grabbed the door. It was darker inside and my eyes needed a moment to adjust. There was a sad quiescence about the shady and quiet Sunday afternoon interior. It was kind of like being in church just after a ... Stop. Nothing. It was kind of like being in a nice apartment on a Sunday afternoon on a nice day. That was all. And never mind that other shit.

I was up the stairs, around the corner and at his door before I knew it. I looked out the window at the end of the hall. It was sunny outside and a few insects tapped against the glass from the outside. I turned to the door and knocked. Will opened the door.

Oh, God. He looked like fuck. Will, was this your grandpa? The Will I knew wore shorts and tank tops into early winter, but this guy wore heavy sweatpants and a sweater. He used to be robust, but now his cheeks were all empty-looking and his wrists seemed brittle, like breadsticks. Shit — bandages on his wrists and hand — had he tried to slash his wrists? And his skin. His previous chestnut brownness had given way to a kind of greyishness, and his kinky black locks had become patchy and even white in certain places.

His eyes. Damn. His eyes.

"Hey, Garth, how ya doin'? Glad you could come over." He offered me his hand.

I really like people who have a firm handshake. Will used to. Now I found myself afraid to shake his hand. My hand seemed drawn on its own. Will's hand slid over and encompassed it, and his skin had a leathery, scrotal feel to it. A wince escaped me. I felt ashamed and tried to cover it up with a hastily composed smile, but I don't think Will noticed, since he'd opened the door wide for me to come in.

I walked in, kicked off my shoes. Will had gone into the kitchenette and was asking me if I wanted something to eat or drink. I accepted his offer of a soft drink and began nervously to going over my mental checklist of conversational topics, wrinkled my nose at the smell, that sick-person cleaning fluid smell of human decay, of mouthwash spilled on an old stained mattress.

"Where's Rachael?" I asked, immediately kicking myself for it. What the hell was I thinking? She wasn't there, she hadn't answered the phone, I couldn't see any of her things — she's left him, she couldn't take the strain of living with a terminal man, she's afraid of his condition, her parents have made her return, he's become too unpleasant in his illness to live with ...

"She's out getting some groceries."

Mental sigh — slow down. Things were just *things.*

Calm.

"So Will," I restarted, "what've you been doing to keep yourself busy? Still working on your projects?"

He came around the corner, offered me my drink while motioning for me to sit down. I figured that he might have fallen into complete inactivity while contemplating the immediacy of his departure from this world.

"Well," he said, slowly easing himself into a comfy chair much more suited to his former litheness, "I've been trying to get a bunch of projects finished ... for understandable reasons."

Will looked at me directly in the eye upon saying that. I was honoured that he was being straight-up with me. I'd rather be honest about bad shit, and not beat around the bush. Good to know he felt the same way. I'd like to be able to count on my friends to let me be as frank.

"I imagine I'd wanna do the same."

"It's funny, Garth," said Will, suppressing a slight shudder in the warm room, "you really get this attitude about everything. Everything seems so important, things that used to be 'Oh, I'll finish that some other day or month or year or whatever.' But things that used to be, like, 'I have *got* to finish this tomorrow,' *that* kinda shit seems so unimportant. I mean, like school for instance.

"Yeah, I finished up last year, but that was enough. Since then" — he gestured with his bandaged hand to the IBM on his desk — "my main concern — well, *one* of my main concerns has been getting published. I used to write, what, five or six short stories a year, plus a longer piece. And since spring, I think I've written forty-five, no, forty-*six* pieces."

"No shit. *Forty-six*?"

"Yeah," he chuckled, "it's amazing how important it's become. It seemed like every thought I got just had to be immortalized. I needed to have some sense that when I was gone, I wouldn't just be some vague memory in people's minds, like 'Didn't I sit next to that guy in Chem?' when people read my obituary in the campus paper. Course," he added slowly, "I'm not likely to see even half the rejection notices until *after* I ..."

"Will ... I ... can we talk straight-up?"

He grinned broadly, and for the first time I noticed how big his teeth seemed, now that his gums had receded as much as they had. The fact that the fat behind his eyes had been eaten up and his eyes seemed to be in oversized sockets, combined with his grim smile, made him look like a well-dressed skeleton. A medical school prank.

"Garth, I'd *love* to be straight-up. You don't know how much people want to avoid the truth. I mean, what the fuck, *I'm* the one with the muthafuckin disease, right? But people are acting like for them to even *mention* the shit is either gonna make me worse or infect *them*. It's hard as shit to deal with this when you can't even have an honest word with someone."

It was really weird to hear Will curse it up so much. It wasn't that he was uptight, it's just that Will usually went for less direct speech. But hey, if he felt the need for more directness at a time like this, I could understand that.

"I'm glad to hear it, Will. First, I wanna tell you ... I feel really bad about not seeing you very much over the last few months ... but, well, I've been *really busy*, and — "

"Hey, I know, you are a student after all — "

"No, but that's no excuse, I mean, I should've made the time. This pretty much qualifies as a special case. I mean, if this doesn't, what does?"

"Yeah, well — "

"Will, maybe *I've* been one of those people who has felt ... some of that. I know it's irrational, and it really sucks to have your friends act like this, but I think I'm one of those people who feels somewhat ... *afraid* ... of it all. It's like ... well ..."

A silence smouldered uncomfortably in the air. Finally Will dashed some water on it. "It's like you're forced to think 'There but for the grace of God ....'"

I paused. I had been looking out the window at something, anything, finally settling on some cocoons at the windowsill. Cocoons in autumn. Bizarre. "Yeah," I finally said.

Will got up with a degree of strain I'd never seen in him, and it frightened and disgusted me. He walked to the kitchenette and had to sort of swing or swivel his hips sometimes to make the legs move in the proper direction. His pants sagged in the ass area over what his girlfriend used to call his "big bodacious butt." Now he was just a sack of fuckin bones. Oh, Will ... how was this possible? You were a young fuckin guy, just like me! This doesn't happen!

I forced myself to get up and follow him into the kitchenette. He seemed a little annoyed, embarrassed even, at this invasion of his privacy. At least, that was what I read on his face. I couldn't understand why he should feel that a kitchen was a place for privacy, until I saw his bandaged handful of multicoloured and multisized pills, like a fistful of costume jewels. He slapped them to his mouth and grimly injected a glass of water down his throat, and his Adam's apple bobbed in a throat gaunt before its years.

Will turned to me. I thought he was going to speak but he said nothing. He just stared out the window that was ringed with cocoons. I put my hands in my pockets. He kept staring out the window. I crossed my arms against my chest. He kept staring.

I didn't know what to do. He was just staring. He seemed extremely pissed off at me, but what had I said? I finally ventured: "Look, Will, if I said anyth — "

"*Don't apologize!*"

I jumped back at the force of his words.

"I mean, that is just the worst, when everybody acts like I'm this frail fuckin flower that can't handle a raindrop. *I'm a man*, and everyone wants to step around me with kid gloves one, like I'm gonna get hurt, and yes, I know, you don't *step* with kid gloves, and it used to be that someone would correct me if I said that, but now? Oh, no, don't upset him, he might become *a-gi-ta-ted!*" He spat out each syllable. "I'm leaving the world forever, and people want it to be as smooth for me as if the universe had taken a cosmic muthafuckin Ex-Lax! Well, I don't need it, I didn't ask for it!"

Will brushed past me, attempting to shoulder me but only bouncing off. His shoulder felt like styrofoam. I felt a pang of guilt for not being rocked or bruised. He walked to the window, gripped the edges of the frame. He didn't look out, but seemed to stare at the edges themselves.

He was silent for a long time.

I considered whether or not I should leave.

Then his body relaxed underneath his ample clothing and he took in a breath. "The biggest pain of all," he said, "is trying to figure out what happens next. Tryin' to figure out what's on the other side." He shook his head, but continued look at the window rim. "That is, assuming there's only one. Some people say it goes on forever, feet in this world, wings in the next, who knows what after that?"

I tried to imagine Will in his skeletal state with a baggy tracksuit and wings, strumming a harp on some cloud. I failed.

"Everyone has an answer, but no one knows the first damn thing they're talkin about from firsthand experience. Except those after-death-experience people. Yeah, I read every one of those I could get my hands on. Great help. Ninety per cent of them talk about a tunnel of light, the others talk about a cyclone of flame, and some doctors say it's the brain in a superactivated trauma state resembling nightmare. Nuthin, nuthin to go on but nuthin.

"The best any of em can do is to see some reflection of themselves ... what they *want* to be, what they think they *are*.

"But you gotta know. You gotta *know*! And even if you gotta go, it would help so much, so much, if you could just see briefly, or reach beyond, and grab a piece of the other side, to know what to expect, what it looks like, *what you look like on the other side ...*"

On the other side of the frail veil.

He sat down next to the sill and continued looking at it. I leaned against the sink. "In the spring, before ... I was happy, or at least I thought I was happy, and people came around and things were good and I could relax enough to let a Saturday afternoon pass without feeling it was wasted if I didn't have some major revelation about life.

"But no more. Nowadays ... you know, in the spring, after I saw the doctor, I began to notice all sorts of things I never saw before. Like things I used to hate, like caterpillars, I used to hate them. Thought they were ugly little furry lumps of jelly. Then I took a really close look one day and saw they weren't so ugly. Kinda neat, actually. Yeah, I know, hardly St. John the Divine on the island of Patmos, but I learned something. Well, I began to notice them change. Spin cocoons and all that. Like most people, I thought butterflies were pretty, but I hated moths. Well, all those cocoons open up and these butterflies come out and flutter around and it's all very nice. But this one cocoon takes a little longer, so I take a special interest in it, start photographing it, drawing it, observing it, trying to figure out what dazzling thing is gonna come forth.

"Well, summer is beginning when the thing finally starts showing signs that something is moving inside. I've got the camera ready for days, just hoping to catch the moment. I'm waiting for the monarch of muthafuckin'-monarchs to come out.

"And you know what? When the thing splits, out comes this fat little brown moth."

He turned to me like he expected an answer to this conundrum of existence. I didn't know what to say, so I just snorted agreement at this allegedly confounding detail.

"*A brown moth*," he repeated for emphasis.

"Huh. Imagine."

"So this *brown moth* flies away, but every once in a while I see it, especially late at night when I'm at the table with the light on and the window is closed, and it's banging against the glass. So one night, a couple of weeks ago, I'm sitting at the table going over details that have to be wrapped up, and the moth, the brown moth, starts banging up against the glass.

"Well, I can't stand the distraction, so I turn off the light hoping it'll go away when the light gets cut, maybe go after the neighbour's balcony light. But it's staying on the window. Why didn't it fly away? It was walking around on the window, walking up a storm, and beating its wings all the time, but not flying. Wings buzzing, fluttering, flapping, but not flying. Why not? Why didn't it go after the light? Why was it flapping its wings while it walked? Why? What was the point in walking on the damn window and trying to fly at the same time? Why? What could its stupid little speck brain hope to gain by flying and walking at the same time?

"So I'm looking out through the thin glass, out *through* it, and I get a chill. I breathe in and close my eyes. When I open them I don't see through the window, the hall light just bounces off it. And I suddenly see the man sitting on the opposite side of the glass, staring back at me. I see the man, this sick little thin stick man, seeing me see him. He's this ugly stick man. And I breathe in a big breath and close my eyes, and when I open them I notice the blood streaming down my forearm because the glass was stuck in my arm because the window was broken because my arm was through the window. I pull my arm back and cold night air pours through, turning my breath white. I'm looking at my arm and I finally hear this voice echoing like it was coming from the top of a well. Rachael comes rushing into the room screaming, 'My God, what happened?'

"I'll tell you what happened. The man was gone. And the brown moth was gone."

Will looked at me solemnly for a long time. I had absolutely no idea what he expected from me. But I was ashamed to admit it. Obviously it meant so much to him. We sat in silence, waiting, until finally the click-clack of a key in the door and Rachel returning to the shattered conversation. With her there, we attempted chatting. She made us some food, but neither Will nor I was hungry. I politely excused myself, pretended I had a paper to write, and left.

Outside, the night air was cold and thick with damp decay, and it poured into my lungs like old bathwater. I biked home through a cold fall night filled with an absence of moths.

# Dionne Brand

## *Three Passages from Elizet*

From the word she speak to me and the sweat running down her in that midday sun, from then I know that I would lose my life. I didn't even raise my head, I finished loving Verlia sweet self, head to toe, looking at her face and her water-black skin so I was to remember what I lose something for. I take my time, I close my eyes and I eat her like rice, like day had no end. Because, you see, I know I was going to lose something, because Verl was surer than anything I see before, surer than the day I get born, because nothing ever happen to me until Verl come along, and when Verl come along I see my chance out of what ordinary. Out of the plenty day, when all it have for a woman to do is lay down and let a man beat against she body, and work cane and chop up she foot and make children and choke on the dryness in she chest and have only one road in and the same road out and know that she tied to the ground and can never lift up. And it wasn't nothing Verl do or say or even what Verl was or what Verl wanted, but is just that I see Verl coming, like a shower of rain coming that could just wash me cool and that was sufficient, and if god or anybody else see fit to spite me for that, is so things is. I abandon everything for Verlia. I sink in Verlia and let her flesh swallow me up. I devour she. She open me up like morning. Limp and stiff and limp. She make me wet and her tongue scorch me up like hot sun. I love that shudder between her legs, love the wash and sea of her, the swell and bloom of her softness. And if is all a woman could do on the earth is sink into another woman like she is the ocean, well, I just meet myself.

Verlia would say, "Open your eyes, I want to see what you're feeling." I don't know what she see in my eyes but she stare into me until I come. Her look said, "Elizet, you are bigger than me by millennia and I can hold you between my legs like rock hold water. You are wearing me away like years and I wonder if you can see me beyond rock and beyond water, but as something human that needs to eat and can die even in your quickness, even as you dive into me today like a fish and want nothing, or so you say." Something say to me, Elizet, you is not big enough for nothing you done live and Verlia is your grace. I never wanted nothing big from the world. Who is me to want anything big or small. Who is me to think I is something. I born to clean Isaiah house and work cane since I was a child and say what you want, Isaiah feed me and all I have to do is lay down under him in the night and work cane in the day. It have plenty woman who waiting their whole blessed life for what I got and maybe is some bad spirit in me, maybe is some bad spirit what make me see Verlia's face spraying sweat in the three o'clock heat.

Had anyone told her she would not have believed that she would wake up in this room. This morning is shed in light and dust. That wooden window will open. The hand opening the wooden window will be the hand of the woman I sleep with in this room. I have never been in such a room. A wooden room. The updraft of air through the floorboards is strafed in slivers of salt and smoke. It is a room where I will open my eyes and the woman opening the window will be the woman I will live with forever. I will not look at her, I know her face, it is melting into the soft sun she lets in with her hand on the window. I do not need to look at her face, it is the face melting into the sun at the window. This morning the Chacalaca birds warn of rain coming. My eyes do not need to open to see her eyes look for rain through the window where her face is melting. I told her I could do the mash potatoes.

She liked the weight of her, solid and permanent, against her. She liked her wayward legs, in sleep they straddled her hips and when they lay plush on their own side of the bed Verlia awoke feeling lonely, pulling the woman towards her, comforted in the thighs lapping against her. It was usually close to morning when she missed her, when she reached over and felt for her, hoping that she was there and sensing another thing, the room full of hoping. She knew that she was safe with a woman who knew how to look for rain, what to listen for in birds in the morning, a woman who loved to feel her face melting in the sun in the morning through a window. She needed a woman so earthbound she would rename every plant she came upon. She needed someone who believed that the world could be made over as simply as that, as simply as deciding to do it, but more, not just knowing that it had to be done but needing it to be done and simply doing it. This is what she wanted to believe and what she had doubts about, and when they'd first met she thought that she was the one who knew and how she was going to change this country-woman into a revolutionary like her, but then something made her notice that she was the one who had doubts and what she was saying she merely said but Elizet felt and knew. When her brightness wore down by four in the afternoon, when wielding a machete blistered her hands and she tried to still keep going, and when she did the wrong thing by working through the midday sun and when her eyes looked longingly at them living their life and not looking at it like she, she had to laugh at her damaged soul. That she could envy hardship, that she could envy the arc of a cutlass in a woman's hand, that she would fall in love with the arc of a woman's arm, long and one with a cutlass, slicing a cane stalk and not stopping but arcing and slicing again, splitting the armour of cane, the sweet juice rushing to the wound of the stem. That the woman would look up and catch her looking and she would hate herself for interrupting such avenging grace.

What made her notice that she was the one needing was that grace, that gesture taking up all the sky, slicing through blue and white and then the green stalk and the black earth. Anyone who did that all day, passed through everything that made up the world, whose body anchored it, arc after arc after arc, who was tied to the compulsion of its swing, who became the whirl of it, blue, white air, green stroke, black dust, black metal, black flesh; anyone with such a memory would know more, be more, than she. Looking up from her exercise in duty and revolutionary comradeship, looking up from the task that she didn't have to do but only did in order to come close to the people, she would watch a whole field, mile after mile of whirling, each person caught up in an arc of metal and dust and flesh until they were a blur, whirring, seeming to change the air around them. Then this world went away from her.

How I reach here is a skill I learn from Adela. The skill of forgetfulness. So I work in this pit in the morning, cut cane when it in season and lay under this man at night until one day I see this woman talking, talking like she know what she is saying and everybody around listening. I walk past because I have no time for no woman talking. It don't mean nothing. It don't matter what woman say in the world. This woman with her mouth flying ... cheups ... I hear something about co-operative. Black people could ever co-operate, this little girl too fast again. Her mouth too fast, her tongue flying ahead of herself. Face plain as day, mouth like a ripe mango, and teeth, teeth like a horse. I don't talk to her then. They tell me she is for the revolution, that she is for taking all the land and giving it to people who work it all their life. Let foolish old people believe her. Is only them have time to sit down and get wrap up in her mouth and think Metiviere and them will let go any land. Is only one thing will fix Metiviere and them and is the devil because them is the devil son self. I pass by her going my way and didn't that woman skin her big teeth for me and look at me so clear is as if she see all my mind clear through to Maracibo, then she say, "Sister," and I could not tell if it was a breeze passing in that heat still day or if I hear the word. 'Sister,' I know I hear it murmuring just enough to seem as if it was said but not something that only have sense in saying. It fly off and touch everything on the road, even that which could not be touched. Things in me. It move like a spirit what clear the road and make it silent. It feel like rum going through my throat, warm and violent, and straight to me . . . Sweet sweet, my tongue sweet to answer her and it surprise me how I want to touch her teeth and hold her mouth on that word. I keep walking. I don't answer. But I regret every minute until I see her next.

The next time she come say she trying to swing cutlass with her mouth moving as fast as you please about strike. strike and demand a share in the estate. Well look at bold face. We navel string bury here, she say, and we mother and we father and everybody before them. Metiviere use it up like manure for the cane, and what we get, one barrack room and credit in he store until we owe he more than he owe we, and is thief he thief this place in the first place. The people listen to she and smile because we know she make sense but she don't know what a hard people these Metiviere is. Is not just people navel string bury here, is their shame and their body. They churn that up in the soil here too. It have people they just shoot and leave for *corbeau* to eat them. What left make the cane fat and juicy. She come from town and God knows where, light, light and easy so. She not ready yet. One for she, she work hard. She body 'ent make for this, well who body make for it, but she do it.

She break my swing. It was the quiet. When I get used to her talking as I bend into the cane, when I done add her up for the swing so I wouldn't miss doing how much I need to do to make the quota, when I make her voice count in the stroke, I don't here her no more. I swing up. What she doing now, like she tired talk. Good Lord! I say to myself, God wasn't joking when he make you. She was in front of me, staring, sweating as if she come out of a river. I wanted to touch the shine of her, to dry off her whole body and say, "Don't work it so hard," show her how to swing, how to tie up her waist so that her back would last, shield her legs so that the sheaf wouldn't cut. That's the first time I feel like licking her neck. She looked like the young in me, the not beaten down and bruised, the not pounded between my legs, the not lost my mother, the not raped, the not bled, the not tired, she looked like me fresh, searching for good luck tea, leave my house broom, come by here weed. A woman can be a bridge, limber and living, breathless, because she don't know where the bridge might lead, she don't need no assurance except that it would lead out with certainty, no assurance except the arch and disappearance. At the end it might be the uptake of air, the leap of what she don't know, the sweep and soar of herself unhandled, making herself a way to cross over. A woman can be a bridge from these bodies whipping cane. A way to cross over. I see in her face how she believe. She glance quick as if unimportant things was in her way, like Metiviere, like fright. Her eyes move as if she was busy going somewhere, busy seeing something, and all this cane, all this whipping and lashing was a hinderance. Then like a purposeful accident her eyes rest on me, and her face open, those big teeth pushed out to laugh for me, sweat flying, she fall again to the cutlass.

# VOICES

*Pull off the mask...and let myself emerge...born into new life, strengthened...and refreshed...*

—Lorris Elliott

Thank you, Lorris, for your great contribution to black literature in Canada.

# Preface

We come from Jamaica, Trinidad, Barbados, Ghana, Haiti, Guyana, Nigeria, Canada, the United States and South Africa. As writers, we push the limits of literature and redefine images of representation. In the process, we create our realities. We are a new generation of *griots*—town criers, or spiritual messengers—whose stories have been transferred to the printed page. Despite the diversity of our cultural backgrounds, we write out of a collective African consciousness—a consciousness embodied in the fabric of oral traditions, woven from one generation to the next, through myths, storytelling, fables, proverbs, rituals, worksongs and sermons meshed with Western literary forms.

African-Canadian literary form has existed for at least two centuries, and began with the importation of slaves in Quebec and the arrival of escaped American slaves in Nova Scotia and southern Ontario. According to George Elliott Clarke's *Fire on the Water: An Anthology of Black Nova Scotian Writings*, the texts of Nova Scotian John Marrant, a former slave, date back to 1785, and are the earliest known writings of a black living in Canada. The more recent influx of immigrants from the Caribbean to

Canada in the nineteen-fifties, sixties and seventies, and lately the arrival of Africans, has created a highly textured literary quilt. This complex history—of a shared heritage on the continent, and the experiences borne of our dispersal to various parts of the world—were very much in my mind when the idea for *Voices* took root.

*Voices* presents new works of poetry and fiction by fifteen Canadian writers of African descent. In compiling this collection, I chose not to force the work into a preconceived moral, political or social framework. Rather, I was interested in providing a less structured, more open frame, to allow for the juxtaposition of individual and unique voices, ideas, styles and forms. I hope that I have acted as a catalyst for the articulation of an individual ethos.

The oral tradition is central to African writing, and so we begin with Molara Ogundipe-Leslie's "Garlands to the Beheaded One," a poem historically linked to the African call-and-response tradition. The poet vocalizes two or more lines alone, and is answered by a chorus. Norma De Haarte's folk tale likewise finds its roots in a more traditional, story-telling form. The latter voices of this collection, notably Claire Harris and Frederick Ward, draw the African aesthetic through an experimental fabric, creating a new texture.

Black writers are now, it seems, struggling between the political and personal landscapes in their work, and this struggle is a strong and recurring theme throughout *Voices*. Two stories, Makeda Silvera's "Her Head a Village" and Dany Laferrière's "Why Must a Negro Writer Always Be Political?" are strong literal depictions of this contemporary struggle. Historically, African-Canadian writing has been overtly political, with little reference to the romantic or erotic. In *Canada in Us Now*, Harold Head writes: "There are no poems on roses or teacups. The love poems have a certain edge to them. Rejecting the teachings of their colonial youth where poetry was placed in some higher metaphysical sphere, Black creative expression is designed to inspire and serve people."

Today, however, such exclusively exterior writing, in which we respond only to the issues that ignore the interior space, the core, is no longer. In *Yearning*, bell hooks points out that "psychological pain is...a central revolutionary frontier for black folks." She correctly identifies the need to heal ourselves, " 'cause you can't effectively resist domination when you are messed up."

*Voices* attempts to balance and to synthesize the exterior and interior spaces: the languages of romantic and sexual love, the languages of lesbianism, sexual abuse and abandonment. In this context, the personal is political, especially when examined from the perspective of a history of oppression. At this stage in the development of an African-Canadian literary aesthetic, the exposure of the deeply personal should be viewed as revolutionary—yes, revolutionary. We all speak passionately, venomously; and we write with immense pride, commitment and confidence. We are, as writers, first and foremost liberators of minds and bodies, not necessarily or primarily political liberators. We have learned true liberation can only be achieved through the freeing of the spirit.

Voices Voiced Voicing
Sounds Images Imagine Compose
mouths speech singing shouting
Drums Incantations Drums

AYANNA BLACK
Editor

# Molara Ogundipe-Leslie

## Garlands to the Beheaded One

praisesong to the true thalaiva
(thoughts after Rajiv Gandhi's assassination)

My thoughts keep coming back to you,
unknown and unsung woman,
sister of wonder, the beheaded one
garlanded with death,
you exploded death like forest pods
to self and others,
exploding yourself in mystery,
shouting: "*thalaiva! thalaiva!*"
My thoughts stop dead at your severed head!

Poet: *Ye-e-pa!*
Audience: *E ma wo o-o-o*

Severed in violence, from love or will or both
what courage lay stubborn within you, held you brave,
as they packed you electrified into a mule of death
what totalness! what zeal!

to so self-scatter to the four winds of the earth
what driving rage! what cause ! what steely need!

Poet: *Iku de!*
Audience: *E ma wo—o-o*

Woman garlanded with death, for death
my garlands of awe petrify here
in faraway Toronto
blow fragrances of awe to you softly
irrelevantly
my song enfolding not the dreams of India
inscribed in Rajiv for him by him or
through him but shrouding you
my song searches only you
forgotten one, unknown soldier
scattered to a charboiled death

Poet: *Ye-e-e pa!*
Audience: *E ma wo o-o-o-o*

Sliced to a staring icon,
your head sitting in formaldehyde
my distant thoughts throw petals
of awe at you and your dare,
woman of will, take petals from
women of your kind, take garlands!
praise the true thalaiva! name her here!
garland the true thalaiva! make way!

Poet: *E ma a wo o-o-o*
Audience: *E ma a wo o-o-o*

Ye—e-e-pa! is a Yoruba exclamation of grief.

*Iku de!* means "Death is here."

*E ma wo* is a prolonged way to say "Don't look at her." It is a ritual cry used in traditional sacred processions to clear the way. When the intonation on *ma* is varied, the meaning of the sentence becomes "Keep your gaze on her."

*Thalaiva* is an indian word for "leader."

## Because We Are Mad
(song to a black sister in Chicago)

Because we dare to love
in a world without love
    in fear of love
    afraid to love
I laugh in weeping down the street
because I know
I met you somewhere before

I always felt that
someone like you lived
not only in the flesh-veils
of my heart but
lurking in the trees
the woods the grasses' hair
laughing somewhere freely
in the winds
free child of Nature
woman

non-threatening soft and true
I know because I know
I met you somewhere before

I laugh quietly through my pores
as I see you now absent
weeping through the skin of my eyes
I know I made my peace with you
a long time ago

a long, long time ago
five thousand years ago
in a green and happy land
where the spirits of light
kiss and dance
with the spirits of grace
and lotuses sit on becalmed water
balanced

They may say
that we are mad
I often think that we are mad
and I know
that we are mad
who seek to romp on
in a green and happy land
set by us in the asphalt sea
set about by jungles of monetary rage
steel and razor hands of global
violences
hands affixed
to the amputated souls

of our barons at home
our barons of home—made death

We are mad
who seek to find a light-filled place
resisting well
who seek to dance in its green and gold
to hug in the joy with which we know
the spirits of grace do melt
into the spirits of life

# Norma De Haarte

## Little Abu, The Boy Who Knew Too Much

Long, long ago in the lush, tropical country of Guyana, land of many waters, there was a boy named Abu. Abu lived on an island in the Esseequibo River in the county of Esseequibo. Hundreds of islands are clustered along the river, especially at the mouth. But many of these islands are uninhabitable. However, Abu lived on one of the largest, called Leguan, situated where the swift-flowing river current meets the Atlantic Ocean.

Abu's parents had been brought to the island as slaves from Africa, but like many others, they remained on the island when they were freed. After Emancipation, most of the people on the island purchased large plots of land from plantation owners and stayed on the island, working as farmers in their own right. Their main crops of sugar cane, rice and coconuts, from which oil was made, were chiefly for export, while vegetables and ground provisions were grown for domestic use. Cattle farmers sold cattle, milk, meat and hides to the region around, as far as the city of Georgetown.

Abu's parents had purchased large plots of land. However, bit by bit, his father leased or sold most of the land and kept only the lot on which the house was built. He also kept a few head of cattle.

Old Abu was not interested in farming. He had learnt the secret nature and effects of certain plants, berries and roots. This knowledge, which he brought from Africa, deepened with the abundance and rich variety of tropical shrubs, vines, berries and flowering plants.

When people had headache, fever, couldn't eat or sleep, and felt depressed, if they were bitten by venomous snakes or insects, scratched by poisonous plants, he administered "bush medicines"—potions, brews and teas. In this manner, he alleviated pain and stress, eliminated poisons from the body and restored his clients to health. Consequently, people travelled for miles from the farthest corner of the island and the far reaches of the coastlands to pay Old Abu a visit and tell him their problems.

In those days, there were no doctors to look after the slaves or indentured servants. Old Abu, therefore, provided an important service, necessary for the survival of the community. Without this service, many people would have died for lack of care, and the population of the island would have been decimated. Therefore, as natural as day is to night, tropical flora is to fauna, Old Abu was essential to the well-being of the people in the region around.

Even as a young boy, Little Abu began to learn these secrets from his father. He was not interested in farming as were the boys in the village. But when the village boys went with parents and relatives down to the "backdam" to work on their farms, Little Abu went and worked alongside them. If anyone was slashed by razor grass or a sharp tool, bitten by poisonous snakes or insects, or injured by cantankerous cattle, Little Abu was as resourceful as his father. He treated the wound with crushed leaves, berries and moss, then bound it securely with special leaves and vines. The boys in the village were in awe of Little Abu. They had the greatest respect for him.

During the planting and harvesting season, children did not attend school. Every child went down to the backdam. Those who were capable worked side by side with parents, until seedlings were sown or the harvest reaped. It was not unusual for neighbours to pitch in and help each other until the work was done. Even though Little Abu's parents did not farm on a large scale, Little Abu accompanied his friends and their parents down to the "back."

Early in the morning, when it was still pitch-dark, the boys would stop near Little Abu's house on their way, to call him with a pre-arranged signal. Hoot...Hoot...Hoot...Hoot...Hoot... Hoot...Hooot...Hoot or Kiss...Kiss...Kiss...Ka...dee! Three times they would utter the throaty cry of the owl or the clear trilling song of the kiskadee. Then they would move on slowly down the country road to wait. In nothing more than a few minutes, Little Abu would join them, shouldering a rice bag like the other boys.

Every boy enjoyed being in the backdam because it wasn't all hard work. The outdoors provided lots of interest and fun. Just before the sun was right overhead, everyone stopped for a meal and a rest. This was the cue the boys were awaiting. The ocean surrounding the island, the inlets and streams, even the waters of the rice or sugar-cane fields were teeming with fish. With bare hands, small baskets or nets, the boys would "catch and toss" fish to each other, returning to the waters the ones that weren't good enough or the right type. This was exciting sport!

On the other hand, some boys preferred the taste of fowl—goose, turkey or pheasant—which roamed wild and in great flocks, abundant on the island. With great care, the boys would set about making snares to entrap their prey. But it was more thrilling to separate a few birds from the wily flock. The plan was to surround the birds infantry style, run them down in one direction, then back again until the birds were tired. Then the boys closed in on the exhausted prey.

While returning from these pursuits, a few boys would spread out to gather fruit. They might collect fruit from their own trees or carry out a raid on their neighbour's, depending on which looked better. In those days no one minded as long as trees weren't damaged or destroyed. They chose from the best mangoes, guavas, pineapples, oranges, tangerines, papaws, dunks, genips, psidium, golden, star, custard and monkey apples, the last along with the luscious purple jamoons that grew wild on the island. They picked whatever took their fancy.

But the real contest began when they decided to pick water coconuts. After suitable trees were selected, they raced to see who would be the first to shinny up the trees, with bare hands. Sometimes each boy mounted the long, straight, barrel-like trunk carrying a short, sharp pointed prod or cutlass between the teeth. Many boys performed this difficult task with great ease and flourish. But it was not unusual for a boy to lose his grasp, fall and become seriously injured.

When fruit was collected from the ground or picked off trees, the boys were very cautious. Care was taken to use long, pliant sticks to prod the ground around the fruit in order to drive away small poisonous snakes, hidden between leaves and fruit. Leaves and branches of trees provide a camouflage for vipers and stinging insects. No boy ventured anywhere without a stick for protection. These boys worked hard on the land, but found ways to make life interesting, while the land yielded its bounty.

Many stories were exchanged, repeated and handed down from one generation to the other, as a result of these experiences and escapades. Sometimes a few did not have happy endings.

Little Abu worked hard alongside his friends, but he was more interested in the animals, insects and plants around him. Sometimes he would lie stretched out on the grassy dam or under a coconut tree, noticeably absorbed as he lay still, listening, hand cupped to his ear. No one teased or laughed at him. His friends were aware of the unique attraction between Little Abu and the creatures around him. As he listened to the chirping of the cricket and the *chirr-chirr* of the grasshopper, a long distance away, he could tell whether the sound was made by a male or a female. He had pointed out and explained these differences to his friends over and over. While they strained their ears to listen without success, they never disputed his knowledge. When Little Abu said it was so, that was enough for them.

Nevertheless, the boys were terrified when a passing scorpion, centipede or the vicious and feared red biting ants crawled across Little Abu's bare arm, body or neck, leaving no marks or stings.

Once, a boy named Noah hit a huge, warty toad, which was sunning itself on the dam, with his stick. All the boys laughed except little Abu. "You fool...!" he growled, flying into a rage, hitting the transgressor with his stick. He sulked for the rest of the day, remaining far away from the group, even though he had taken the toad back to the trench and they had seen it swim away. After that incident, his friends were careful not to hit a frog, toad or any creature while he was around. They were frightened of Little Abu's anger.

However, his companions were spellbound when he mimicked the mating call and song of every bird on the island. He knew each bird's identity from its call. It was not uncommon for a thrush or kiskadee, attracted by his call, to sit on his outstretched arm, trilling and singing as if its chest would burst. Many birds came to his call. And the boys never ceased to be amazed at these performances.

As the afternoon sun started to set, large flocks of showy macaws, parrots and parakeets congregated. Moving from tree to tree, they set up a chattering and squalling. Then upwards they would fly again, colourful in the dazzling light. Joined by flocks of herons, mallards, sea gulls and cranes that nestled on the seashore, they fluttered, picturesque against the sky-blue canvas, plumes bathed in the golden rays of sunset. Together, the birds filled the air with a warlike chattering, screeching, screaming, chirping, chirring. Swirling forward, then backward, then forward again, they would race westward, home.

One late afternoon, when the birds were at their loudest, everyone was preparing to leave. In the gathering twilight, the six o'clock bee kept up a tiresome buzzing and the howling monkeys, invisible to the eye, smote the air with their doleful, impulsive call, without a break or pause. The boys had already mustered the herds together and were chasing the obedient cattle homeward. Each boy was well aware his cows would instinctively stop off and like homing pigeons enter their own yards.

But the day was far from over. Stealthily, the boys advanced towards the seashore. They were exceptionally quiet, knowing the snapping sound of breaking twigs, the *thud, thud* of footsteps would scare away the prizes. Their faces were a study in pure delight, as giant blue crabs, following the leader in soldier-like files, marched entranced towards the ocean and into the ready and waiting rice bags. Satisfied, the companions moved off without the slightest sound. There was a chance they might discover a turtle or two burrowing in the sand. With a quick flip, the unsuspecting creatures were turned over on their backs. Then hurriedly but carefully, the boys searched for eggs in the sand.

"Listen! What was that unearthly hissing?" With quick, light steps, the friends rushed over to help two of their companions who caught a couple of iguanas, hissing and struggling to get free. The creatures thrashed about wildly, using their tails as whipcords and baring sharp, ugly teeth. But with dexterity the boys tied the tails securely to the iguana's scaly backs, while the captors grinned in triumph. These catches, highly esteemed, were sought after as delicacies.

But Little Abu had not joined the high-spirited group. Like the blue crab, he marched as though entranced over the shifting sand towards the Atlantic Ocean. With ears cocked, body alert, he appeared to be listening. He listened to the dreary, haunting echoes of the wind as it rose and fell, swelling the tide into giant waves, crashing, lashing against each other, furiously rolling into one, only to be spent gradually on the seashore. The boys stared at Little Abu, then from one to the other, speechless, helpless, scared. Little Abu was now standing in the water, knee-deep in the slowly sinking sand, trancelike, muttering. His mutterings grew louder and clearer as he repeated, over and over in singsong, words his friends could not recognize.

Then Little Abu screamed, and immediately the spell he was under seemed to be broken. But only for a moment, as he stumbled out of the water towards them, reeling from side to side.

"You hear...!" he cried out. It was more a statement than a question. For a fleeting moment he gazed at his companions, searching their faces, looking into each one's eyes, expectant, as if they could comprehend or divine the significance of his sudden penetration. He stood before them, breathless, chest heaving, then charged past in the direction of home.

The boys stared after Little Abu, stupified, eyeing each other. They had seen his brown face strained with distress, his dark eyes bright with a knowledge that confused them. As he spoke, they too had leaned forward, listening. But no one responded. They dared not reveal their own thoughts. All they heard was the sighing of the wind. They stood there, hesitating, looking bleak and bewildered, eyes following Little Abu, who had already become a trail of dust in the darkness.

That was the last afternoon Little Abu and his companions spent together as boys. It was a time they would remember for the rest of their lives, because of the things they did together, and the unusual event that brought their relationship to a dramatic, if not abrupt, ending. Later that evening, the news spread around the village: Old Abu was dying.

The boys could not explain why Little Abu's absence created such a void in their daily activities. He had little interest in field work. He was eternally drawn to the plants and animals, spending most of his time observing them. Yet, as the boys passed Little Abu's house the very next morning, they gave the signal, but didn't wait for him down the road. As they ambled along, they gazed back every now and then, wistful, though deep in their hearts they knew he would never join them again.

Death hung over the Abus' household for a little more than a week. As was customary, villagers knocked on the Abus' door during this time but were never successful in seeing any one of the family. No one was admitted. No one ever left the house and no fire was lit for days in the kitchen, which stood apart from the house. The villagers started to whisper among themselves. They claimed they recognized Little Abu's mother's muted, mournful wailings and Little Abu's voice above the weakened chants of his father. At times, they gossiped about the eerie and mysterious silences inside the house. A shadow of suspicion and tension hung over the village.

But curiosity whetted the villagers' appetites for more information, so they continued to knock at the Abus'. They left gifts of food and fresh fruit. There was nothing else they could do, so they waited. Then one morning, a villager passed by and saw the flag. Soon it was all over the island: Old Abu was dead! This time, when the villagers called on the Abus, they were welcomed inside and allowed to share in the family's grief.

Sometime afterwards, the people realized Abu was no longer a boy, though he was no more than fifteen years old at the time. "Abu's now head of our family.... He will provide for us!" Abu's mother, plump and half smiling, announced pleasantly to a villager who called. This announcement troubled the villagers. They had kept a respectful distance after the funeral, while still sharing their bounty of fruit and fish.

"But is how they goin' to make out at all?"

"De poor boy is too young...ow, ow!"

"Is not only dat...man, you ain't see de boy is a dreamer!" they whispered, scoffing at the idea among themselves.

These snatches of conversation took place among neighbours whenever Mrs. Abu appeared in the yard, minding the stock or tending the kitchen garden. Then one day, Mrs. Abu went to the village shop a few miles away. She purchased a large quantity of groceries, cotton fabrics and familiar household items, for which she paid with a handsome sovereign. The shopkeeper was amazed! The gold piece overwhelmed him. He nodded his head as he considered the situation. Mrs. Abu was not a regular customer, that was true. She was one of a breed of quiet, thrifty women. Then Old Abu must have had quite a mint tucked away.

Of course! Indeed, it had slipped his memory. Old Abu made a good trade from his bush medicine and chants! Why, at one time or another, many of the villagers, not excluding himself, had cause to visit Old Abu. The old man never took money but accepted gifts: a calf, a lamb or a young goat, even a half bag of rice. And he was careful to keep no more than five or six head of cattle. Cattle always fetched a good price. Real clever...me buddy smart man! The shopkeeper smiled triumphantly while he busied himself, helping Mrs. Abu pack her many purchases in a huge basket, set it on her head and then with characteristic ease and friendliness, he saw her off. By nightfall, the news had spread like wildfire. The whole island was bubbling with excitement, predicting and calculating the Abus' worth.

When the topic was exhausted, the villagers turned to young Abu. They talked, adding new details, giving new dimension to stories about his "bewitchment" of animals. Of course, during the time he was locked in with his father, they knew exactly what went on and elaborated their views on the subject. The fact that no one was allowed to enter the house, while it was reported that the young lad's and his father's feeble chantings were heard, added more fuel to their imaginations. They recounted the unusual things, things such a "little, little" boy had done, which they had seen with their very own eyes! They babbled, hmmed, ahaaed, shook with displeasure, appeared shocked, and the village buzzed.

Then one day, the boy Noah, who had struck the toad, carried his sick little sister, wrapped in a blanket, to see his friend Abu. Noah waited in the outer room while Abu's mother went inside to fetch him. Abu appeared and Noah was amazed at the change in him. Abu was no longer the boy he had known. He was at least a head taller. Reposed, he stood before his friend, magnificent in a long, flowing white robe, hair closely cropped, fingers entwined across his stomach. Abu moved with the same smooth grace, which had seemed womanish and unfavourable when they romped together as boys. Noah, so taken aback by the change, forgot for a moment the rigid bundle in his arms.

"My friend!" Abu greeted them. His voice sounded different to Noah, yet it stirred strong feelings, reminding him of the not too dim past, reflecting confidence, spirit and humility.

"I see you are well...but your little sister, Beatrice?" Abu's words hung in the air, stunning Noah. Abu could not have known her! Even now, the little body was well wrapped because of the fever, and her face was covered, save for a little opening for breathing. It was really incredible. Beatrice, one of fifteen-month-old twins, was difficult to identify. Yet Abu called her name without removing the blanket.

Abu unwrapped the covering, then placed the rigid infant down gently on the pallet bed. The child lay scarcely moving; only the slight heaving of her chest, followed by a weak moan, signalled she was alive.

"You must leave her...maybe two days!" Abu gestured, nodding his head, touching the distended stomach. "My mother and I..."

"No, no...!" gasped Noah in despair, rushing to his sister's bedside. At that moment Beatrice made a low, whining sound, opening her eyes, which were dark and sunken. "What will I tell my mother?" His voice quavered; he wrung his hands in wild panic.

Abu said nothing. He was already soothing the fevered brow with a piece of cotton dipped in a calabash of pleasant-smelling liquid. Noah was in a dilemma. There was no one else to help his sister. Yet he feared leaving her, a mere infant, with this boy who had developed overnight into the mysterious stranger standing before him. Suddenly, it was clear to him what to do.

He backed towards the wall. Whatever happened, he would remain in the room with Beatrice.

"If you trust me...you must go!" Abu spoke softly but his tone, though compassionate, conveyed a command, startling Noah to his feet as he was about to sit down. He wrung his hands, moaning again and again. However, head bent and without a word, he went through the door, thoroughly perplexed.

Mrs. Abu silently closed it behind him.

By the end of the day, the news had spread and people gathered outside the Abus', watchful, sullen and expectant.

"But is why they keep the people's chile atall?"

"Don't ask me, my girl...dat's what I come to find out!"

"Old Abu nefer do that...he used to gi'e you good good medicine an' send you away!"

"Girl, a time he gi'e me something...ah tell you when ah tek it ah was sick sick sick...but since then awright!"

"Is wha' they doing so long...is wha' they keep de people chile for?"

"To carry on with dey rigmarole...what else!"

Talking loudly, they ridiculed, praised and blamed the Abus. They gossiped nonstop until someone shouted, "All you bettah fetch the police!" And everything grew suddenly quiet.

The Abus ignored the disturbance. They continued with what they were doing as if no one was in their front yard. By nightfall, Abu thought half of the village was camped outside his door. He could see the flicker of their bottle lamps through the cracks in the wall, and he had recognized many of his father's visitors, who had stayed over on countless occasions. Their children too were left quite willingly for his parents to care for. At times, he thought the noise would never end. He pondered the sudden opposition, but was indifferent to their protestations. A few more hours and the child would be well.

He was not afraid of the police, and, besides, they were miles away.

"Eh eh...look de police comin'!" Someone shouted. It was the afternoon of the second day. The villagers, quiet from their watch since the day before, eyed each other awkwardly and with unease. The policeman came into the yard. Everyone remained quiet, making way for him to get through. But before he could, the door was opened by Mrs. Abu, who appeared with a blanket folded and draped over her left arm, leading Beatrice with the other.

"Give her plenty young coconut water," Mrs. Abu said to Beatrice's mother and father, who had instinctively moved forward; she hesitated a moment.

"Ma...Ma!" Beatrice called cheerfully as she hurried to her mother's outstretched arms. The mother came forward, eyes downcast, caught her, looked up, embarrassed, to the open door, but Mrs. Abu made a graceful nod, then closed it.

"Look...the chile get better already!" The mob pushed forward to get a better look at Beatrice in her mother's arms.

"She really looking better!"

"She never look so sprightly before!"

"She was always sickly lookin'!"

"The Abus is decent people...Old Abu was good good man, ah don't know what get into all you head foh sen' foh de police!"

"The young man do a very good job...you all should thank de people," a thoughtful villager said loudly. The mob babbled on without shame.

"The police got no right here!"

That did it. Constable Moriah was exasperated more than he was confused, as he pushed his way back through the crowd and stood aside, mopping his brow. He was the one to give up his lunch hour. He had just finished cooking and left the comfortable shelter of the tiny outpost, walked five miles through the broiling midday sun, and for what! He was supposed to question the Abus about the child. The same child who was right before his eyes, unharmed. He looked about to see if he could identify any of the instigators who had crowded into the small outpost, but couldn't recognize any of them, and wished he had taken down a few names. How he disliked writing long statements! The truth was, he disliked police work more!

"Mr. Policeman! Drink this water coconut; it will cool you down." Out of the blue, a woman, head wrapped with a large colourful head-tie, lopped off the top of a coconut, chipped a small hole in it and thrust it at him.

"You all get off these people property," he barked with forced authority, and the crowd began shuffling off.

Early the next morning, Mrs. Abu went out to milk the cow. She discovered, much to her surprise, a pair of ewes tethered in the yard. She stared at the ungainly creatures for a moment. Then, smiling to herself, she placed them with the other stock and went on with her work. She would tell Abu later, but was certain he already knew about it.

After the healing of Beatrice, word about young Abu grew like lush paddy plants. He was openly approved, his authority accepted and he became highly respected. Consequently, his influence extended to people of diverse persuasions and interests.

A few weeks later a farmer, jealous of his wife, ended her life in a savage manner. The neighbours had always gossiped about his unreasonable attitude and deplored his regular assaults. They had heard her cries against his violent abuse and were outraged; but had kept their distance. On the night in question her cries were unbearable, and therefore a report was made to the police. Early the next morning, Constable Moriah appeared on the scene to investigate the matter. The husband invited him in but maintained his wife had left earlier in the morning to catch the first ferry. She had gone to visit her parents on the coastland. Constable Moriah's suspicion was aroused when he noted a baby among a brood of children, all too young to be taken care of by the father. Unsatisfied, the constable questioned the farmer at length, but the man could not explain why his wife had left the baby.

Then the constable talked to the neighbours, who agreed the woman would never leave the children. The policeman checked the ferry and, convinced the woman never left the island, returned with a warrant to search the house and grounds. He went over every inch of the farmer's house and yard, but found nothing. However, fearful the man would disappear, Constable Moriah arrested him.

Because of the murder investigation and the diggings, the police force on the island was strengthened. They needed a body in order to establish a case against the husband. Also, by this time the woman's distressed parents reported they had not seen her. The investigation was now in the hands of an inspector from the coastland.

Constable Moriah was tired of digging. He argued about the time being wasted and made a suggestion that the body was not anywhere around, hinting they might have to let the man go. Cautiously, he proposed they get young Abu's help. The inspector and the rest of the crew were shocked the constable would venture to make a joke out of the investigation. They turned on him with jibes and taunts. He challenged them with what he had heard about Abu, but they took no notice of him.

The search became extensive, spreading to farmlands down in the backdam. The task was impossible and the crew was exhausted. The inspector threw sideways glances at the men as they mumbled, whispering among themselves, sucking their teeth and yawning unabashed. He was uneasy. He knew what was on their minds and later that evening went to see Abu in secret.

"Tomorrow morning at half-past four, meet me on the bridge. I'll be waiting!" Abu greeted the inspector, who gazed at him speechless. How could Abu know? The inspector hadn't said a word!

Next morning, the inspector and his party arrived some time after four to find Abu waiting on the bridge in front of the yard. As they started off, Abu insisted he walk ahead of them. In this manner they walked, Abu twenty yards or more ahead in long flowing robes with the hood covering his head and bare feet.

Abu led the party straight for the backdam. They walked for miles across farms, trenches and dams. The inspector checked his watch at intervals. It was still dark but the men were sweating and tiring. Through rice fields and cane fields they went on a long and arduous journey. By this time the inspector was sure it was a wild goose chase. The men puffed and sweated as they tried to keep up with Abu.

"What dis man tink itis atall? We working hard all day, while he sitting down in the house!"

"I can't understand why he flying like dat and at four in the mornin'!"

"Watch where you goin', man—you nearly trip me up!"

"Jesus, man, I cyna keep up atall!"

"What de hell is this? Some force driving he, man!'

"You notice too...Look at he, man like he foot ain't touching de ground!"

"And he ain't even looking back!"

"This ain't natural, cyna be natural...this man ain't human!"

Baffled by the mysterious figure ahead, the men tramped laboriously behind, fretting and swearing. But Abu never looked back and he moved like the wind.

Suddenly, Abu stopped and would go no farther. Beckoning to the inspector, he pointed, describing a spot ahead on the dam and insisting the men would discover there what they wanted.

The inspector rushed forward, keeping the men at a distance while he looked for the clues Abu spoke about. In an instant, he called excitedly to the men and, pointing to a spot, instructed them to dig. Within minutes of digging, there was a chorus of enthusiastic cries. The men had found the body, the search was over.

Jubilant, the inspector called loudly, summoning Abu. Getting no response, he hurried forward with expressions of praise. He stared ahead, but Abu was nowhere around. He gazed into the distance. Abu could not have gone far. In excitement, the inspector ran down the dam until he was out of breath, then stopped and took in stretches of the dam as far as the eye could see.

Abu had disappeared completely.

---

Many people continue to use bush medicine to this day. What began as a matter of survival became an indispensable part of a culture. The same is true for other West Indian territories.

# Afua Cooper

## And I Remember

And I remember
standing
in the churchyard on Wesleyan Hill
standing and looking down on the plains
that stretch before me
like a wide green carpet
the plains full with sugar cane and rice
the plains that lead to the sea

And I remember
walking
as a little girl to school
on the savannahs of Westmoreland
walking from our hillbound village
walking along steep hillsides
walking carefully so as not to trip and plunge
walking into the valley

And I remember
running
to school on the road that cuts into the green carpet
running past laughing waters
running to school that rose like a concrete castle
out of my carpet of green
running with a golden Westmoreland breeze

And I remember
breathing
the smell of the earth plowed by rain and tractors
breathing the scent of freshly cut cane
breathing the scent of rice plants as they send
their roots into the soft mud
Yes, and I remember
thinking
this is mine this is mine
this sweetness of mountains
valleys
rivers
and plains
is mine
mine
mine

## Memories Have Tongue

My granny say she have a bad memory when I ask her to tell
me some of her life
say she can't remember much but
she did remember the 1910 storm and how dem house blow down
an dey had to go live with her granny down bottom house
Say she have a bad memory, but she remember
that when her husband died, both of them were thirty,
she had three little children, one in her womb,
one in her arms, one at her frocktail. She remember when
they bury him how the earth buss up under her foot
and her heart bruk inside
that when the baby born she had no milk
her breasts refused to yield.
She remember how she wanted her daughter to grow up and be
a postmistress but the daughter died at an early age
she point to the croton-covered grave at the bottom of the
yard. Say her memory bad, but she remember
1938
Frome
the riot
Busta
Manley
but what she memba most of all is that a pregnant woman,
one of the protesters, was shot an' killed by soldiers.
Say she old now her brains gathering water
but she remember
that she liked dancing as a young woman
and yellow was her favourite colour. She remember
too that it was her husband's father who asked

for her hand. The Parents sat in the hall and discussed
the matter. Her father finally concluded that her man was
an honourable person and so gave his consent.
Her memory bad but she remember
on her wedding day how some of her relatives
nearly eat off all the food. It was all right though, she
said, I was too nervous to eat anyway.

---

In 1938, workers all over the island of Jamaica struck and demonstrated against deplorable working and living conditions. One of the centres of these activities was Frome Estate in Westmoreland.

When the colonial militia was called in to put down the Frome demonstrations, the militia killed four people. Alexander Bustamante and Norman Manley were labour and political activists who led the people, and later became leaders of the country.

## Lovetalk

My love enfolds you
my love encircles you
I am the river from which all sweetness flows

My breasts your milkpots
from which you refuse to be weaned
my navel, your centre

You smell my particular smell
and your whole self begins to quiver
I am the tree of life
the giver of your knowledge

You want to remain for ever
in the shadow of my moonglow
to taste its essence
and wonder at its sweetness
I am the river from which all good things flow

# Cyril Dabydeen

## Phoenix

This bird,
alighting

On blacksage brush
when I fired—

The entire forest
ablaze...

Feathers floating
in the wind—

Leaves scattering
like ash.

Swarthier than ever,
skin burning—

Closer to the ground,
as I experience

Birdsong and wail...
such rememberances

In the night,
flesh of fire,

The tropical wind
patterning

A life—
moulding the sun,

Singeing the years.

## Multiculturalism

I continue to sing of other loves,
Places...moments when I am furious;
When you are pale and I am strong—
As we come one to another.

The ethnics at our door
Malingering with heritage,
My solid breath—like stones breaking;
At a railway station making much ado about much,
This boulder and Rocky Mountain,

CPR heaving with a head tax
As I am Chinese in a crowd,
Japanese at the camps,
It is also World War II.
Panting, I am out of breath.

So I keep on talking
With blood coursing through my veins,
The heart's call for employment equity,
The rhapsody of police shootings in Toronto,
This gathering of the stars one by one, codifying them
And calling them planets, one country, really...

Or galaxies of province after province,
A distinct society too:
Québec or Newfoundland; the Territories...
How far we make a map out of our solitudes
As we are still Europe, Asia,
Africa; and the Aborigine in me
Suggests love above all else—
The bear's configuration in the sky;
Other places, events; a turbanned RCMP,
These miracles—

My heritage and quest, heart throbbing;
Voices telling me how much I love you.
YOU LOVE ME; and we're always springing surprises,
Like vandalism at a Jewish cemetery
Or Nelson Mandela's visit to Ottawa
As I raise a banner high on Parliament Hill
Crying "Welcome!"—we are, you are—
OH CANADA!

## I am not

1

i am not West Indian
i am not—
let me tell you again and again
let Lamming and Selvon talk of places
            too distant from me;
let me also recover and seethe
& shout with a false tongue
if I must—
that i am here
nowhere else

let me also conjure up other places
as i cry out that all cities are the same,
rivers, seas, oceans—
how they swell or surrender
            at the same source

2

i breathe in the new soil
engorging myself with wind,
yet flaccid—

i inhale the odour
of rice paddy
cane leaves in the sun
& birds blacker than the familiar vulture

circling my father's house
with a vague promise

          amidst other voices
i come together with you,
crying out
that there are hinterlands,
other terrain

3

we fashion new boundaries
          and still i do not know,
i do not know,
in the cold, this heat
of the insides—
wetness at the corners of the mouth

skin grown lighter,
& once the giant lake,
foamy whiteness of my Ottawa river—
          now Mohawk or Algonquin...
whither Carib or Arawak?

i breathe harder
with my many selves,
          turning back

# Lawrence Hill

## So What Are You, Anyway?

Carole settles in Seat 12A, beside the window, puts her doll on a vacant seat and snaps open her purse. She holds up a mirror. She looks into her own dark eyes. She examines her handful of freckles, which are tiny ink spots dotting her cheeks. She checks for pimples, but finds none. Only the clear complexion that her father sometimes calls "milk milk milk milk chocolate" as he burrows into her neck with kisses.

"This is yours, I believe." A big man with a sunburnt face is holding her doll upside down.

"May I have her, please?" Carole says.

He turns the doll right side up. "A black doll! I never saw such a thing!"

"Her name's Amy. May I have her, please?"

"Henry Norton!" cries the man's wife. "Give that doll back this instant!"

Carole tucks the doll close to the window.

The man sits beside Carole. The woman takes the aisle seat.

"Don't mind him," the woman says, leaning towards Carole.

"By the way, I'm Betty Norton, and he's my husband, Henry."

The man next to Carole hogs the armrest. His feet sprawl onto her side. And he keeps looking at her.

The stewardess passes by, checking seat belts. "Everything okay?"

"May I go to the bathroom?" Carole asks.

"Do you think you could wait? We're about to take off."

"Okay."

Carole looks out the window, sees the Toronto airport buildings fall behind and wonders if her parents are watching. Say goodbye, she instructs Amy, waving the doll's hand, say goodbye to Mom and Dad. The engines charge to life. Her seat hums. They taxi down the runway. She feels a hollowness in her stomach when they lift into the air. Her ears plug and stay that way until the plane levels out over pillows of cotton. They burn as bright as the sun. So that is what the other side of clouds look like!

"Excuse me. *Excuse me!*" The man is talking to her. "You can go to the bathroom now, you know."

"No, that's all right," Carole says.

"Travelling all alone, are you?"

Carole swallows with difficulty.

"Where do you live?" he asks.

"Don Mills."

"Oh, really?" he says. "Were you born there?"

"Yes."

"And your parents?"

"My mother was born in Chicago and my father was born in Tucson."

"And you're going to visit your grandparents?"

She nods.

"And your parents let you travel alone!"

"It's only an airplane! And I'm a big girl."

The man lowers the back of his seat, chuckling. He whispers to his wife. "No!" Carole hears her whisper back, "*You* ask her!"

Carole yawns, holds Amy's hand and goes to sleep. The clinking of silverware wakens her, but she hears the man and woman talking about her, so she keeps her eyes shut.

"I don't know, Henry," says the woman. "Don't ask me. Ask *her*."

"I'm kind of curious," he says. "Aren't you?"

Carole can't make out the woman's answer. But then she hears her say:

"I just can't see it. It's not fair to children. I don't mind them mixed, but the world isn't ready for it. They're neither one thing nor the other. Henry, wake that child and see if she wants to eat."

When the man taps her shoulder, Carole opens her eyes. "I have to go to the bathroom," she says.

"But they're going to serve the meal," the man says.

"Henry! If she wants out, let her out. She's only a child."

Carole grimaces. She is definitely not a child. She is a young lady! She can identify Drambuie, Kahlua, and Grand Marnier by smell!

Once in the aisle, Carole realizes that she has forgotten Amy.

Henry Norton hands her the doll. "There you go. And don't fall out of the plane, now. There's a big hole down by the toilet."

"There is not!" Carole says. "There isn't any such thing!" She heads down the aisle with an eye out just in case there is a hole, after all.

Coming out of the toilet, Carole finds the stewardess. "Excuse me, miss. Could I sit somewhere else?"

The woman frowns. "Why?"

"I don't like the window."

"Is that it? Is that the only reason?"

"Well...yes."

"I'm sorry, but we don't have time to move you now. We're serving a meal. Ask me later, if you like."

After Carole had eaten and had her tray taken and been served a hot face towel, the man says: "What *are* you, anyway? My wife and I were wondering."

Carole blinks, sees the man's clear blue eyes and drops her head.

"What do you mean?" she says.

"You know, what are you? What race?"

Carole's mouth drops. Race? What is that? She doesn't understand. Yet she senses that the man is asking a bad question. It is as if he is asking her something dirty, or touching her in a bad place. She wishes her Mom and Dad were there. They could tell her what "race" meant.

"That doll of yours is black," Henry Norton says. "That's a Negro doll. That's race. Negro. What's your race?"

The question still confuses her.

"Put it this way," the man says. "What is your father?"

The question baffles her. What is her father? He is her Dad! He is her Dad and every Sunday morning he makes pancakes for the whole family and lets Carole pour hot syrup on them and afterwards he sits her on his lap and tells stories.

Mrs. Norton leans towards Carole. "Say you had a colouring book. What colour would you make your Dad?"

"I never use just one colour."

"Okay. What colour would you make his face?"

"Brown."

"And your mother?"

Carole imagines a blank page. What would she put in her

mother's face? She has to put something in there. She can't just leave it blank. "I don't know."

"Sure you do," Mrs. Norton says. "How would you colour your mother's face?"

"Yellow."

Carole sees Mr. and Mrs. Norton look at each other.

"Is your mother Chinese?" Mrs. Norton asks.

"No."

"Are you sure you'd colour her yellow?"

"No."

"What else might you colour her?"

What else? Carole feels ashamed at her stupidity. A tear races down her cheek. "Red," she says, finally.

"Red! You can't colour a face red! Is your mother white? Is she like me? Her face! Is it the same colour as mine?"

"Yes."

"And your father's brown?"

Carole nods.

"When you say brown, do you mean he is a Negro?"

"Yes." Of course her father is a Negro. If Mrs. Norton wanted to know all along if her Dad was a Negro, why didn't she just ask?

"So you're mixed?" Mrs. Norton says. "You're a mulatto!"

Carole's lip quivers. What is mulatto? Why do they keep asking her what she is? She isn't anything!

"So is that it? You're a mulatto? You know what a mulatto is, don't you? Haven't your parents taught you that word?"

Approaching with a cart of juice, the stewardess looks up and smiles at Carole. That gives her a rush of courage.

"Leave me alone!" she screams at Mrs. Norton.

Passengers stare. The stewardess spills a drink. Mrs. Norton sits back hard in her seat, her hands raised, fingers spread. Carole sees people watching.

"Why do you keep asking me if my Dad is Negro? Yes, he's a Negro! Okay? OKAY? Negro Negro Negro!"

"Calm down," Mrs. Norton says, reaching over.

"Don't touch her," the stewardess says.

"Who are these people?" someone says from across the aisle. "Imagine, talking to a child like that, and in 1970!"

One woman sitting in front of Carole stands up and turns around.

"Would you like to come and sit with me, little girl?"

"No!" Carole shouts. "I don't like all these questions. She keeps asking me how I would colour my parents in a colouring book! Why do you keep asking me that?"

Mrs. Norton pleads with Carole to stop.

"How would you like it if that happened to you?" Carole says. "So what are you, anyway? What are your parents? How would you colour them? Well, I don't care! I don't even care!"

"How would you like to come and sit with me?" the stewardess says, smiling. "I'll make you a special drink. Have you ever had a Shirley Temple?"

Carole nods enthusiastically. Already she feels better. Clutching Amy, she passes by the Nortons, who swing their legs to let her out.

"My God," Carole hears Mrs. Norton tell her husband, "talk about sensitive."

# George Elliott Clarke

## Casualties
*January 16, 1991*

Snow annihilates all beauty
this merciless January.
A white blitzkrieg, Klan—cruel,
arsons and obliterates.

Piercing lies numb us to pain.
Nerves and words fail so we
can't feel agony or passion,
so we can't flinch or cry,

when we spy blurred children's
charred bodies protruding
from the smoking rubble
of statistics or see a man

stumbling in a blizzard
of bullets. Everything is
normal, absurdly normal.
We see, as if through a snow-

storm, darkly. Reporters
rat-a-tat-tat tactics,
stratagems. Missiles bristle
behind newspaper lines.

Our minds chill; we weather
the storm, huddle in dreams.
Exposed, though, a woman,
lashed by lightning, repents

of her flesh, becomes a living
X-ray, "collateral damage."
The first casualty of war
is language.

## April in Paris

Elms etch against the watercolour sky.
I exult in sprays of green—vines and leaves
Leaping up walls, occupying *les rues*.
Africans on the white steps of Sacre Coeur
Sell gold tinted by barter and banter;
They curry a spicy callaloo
Of currencies into francs. The pigeons are
Up to no good, dreaming of July's heat.
*Une beauté* peels a newspaper from cool
And steady wind. We are home in April.
The pigeons startle at my too-loud thought
And wheel into the pale heaven. Verdant

*Messieurs* wielding long brooms, sweep shit—
And old manuscripts—from the cobblestones.
    I wander among the graves of poets,
Stalk inspiration with a loaded pen,
And collect bunches of fresh, cold lilies.
I keep thinking of you, so, so lovely,
Rambling the ramparts of the Citadel
Of Quebec. I want to drape you in silks,
Array you in beautiful, gaudy flags,
But you've kept me drifting all of this time.
    If you will offer me another home—
A balcony where I may type this poem,
I will bring you wine and albescent honey.
I will bring you kisses of albescent honey.
I'll name you with the most beautiful nouns:
Carnation, orchid, rose, iris, trillium, anemone.

## April 19, 19__

    He was falling apart under the pressure of love;
his blood gelled slowly into honey:
nectar was accumulating in his veins.
Becoming fierce and fiercer for her, his measures
broke up sonnets because they couldn't accommodate
the immense pleasure of her kiss.
    Troubadours and toreadors sang of her all night
so he couldn't sleep. Her name quarried *corrida*
and *querida*. She seemed to have been born in silk,
a liquid, icy fire that chilled her skin,

inciting her nerves to gasp at the caress.
Her kisses were rain upon his face.
    He brought her lilies and the bluesiest
albas ever strummed by a Nova Scotian,
yielding their private language to a public form,
because of the night she lay beside him
and the day they lolled in apple blossoms.
They were guilty of unspeakable love.
    There was the beginning and that only:
the first poem that made her gasp; the first embrace
that made him echo a millennium of songs
By entombed, regretful poets who wished
They had known lips as full and soft as hers.
Their love survives now only in this poem.

## Marina: The Love Song of Lee Harvey Oswald

    Here are some early narcissus for your blue eyes,
Marina Prusakova.
Let's mose beside the River Minsk—you, nineteen and perfect,
And I just twenty-one.
Look, in still life, Father Lenin smiles upon us.
Take these blue plums and some hot, black tea.
    I've scribbled in my Historic Diary
About the workers's future—sunlight sifting
Through birch branches and hydroelectric towers,
Silvering everything, everything.
I promise you we'll blind history!

Taste these sweet plums, Marina.
    Let's dawdle in doorways while the snow mills:
This world is like a coming storm.
Peasants will throw flowers when our steamer aways,
Silver narcissus petals snow through air,
When we embark for glimmering America
To become its shining President and First Lady.

## To Milton Acorn

    Death's plain idiocy, maker. There's no
Music in it, only suspires of rain
And sighs of dumb, worm-ravished earth. Naive
Carpenter, where's your voice now that once sang
Of love and anger in jack-pine meters
That couldn't be planed to fit pre-fab verse?
    You were our Miltonic, Atlantic Lear,
A raging, white-bearded, word-weathered bard,
Who howled against the liars' legislatures.
How can I speak of you?
    I break!
I break from the tension of the iambic line.
    Craftsman, does your voice cry through crows
Or does the grave open its mouth and sing?

# April 3–4, 1968

A century of rain crashes home in night,
Dark richness. He sojourns through wet lightning
To the church to sing his death. He feels it
Like sparks, something blazing the shrouded air.
He unveils the bright Bible in his head;
Sudden lightning enraptures the black church.
To the pulpit he rises, thundering
Justice, Jesus, and John, because God has
Shown him The Promised Land; his voice crackles,
"I've been to the mountaintop." The next day,
After the rain, he steps into the cool
Evening, into the cool, April evening.
Andy dreams he hears an engine crackle.
Ralph jumps "instinctively," then turns, then turns,
And sees King, arms outstretched, the blood crashing
From the hole the bullet's punched through his neck.

# Austin Clarke

## Letter of the Law of Black

Edgehill House,
Edgehill Road,
Edgehill Gap,
Edgehill Lane,
Edgehill Hill,
Barbados

My dear only Son,

I take up my pen in hand to send you these salutations, hoping that the reaches of them will find you in a perfect state of good health, as they leave me feeling fairly well, at present.

I am telling you this now, at this rather late time, because when you left Barbados to go away, there was too much emotion in the air to talk to you and make sense. Most of the things said were what I call emotion; and all that emotion was good for someone as young as you, taking up a journey in life, to a country which is strange to you, although you were born there. The emotion itself was not complete, was not real emotion, and it rang a bit empty because the one person who could have made the rafters ring for joy, that you, her child, were going to a place where she had so many happy years, was not there. Then was not the time. Then was not the occasion to bring back memories whose only meaning and point in bringing them up would have demanded the bringing up also of the tragedy which defines those memories of happiness. Your mother.

I waited also because I wanted to be sure that you got through your first year in Toronto. The first year is always the hardest. It is the happiest and the saddest. You are free from whatever responsibilities being at home assumes you should carry; and you are alone in a new freedom; and very often you need someone to help you confine yourself within that very freedom. And if I remember correctly, from my own days at Trinity College, the first year demands complete attention to details that prove later to be a complete waste of time. You have to watch your allowance and be a banker; an economist; an investor; and, worst of all, a hoarder. God help you that you do not, like me, have to be a hoarder. You see a shirt for ten dollars, and you buy it because you think it is a saving: but, the next day, you pass a shop window and you see the same shirt, on sale, for half the price. And being new, you do not know and would never think that you could take the ten-dollar shirt off your back, and put it in a nice parcel, and return it, because you could say, had you learned, "This shirt is too small for me."

Is Stollery's Emporium for Men still at the intersection of Bloor and Yonge streets? I spent many dollars and more hours in that store, getting the wrong advice and the proper fit from the male clerks, than I can recount. Their shirts are not bad. But the best ones I wore, and still have some of, were obtained either at the Annual Jewish Sale of clothes in the Exhibition

Gardens down at the Ex, or at a second-hand establishment named the Royal Ex-Toggery, near the Anglo-Saxon residential district of Rosedale. So, you see, I took the best—the best of second-hand!—from the best of both Toronto worlds, at the time. I am talking about the fifties. Now, as I have been reading from the clippings you have sent down, the place is a virtual potpourri of nationalities and something called multiculturalisms.

I noticed the titles of your small but well-chosen library of books. I was pleased to see that although you read the Classics, you still had time besides Latin and Greek for good literature. You should, whilst you are there and during the term breaks, look at the Russians, especially Pushkin. You know, he was one of us! By that I mean a colonial man, more than I mean the obvious: that he was black. Even in your position of being in a minority amongst all this multiculturalism, through colour, in a country like Canada, whose immigration policy was officially white up until 1950, the fact of being a colonial—you young intellectuals would say "post-colonial" or "neo-colonial," but I am old, and old-fashioned, and I say colonial—the colonial is the fact that transcends blackness. Blackness may change when you are amongst all black students; or it may change when you are in the company of good white people. (Have you had the chance to look up Mr. Avrom Lampert yet, as I have asked you to do, and pay him your respects? He was extremely kind to me, and most helpful. I have eaten more bagels and lackeyes, or latkees—do you spell it so?—in his home during my time in Toronto, than I have eaten flying fish and peas and jerk pork. I hope he is still in the quick. I still owe him the fifty dollars he lent me, thirty years ago, to pay a bill. Shirts, I think. Definitely, pay him my respects. But use your discretion in paying him that old obligation.)

You should browse through some Russian literature. In addition to Pushkin, I would think that Dostoyevski's *Crime and Punishment* would be worthwhile.

One winter, when I was flat on my back with fever, indisposed through health, in a small attic room on College Street near where the main Public Library used to be, I took out and read *Crime and Punishment* in two days of delirium and high temperature. I got worse. They rushed me to the Toronto General Hospital, they meaning two Canadian students who rented rooms that summer in the same house. Dr. Guile, the physician who saw me in Emergency, just smiled and told me to get a bottle of Gordon's Dry Gin. I had told him of Dostoyevski. I hope you won't have that kind of relapse when you seek to broaden your literary horizons. If you were to read *Das Kapital* or *The Communist Manifesto*, even though you were reading for your degree in Political Science and Economics, polly-si-and-ec, they will say you are a communist. You may, if you read these two ideologies, have to hide their tolerance under your academic gown. But if you are seen reading Pushkin, or Dostoyevski or Tolstoy, they will say you are an intellectual. Even if they called you a colonial intellectual, it would be different. You would be more dangerous to them; and they would not be able to despise, or, worse still, ignore, your presence.

Who are these "they"? "They" are all the unmentionable spies, the unnameable people, people who watch you when you do not know they're watching you, when you do not feel they are, or should; and who take it upon themselves to be your sponsors. Beware of sponsors. Beware of liberals. Beware of patronage. Beware of fools.

One day, Kay called me. She was crying. Her fiancé had met a Canadian woman, much older than she, and older than he, who had a child, nine years old. You know who Kay is. He told his colleagues in the Sociology of Violence As It Affects course that he was going to marry this Canadian girl. And he did. And Kay killed herself. But before she killed herself, he never apologized to her. Never called. Never wrote a letter to avoid breach of promise. Never sent a message. Was not mortified by the mortification of Breacher of Promise, or by the violence Kay's stepfather had promised him as a new wedding gift, or by the violent sociology of the jilter.

The church had been booked, she said. The reception, in a rec room—what a doleful term! A rec...could it be a wrecked room?—was booked for the reception, she said. Flowers were ordered, she said. Her girlfriends at the bank, all tellers, and of lies, presumably, were invited, she said; and had bought their wedding dresses, she said. Everything was arranged, she said. The "wrecked" room was vacuumed twice by the superintendent of the apartment building, she said. It was situated in a dreary district of Toronto, where there were five factories and one slaughterhouse, for cows and for pigs.

I don't know why and how I got started on Kay. But having begun, you shall hear the end of that part of my life. I do intend, however, that the end of my life shall be slightly postponed. At seventy-one, I intend, as I have said before you left Barbados, to begin at Genesis, and word-for-work, word-for-worm, work my way through until I reach Revelation and the Concordance. Another poetical word. I feel I have reached concordance with you, my son, in the writing of this letter, at this stage; for after Hitler has been fed his rice and fishheads—hoping no bones are caught in his swallow pipe!—and I have read a few chapters of Exodus, I shall retire for the night, and join you again, soon, in a concordance of love and of deep nostalgia. I hope to complete both: this letter, and the Good Book; and I wonder which of the three remaining duties of my remaining days shall have been dispatched first? The Good Book? The letter? Or my life?

The feelings which I have been expressing to you, and which I have been expressing particularly with more emotion and honesty, are taking hold of me; because all of a sudden, you are not here, not here in this big old house, whose emptiness echoes as if it were a rock quarry, and I myself dynamiting coral stone. It is an old house. And it is larger, too large for one man who spends almost every hour of the day and night inside it, alone. But it is a happy house. A warm house. A museum of memories and events and things which have been ourselves and our past and our aspirations. Your absence gives me the joyful opportunity both to view these things and to rearrange them. Your absence, I hope, is merely temporary—four years of study in that city which, at this time of year, must be forgetting the lifefulness of summer. I was talking about feelings. Yes, these new feelings which I must be expressing to you with a vengeance you had not known before, are feelings more characteristic of a mother; a woman who follows her child into another land with words of love and of reminiscence. And in the case of most women, this kind of love and reminiscence need not be pure love. It could be a transmitting of the cord of birth, the maternal cord, the umbilical restriction that reminds the child, the daughter, that she owes an unpayable debt for being born. It is important that you understand. I do not wish you to miscalculate my motives, even if they are devious.

I have, and I probably transmit, feelings to you that state I am not only your old, irreverent father, but am behaving as if there were a piece of the woman, the mother, inside my advice and words. And I hope that, as a wise man, with the blood of your dead mother's veins inside you, an Edgehill, that you will disregard all the advice I have been giving you, because I am speaking a different language, and breathing in a different air. Disregard it as a modus vivendi: but regard it as a piece of history, to be used as a comparison. Having now absolved you from all filial encumbrances of the mind, let me now incarcerate you immediately for your choice of a philosophical position which is not valid, or tenable, precisely because, as I have said earlier, you have not assumed that there was a history before your time at Trinity College.

You said you wrote a paper on the British Constitution, and your professor gave you a B. You said you showed your paper to a Canadian friend, and he asked you to let him use it as his own submission. In the same course, you said. To the same professor, you said. The same length, you said. The identical paper, you said. The only change in the paper, you said, was that your Canadian friend put his name, a name different from yours, on the paper. You said all these things. These are the facts of the case. And your Canadian friend got an A for the paper, you said. And you ask me now, if this is not racial discrimination, or bigotry, or unfairness? It is not so much your shock that it happened, and to you, as that there was no explanation, no regret, no forgiveness from anyone, when you pointed it out to the two of them.

I myself am shocked that you would have confronted the professor with his own bigotry. I am also shocked that you expected, and did not get, an apology from him. You seem to feel that all these incidents of bad manners, all these expressions of a lower-class, peasant syndrome and mentality, have begun with your presence at Trinity College, and that Trinity College is above that rawness of disposition. Had you an eye to history, to the reality and the logic, that other black men before you have passed through Trinity College, you would not now be so smitten by your paltry experience. Have you ever thought of a day in their lives, in the year 1931?

You are, in spite of the black American Ralph Ellison, who would claim that you are "invisible," you are rather outstanding and conspicuous, and as they say, nowadays, through that thing called multiculturalism, most visible. You are also a conscience. And you should also know that part of our make-up, of our psyche, is hidden, is dark, is criminal, is Christian, is pure, is degenerate and is beautiful.

There was a group of West Indians at a place in Montreal, a second-rate place, called Sir George Williams. Montreal, as you know, and in spite of what you may be hearing amongst the Anglophones at Trinity College, is essentially a French city. Why did I say this, when I am really speaking about the West Indians, and a bigoted professor of Biology, and not about the culture of the place? Anyhow. The West Indians protested. And the administration at Sir George, which had become during these protests a most determinedly third-rate institution, ignored their pleas. The West Indians then held a demonstration. They held it in a room where there was a computer. I never could understand that computer. Why did they not demonstrate in the department of Biology? Or at the professor's home? In my estimation, it would have been better to have done one or the other. However, the computer was damaged. Allegedly damaged by the West Indians, they said. The West Indians were arrested. The West Indians were charged. The West Indians were later sentenced. To various prisons. And to various prison terms. One of them is now a Senator down here. Another is a Senator up there. Does Trinity College have a computer? Do you wish to be a Senator? Up there? Or down here?

In my own experience at Trinity College, I fought that kind of bigotry, in a humorous manner. When I felt it was in the college, and that I was a victim of it, that I was, as I have said of you, a conscience, I merely copied my paper in Political Science (it was also on the British Constitution!) and on one copy I put the name of a student who I knew was getting the best grades, undeservedly so. I submitted that copy with his name first. I had arranged with this person that he would not submit a paper and spoil my stratagem. He was, moreover, lazy. When the professor had read that paper, and had given him an A, I then submitted the other copy. Of the same paper. But with my name. The professor gave me a B-minus. I took both papers, and without talking to anyone, I reread them to reassure myself that they were identical, word for word. When I was convinced of this, I took the first page with my name on it, and pinned it onto the other pages of the other paper—the professor always wrote his comments and the grade on the last page—and then I asked for an appointment. He registered an A in his book for me; and for the other student, who had by now not submitted a paper at all, he gave an A-minus. I had made certain, however, that this was the last course and the last examination I had to take with this gentleman. He was an Englishman. He spoke with a Cockney accent. He came from Cork. His shirts were always dirty at the neck and at the cuffs. He did not buy them at Stollery's Emporium for Men; and he did not know about the Annual Jewish Sale, or the Royal Ex-Toggery. He didn't even know a latkey from a lackey.

These are not the same sentiments I like to send, in a red-white-and-blue airmail envelope, with a fifty-cent stamp on it, all the way from this island of Barbados to you, up there, buried almost up to your knees in snow; and in hostility. I thank you for sending me the phonograph record by Lionel Richie, *Games People Play*. It is also the title of a book by a man named Toffler. I could never understand why so much attention was given to Toffler's book, which I have not read, and so little to Lionel Richie's song. The Third Symphony of Beethoven's arrived without a scratch or a warp.

Unfortunately, the music that the Government Radio in this place plays is like the voices of the politicians: vulgar. "Games People Play," which I remember dancing to, with Kay, almost every Saturday night at a West Indian calypso club where the notorious civil rights lawyer, Charlie Roach, played guitar, badly, fifty years ago, is still fresh and contemporary in my mind, and very sensual. Is it the same "Games People Play?" If Hitler were a woman, Hitler and I would make a few steps.

It is the kind of music that makes you want to dance with a dog! Timeless. Incidentally, although I do not advocate that you become a Christian, I do insist that you sit in a church at least once a month. But preferably in the Church of England. If you could stumble into a Catholic church, or if you are taken there, choose the best: the old cathedral at the corner of King and Church. Sit inside a church. Listen to the music. Pay less attention to the sermon. The sermon is not meant for you, for us, for our people. But the liturgy and the ritual are artistically rewarding. And so is the liturgical music. So far as Trinity College is concerned, and in case you are hung over and desperate on Saturday nights, and cannot rise for breakfast before the dining hall closes, slip into the Chapel; take a seat in the rear; find the hymn; sing it loudly; but not as if you are the soloist; and before the worms in your unrepentant stomach growl you out of favour amongst the "denines," as we called the Theological students, and amongst the sincere worshippers, who are there because of the breakfast that is served after the collection plate, you may find yourself amongst the blessed—meaning the hungry poor. For the rich would not have risen so early on a Sunday morning; and when they do not rise, instead of oranges and bran flakes and soft honey that is grey in colour and bran bread and bran toast and warm milk and bacon done too hard and soft-boiled eggs, they would rather soothe their constitution with caviar and champagne. If you were here, at Edgehill House, you would be partaking of our Sunday breakfast: crab backs stuffed with pork and champagne. (I found a bottle dated 1943. Dom-Pee.) A pity it is that I cannot fold a crab into this red-white-and-blue airmail envelope, and send it to you!

"Games People Play" is old. It is also a song that keeps coming back to my ears, and whose emotion will not let me forget the sadness of love spent in Toronto. But I have to begin to scratch my way through Genesis, in this concordance of journey, and watch for the bones in Hitler's supper.

Hoping that the reaches of these few lines have found you with your own concordance,

I remain...

# Nigel Darbasie

## Winter Stroll in Tipaskan

The schoolyard provides visual relief
yet not without its own clutter.
A large open space covered in snow
packed and cratered under millions of footprints.

In every direction, rows of houses and apartments
rectangular in stucco and aluminum siding
with sloped rooftops shingled brown, grey, black.
Metal chimneys glinting in the sun.

The eye wanders. Sights along crooked fences
studies the thin nakedness of backyard trees.
Then returning to the horizon
is caught unexpectedly
by rounded minarets with arched portals
a crescent moon and star.

## The Oracle of Babylon

Tear up this wonderful city
burn it to the ground?
Man, all you crazy yes.
Better out the flambeau
rest the pickaxe and sledgehammer
before somebody damage the place.

What happen, you don't like nice thing?
Look this fancy dining set
you could be eatin from
in yuh split-level luxury home
with swimming pool, up in the Heights.
Then imagine the two-car garage
with Porsche and Mercedes inside.

On a winter's night, step out
in a fur coat sweepin to yuh ankle.
Accent with some gold chain
a scatter of diamonds.
But don't tell nobody
we love glitter just like white folks.
And when they roll their eye
in yuh purse or wallet
is fifty-dollar bills
padding a line-up of credit card.
Now that's a good feeling.

Bring down Western society?
Well is book learnin you go need
to convert these millions of worshippers.
And don't let me hear
all you break some showcase on mainstreet.
Throw a big TV on yuh back
run up the road
call that a cultural revolution.

## Conceiving the Stranger

First define the tribal self
in skin colour, language
religion, culture.
Add to that
boundaries
of nation, city
village or street.
And there you are:
out of place
a foreigner
the strange other
a moving violation
of tribal differences.

# Rozena Maart

## Conceptualizing the Immaculate

It was at this occasion when Sarah thought it appropriate to announce her dissatisfaction with the priest. She proceeded with no paper in her hand, unlike the many attendants, to voice what might be the most dissatisfying news for the whole committee. She ruffled her skirt and walked towards the door, where several women were gathering to plan the upcoming Sunday school festival. Many mothers complained about Father John's methods of organizing, and others objected to his somewhat abusive manner. Looking ruffled, she thought, may cause the women to pay her some attention. Father John had been away and the determined twelve-year-old female child was more than pleased about his absence. She paced the wooden floor, sometimes glancing at the ceiling and looking for places where she had previously hidden and gathered her strength.

Before approaching the door, she watched and touched the wooden image of Mary, still rigid and in place in the Nativity scene. Mary's makers had ensured that she was gracefully endowed with fine features: her lips slim and silent, her eyes indirect and wondering, her expression angelic, with an air of gracefulness that only a painful heart like Sarah's could erase. Sarah did not know that the colour of the wood had been selected by Father John. He, the priest fulfilling his mission, had selected the carvings because, surely, he could not allow his Nova Scotian Natives to ever think that Mary was remotely as dark as the wood suggested. The carvings were smooth. They had an air about them, a sense of superiority, as if placing them in the church endowed them with biblical powers.

Caught between the almost seductive Mary and her decision to disclose her own immaculate conception, Sarah wondered whether her testimony would be so well received: whether others would bow before her and praise her and the child she was to bring forth into her black world. Mesmerized by Mary's presence, Sarah stared at the statue in front of her with hypnotic fervour. Suddenly, it seemed alive. She caressed Mary's arms and touched her erect wooden breasts, fondling them the way she had had her own protruding nippled flesh fondled by both her biological father and Father John. They had started touching her at the same time. When, she could hardly remember.

Then she anxiously started searching the wooden Mary, looking for an expected part that she had waited and wanted to touch. She searched without hesitation beneath the cloth that was Mary's dress and opened Mary's rigid wooden legs. "It's not here," she gasped. "It's not here." She searched again, turning Mary upside down in the hope that what she was looking for may have gone somewhere else. "There is no vagina," she whispered. "No vagina." Sarah found not one trace that Mary had ever borne a child.

The infuriated young female child undid her skirt and searched for the large silver pin that kept her clothing together. Her first entry was fierce. And, like her own first entry, there was no foreplay, no preparation, only a few stolen moments to ease the need for unlawful, immediate, sexual gratification. She pierced and cursed and swore and bled as she vaginized the Mother of Jesus. She stuck her pricked fingers deep into the wooden image thousands had observed. As she panted and carved and panted and nail-scratched Mary a vagina, the tears clouded her vision of a Nativity that was of no relation to her as a Native. Her fingers bled all over Mary until the statue was covered in blood and tears, the fluids of her womanhood. As she dug and carved anxiously, Mary's body disappeared into the ground and chips of wood splintered their way onto the floor and her face. Sarah's skirt was hanging loosely about her straight-waisted, protruding stomach. Finally, she sighed in exultation. The perfect image of Mary had been destroyed. Mary now had a vagina, but she was of no use to the packaged scene that bore the memory of the birth of Jesus and signalled the sacrifices of millions of people, who had to abdicate all sense of inner power and submit to Christianity for the sake of survival.

Sarah stared long and hard at the door to the meeting room and wondered whether anyone had heard her crying. The door stayed shut and Sarah remained crouched on the wooden floor, sucking at her bloody fingers. She was familiar with the taste, although this time she clenched her hands with pleasure. These stains she had sustained during a fight with Mary, unlike other times when she had sucked her blood-stained fingers in the hope of swallowing the memories. On the kitchen floor of her home and the kitchen floor of the rectory, she had crouched and sucked the flesh she wore like a stamp. Which one was it first? she thought almost aloud, and jolted into an upright position as she heard a door slam behind her. She crept under the rows of wooden pews and lay watching Mary, listening to Father John's bold biblical steps and observing his strides of confidence as he entered the church. Sarah lay silent and in pain, clenching both her hands, folding them helplessly into her mouth. Two more steps and he'll see me, she thought.

Father John had played hide-and-seek before, and when he had found his unwilling hider, he had ejaculated almost immediately, as though all his libidinous desires were centred on the search. Sarah was his prize. It was late one afternoon after the girls' choir had returned from an outing in the woods when Father John had first started playing his games. It was not unusual for him to request that Sarah stay behind. The choir outings were a joy to Sarah because they were a time for her to be with female children her own age. She laughed and giggled as they did, imitating the gestures that her father silenced, indulging in stories and jokes about boys who wanted peeks under their dresses, until her face hardened when she learned that the girlish desires of her peers, practised in this atmosphere of fantasy and comfort, were already a reality for her. To her peers Sarah was a respected female child who had earned the reputation of an honorary adult. Motherless since the tender age of seven, she took care of her father and four brothers, each delighting in motherly attention from a child who needed it herself so dearly. At breakfast, she prepared three different cereals and poured endless cups of tea, as each brother demonstrated his desire to have his cup filled and dear old father gestured with stares, moving his eyes in the direction of what he desired. His boots were securely tied and his face was patted as Sarah lifted herself from the ground, just as her mother used to do. The four boys had their sandwiches wrapped in particular ways so that each could identify which was his. By the time Sarah was ten years old, she had managed to run a house without ever knowing the joy of learning to read a book. Sarah's admiration of books gave Father John many clues. He knew that she cherished the unknown. Father John would motion for her from the desk to his lap—each time teaching Sarah about his own misguided and deceitful desires. His long black robe twirled itself around him more times than he deserved. It embarrassed him with righteousness and hid his fondling abusive hands, which covered every detail of Sarah's black body. It camouflaged a priest who hid his carnal desires and performed them regularly upon an unwilling child.

One day, Father John overheard the giggling conversation of the girls and forbade it, warning that it stole time away from God's work: that girls ought to be girls and give their souls and hearts to the Lord, who would cleanse them and keep them protected from the evils of the devil. As he gripped her hand, Father John showed Sarah that he favoured her. Her peers watched with envy as Father John explained to Sarah how the cow had given birth to the calf. She knew that something was already growing inside her and soon her calf would want to leave too. That day, she remained silent on the bus and protested not a word when her father mounted her upon his bed that same evening, but listened to the crying calf and the swaying trees vomiting inside her stomach.

Lying silently under the pews, Sarah watched the boots of Father John, cursing the moment of his entry. She wondered if he could smell her, as he had complained on occasion, and offered holy waters to clean her soiled and unbathed parts. But no. Father John checked his wristwatch and proceeded into the meeting room, where disapproving voices announced his arrival. He commanded the attention of the women and held it for a long time. Sarah rolled over to the end of the pew and lifted herself without erasing the traces of her presence. She remained silent as she realized the fear of the women she so admired. It was clear where their commitments lay. Their Christian duty had forbidden them to challenge the man who preached the gospel of obedience. To Sarah, it marked a moment of defeat. It was clear to her that she could no longer rely on their goodwill. The tears stuck in the corners of her eyes, refusing to fall. She gripped her lips with her teeth, sealing her resentment for the women who amongst themselves disapproved of Father John, but who, when confronted by their Father, remained as children—obedient to the one they served.

Sarah stood before the Nativity scene that, during the first week of January, still urged a genuflection. She did bow, and bowed again, and again, until her body fell to the ground. She realized that Jesus, hanging on the cross above the altar, was staring at her. Should she confront him? "It may be a good idea," she murmured to herself. She moved towards the cross and stared at the man with whom she was going to converse.

Their silence fell upon the church and Sarah stared at the walls as she heard her thoughts being echoed. She saw him smile. Saw him smile as her silence spoke. It was time for her to raise her objections to the man who witnessed her rape, her rage, her unwilling submission. "You are dead, aren't you?" she asked. Sarah moved towards the figure hanging on the cross. She refused to touch him, although her temptation was greater than she had anticipated. She gestured towards his lame, dead body and touched his bloody feet. The nails stuck deep into the wooden flesh and a cloth covered the genitals she motioned to see. She could not reach that high and had to fetch a ladder from the downstairs room. Standing on the ladder, Sarah could reach her right hand up and touch the statue of Jesus. The cloth around his waist was hard, like the rest of the wood, and his blue eyes warned against the atrocities she was about to commit. She stroked his one breast, but could not reach the other. Her hands covered all the areas they could reach. In an attempt to understand her forced genuflection, she giggled, then laughed so loud that the meeting room door swung open. "Get off there at once," shouted Father John. "Oh, no, what a terrible thing to do," echoed Mrs. Brown. Her voice filled the room and the emptiness of the church made it appear blasphemous. Mrs. Brown massaged her pregnant stomach and no sooner had Sarah's eyes grown still when she collapsed. Mrs. Thomas rushed to her aid and assisted Sarah with a scented handkerchief. Within seconds, Sarah knew what had happened and cried no more. She looked around the room, identified each of her onlookers and raised her body from their disgusted stares. She walked straight ahead and left the church without looking back.

Sarah knew then that her options were few. None of the women at the mothers' union could assist her. Only her own actions could save her dignity and ensure her future. As she walked briskly towards the house of her friend, she recollected her thoughts on the days she had spent at the child-care room.

She could only go to Alice and together they could work something out. Alice had encouraged Sarah to disclose her pregnancy at the mothers' meeting, and claimed that Sarah's pregnancy gave her the right to be there: she was a mother-to-be. Alice was older and lived with her mother, two sisters and her four-year-old brother. She had lost her father when she was ten years old. It was still mid-afternoon when Sarah arrived and found Alice in the company of four others. The female children were known to Sarah, and they greeted her respectfully, even though they were all the same age. They groomed each other, picking away with their afro combs and talking in soft voices about Father John and his hide-and-seek games. To Sarah's surprise, she was not Father John's treasured jewel but only his pregnant one. Each told her story while the others assisted with embraces and handkerchiefs until their voices grew louder and fiercer. Their silence had reigned for too long. Father John had to be dethroned from his kingdom of abuse: of rape and brutality; of destruction and robbery; of the helpings he took from their bodies in order to do his manly job.

The female children decided upon their plan. Their combs lay silent and patiently awaited the outcome of their courage. Sarah left first, clenching the scribbled note that Alice obliged her with. Each accomplice left on her own journey, in search of the items they had all decided upon. In two hours time it would be dark, and each would have to attend choir practice. The boys would be with their instructor and Sarah's father would be at home. Sarah went home to cook. She placed the note in her panties, then removed it with the knowledge that it was not a safe place and tied the note around her stomach. It lay crumpled and fearless as she shivered no more.

Promptly, all the female children arrived for choir practice. Sarah was expectedly late and presented her note to Father John. Father John did not complain about Sarah's late arrival since it was a usual occurrence; nor did he voice any objections to the note requesting his urgent presence at the home of her father. He asked that the girls sing along while he attended to his duties and that Sarah take charge of the choir. As Father John left, the female children all asked Sarah whether they could leave since everybody knew that it would be some time before Father John returned from house calls. This was, of course, part of the plan, and Sarah granted her peers their wish while she and Alice waited for them all to leave.

Their accomplices had already taken the shortcut to Sarah's house where Father John would soon respond to a false house call. At the back of the house, the female children gathered with their cans of petroleum. Within seconds the scattered liquid surrounded the house. Sarah's father and Father John were shaking hands and exchanging godly words of wisdom when Sarah's accomplices secured the door from the outside. Father John turned down the loud music but all was set for the final departure. As the flames ascended into the heavens and the screams of two trapped males echoed in the distance, the female children all gazed into the burning flames. Each recalled the times of their rape, their thoughts plunging into the eager fire.

When the screams of the men could no longer be heard, the female children informed the neighbours about the unfortunate event. The buckets of water, the screams and yells from churchgoers who questioned the carelessness of Sarah's father with his oil lamp and cigarettes eased the pain of the younger children as they glanced at one another for support. Older men forbade the children to see the burnt bodies and several of the women cuddled Sarah and stroked her stiff body.

Sarah looked pale in comparison and her shock was not as severe as they had anticipated.

# Ayanna Black

## I Write Imaginary Stories

1. seed

going it alone was never my ambition
I knew at 13 yrs old
I knew
I knew it was
not fashionable like the contents of *Vogue*
today she writes she's going it alone—
single motherhood by     choice
or despair?     the sperm bank is her obsession
and seduction
technicalizing the perfect seed for sprouting

what about the history?
smelling father's odour     smell touch and touch
like my cat Zwardi mews and mews and cuddles
up in my lap for my smell     my body contact

2. cloud

I never learned fatherly games
like my friends Carol Nerissa Pauline
when the pain was
too much for my body
to resist     I fell
in love with his absence     seven years old
and I buried him over and over
his glass casket covered
with white purple black
clouds
I write
I write imaginary
stories

3. rain

black hole
this is not your crude joke
this is a celestial reality
emptiness longings
my grandma agnes knew :
she fills me
with old photographs     him holding
me     six months old     him feeding
me     him feeding     feeding     photographs
photographs and letters and words
I cannot read words that make rain
drops I hear the sound
of raindrops I don't need raindrops
too much pain too much

grandma agnes howling sound level
with wind I'm inside
the sun his voice the healer
his face a sun
flower

4. feminism

he says feminism is not our problem
not for us it's dividing the race
I say I'm piecing
my world together already divided
before me years ago
divided
she sits regal
passionately pushing the right keys
re: feminism interspersing
her attitudes re: men
this is my centre        centre
my politics calling upon
within my healer        my survival
I write stories
I write

# Claire Harris

## Under Black Light

on the first saturday of every month                    no
                    matter what is/   or hoarfrost nestings
                    scent of lilacs   rain   sky bled white
                                                sky bruised
                                                  shedding

on the first saturday of every month                    at
                                              eight O'clock

the girl is yOurs
the boy is yOurs

that first night my daughter shines
down to the basement
dancing for dad   the mayor
his friends   our son playing
the flute         excited
footsteps clatter   high voices proud
laughing   i say sh! break a leg!
their shimmering...

yOur friends    bottles of rye
cameras in place

downstairs low
growls    scattered laughter
shouts    men clubbing
jubilant    below sealed doors
in darkness    be
yOnd firelight    perimeters

no matter what
season    the girl
the bOy

upstairs    on the edge    i keep
house    on an acreage
creeping towards abandoned
prairie    grasses waist high    yellow
mustard flogging bright stalks    bearded
oats    the blasted rock
young under blue blue skies i
think    we are like all the best things
commonplace    simple    so we
played there slithering up on gopher
holes to smash the young    unwary    hot &
laughing    on on to the grey broken
house    hollow despite
empire table    chairs leaning in s/ashed
conversion    rosebuds straining from
the stalk    ghosts of windbreak
poplars    & there you played the fiddle
threw sharp stones    till
i danced

yOurs

when the house next door burnt down
we stood like a family
in the roar and bitter air
yOur hand on the girl's
shoulder    my arm around the boy
you said "finally privacy"    startled i
turned to look    yOur eyes holes
where something leapt    writhed
    boy so still
    girl rigid
i turned back to the fire    understood
i had seen flames
reflected
on the first saturday of every month    the girl
is eleven    the boy
is nine

slowly
slowly down stairs
    boy in white    & flute
    girl in pink tutu &
slippers    i remember so much
what they feared    what they dreamt:
the boy a bat carved into his hair
a red bicycle        a real easel
for the girl and one long jangling earring
hand-in-hand    they
drift    to the first landing
below tretchikoff's
cockfight    they turn
look up at
me

hOw beautiful they are    i fear the wOrld

some nights the boy gleams
for a moment    then falls into shadow
the girl is always in half
light her profile rusty    an artifact
newly unburied    their thin backs
winged    reluctant bodies foreshortened
when they look up their eyes
are caves    in the dream i lean over
banisters    in the dream i am falling towards
i am saying    go on
i am saying    you'll be all right
in the dream i am saying    make your dad
proud    i am falling through    in the dream i
wave shoo shoo    go    go on
go on in the dream    i always wake up

yOurs
you deposit them on the bed    you
put five dollars
under the pillow
yOu say    she sure can dance
i say    this is too late    troubled as
if by memory    i say they're exhausted
you say it's only the first saturday of every month
yOurs

minutes or months later
Mama    i'm tucking in a corner    Mama i
want to stop...
ballet

her face to the wall

i say the kids want to stop
you turn their lessons your eyes
flare air is begging my body hovers
over your buckle the belt circles
that room knuckles dance a two-step around
me light alive with thwacking air
burns your brown shoes scarred like my father's
someone cries cries the ceiling swings
open in the mirror corners scream
door snakes through air i am
on my knees head covered by my arms
walls sobbing sobbing

INTERIOR: COURTROOM DAY

Judge, lawyers, witnesses, jury, court officials.
The children sit together. On either side of them
a social worker. They are wards of the court.
There are no spectators. i am grateful.

*the room*
*muffles*
*your*
*secrets burn*
*naked*
*i didn't know*
*floors*
*hover the air*
*is a dead*
*zone my*

Q:
You are under oath. Surely at that point you
knew that something was terribly wrong?

A:
it was not the first time i had been beaten.

Q:
You expect us to believe that your husband would beat you simply for saying

*courtswells*
*shimmer*
*discordant*
*a nutcracker*
*seizes*
*how could i*
*know*
*the judge's*
*webbed wings*
*cling*

*father's faces*
*are bear*
*traps faces*
*swing crazily*
*towards me*
*ceilings*
*pulse   flow*
*prosecutor's face*
*a funnel*
*chandeliers*
*ping small hail*
*pitching off*
*bins in the*
*barn my*
*mother's faces*
*spring at*
*me*
*i didn't know*
*nobody*
*told me*
*nobody you women*
*i am dead*
*centre*
*i am in*
*you women who*
*now live*
*who stare*
*your daughters*
*mark me*
*without care*
*at ease now*
*quake*
*be terrified*
*you women*
*tremble*
*your happy homes*

that your children no longer wished to take ballet/to play the flute?

A:
yes.

Q:
I put it to you that you enjoyed those beatings. That you were a willing participant...

A:
no! no!

Q:
What happened the next day?

A:
i did what women do.

Q:
Why didn't you leave him? Take the kids...

A:
i got up to prepare supper. when he came in, we sat down to eat...

Q:
Answer the question!

A:
where could I go that he couldn't find me? how would we live? i phoned the police   they said no lock could keep a man out. would they be better off if i were dead?

*to my hair*
*frozen*
*i*
*lungs stuffed*
*accusation*
*drips down*
*window panes*
*walls twist*
*the chair*
*dissolves under*
*faces flap*
*over benches*
*tectonic*
*plates shift*
*in cracks a type*
*writer plays*
*Tchaikovsky*
*my mother's spin*
*past windows*
*the jury*
*the flute*
*dances past*
*my lips*
*rest on the box*
*without care*
*for the moment*
*i am dead*
*you burn*
*vultures*
*fly from your*
*mouths*
*flap*
*in court-air*
*wings*
*brushing*
*against*

*tremble*
*see clearly*
*your eyes*
*whirlpools i*
*swirl drown*
*your polar*
*eyes*
*the liar speaks*
*sweetly*
*the devil does*
*not stammer*
*he smiles & smiles*
*and listens*
*and speaks of love*
*and listens*
*the creak in*
*the heart* O
*the thirst in*
*the heart*
*you women your*
*grim teeth*
*your daughters*
*your babies*
O

Q:
You said yourself you could not protect
them!

A:
i wanted to live... i tired
...hurt.

Q:
You have testified that you lied on the two
occasions that you went to the hospital...

A:
i was ashamed...i thought every wo...

Q:
Your pride wouldn't allow you to protect
yourself, or your children. Do you consider
yourself a fit mother?

A:
i didn't know what was happening to the
children. i didn't know...

*i am a cliff*
*i am*
*granite*
*i live even*
*with your nests*
*on my ledges*
*my breasts*
*no*
*longer ache*
*my mouth*
*is a crack*
*i am*
*white cliffs*
*my voice:*
*small stones*
*you women*
O
*your daughters*
*will mourn*
*will tremble*
*will dissolve*
*your daughters*
*your babies*
O

my eyes beg the children
become stone

yOurs
light-years ago
you are a bolt in the sky
and you are molten brass
volcanic
you swallow the world:
look these are hands of
a man who works hard for his family

a man    who protects
light-years ago
we shrivel        girl
is a wound        boy
ash
on the first saturday of every month
at eight O'clock

in the locked
basement
girl is yOurs
boy is yOurs

brown stains on her pants
she is hesitant
i take her in my arms
this is what it means to be a woman
she is a woman now a woman    i
rock her a woman i rock and rock
now    woe woe woeman

i say    she is
i say she is woman now
too old to dance

relief draws its map
into your face    never
never too old to dance for Papa
he puts his arm around her
she is bone
he kisses    loudly
laughs dances her

pats her bottom    slips
her twenty dollars
it flutters to the floor

it is then i know
she is an absence
i remember

on the first saturday of every month                at eight
mirrors gleaming    mums in the windOw
house a beacon on the edge    i host
a card party    wives of all yOur
friends    later the doctor    the minister's
wife    it was a test
how could anyOne believe

in the basement        girl
danced in her slippers
wooden zest on
her face    herself
curled tight
in her own womb    hiding
from the lascivious
gleam of their husbands    while
in the corner    nude
boy played the flute

on the first saturday of every month    you
auctioned yOur tender
flesh

i am no longer

mama no no    nor mummy
no!    and beneath
such wrappings there is
fine dry muscle
i am a shelled thing
eaten    left is the husk    white
calcareous

i am all there is

on the first saturday of every month
the procedures are simple    dignified
greetings    conversation    Tchaikovsky
a wine punch in silver wedding bowls
hors d'oeuvres    we wait on Sylvie    my
throat taut    our mayor's wife always
late if she doesn't come i will knOw
if she doesn't come    the world ended
meanwhile    there are fresh blossoms
on the table    meanwhile varied linen
wild rOse china cut glass shimmering
i wait    white seethe of hope/no/hope
she comes chattering    garnished with
pearls and the night is not rags not
flaming despite    girl palely pink
and delicate curves    bOy in white &
flute    no dogs howl    air comes back
in cat's yawn    in the whispering of
cards    the even rhythm of cakes and
coffee    i am not Jael    i do not take
hammer    or nail    downstairs they
divide the spoils    to each in turn
the girl    the boy

on the first saturday of every mOnth nO
matter the season
girl is thirteen
boy is eleven

for me there is nO
longer
a name

Uh um the girl stares through the open
window in the scent of dust and hedges um
I haven't had a period
my hands clench the dough
it swells through my fingers
for three months
bees in the lilacs
for this moment was i born
for this moment my mother's silence
the handy man's fingers her rage
my father's clogging games
for this moment this girl
who never mouthed a refusal

if there were rage it would stalk this page rend/rip

she moves away a watchful teasing
malevolence i saw your friend
the doctor she wants to see
you tomorrow
it can't wait till the first saturday
i breathe in
does she want to see your father

no....just my mother

she stares and stares
cabbage whites dance in the arbour
                                        i will not split
                                        along seams    i wait
the door bangs shut

i laugh and laugh and lau.....

Now seventeen months later    I stand on the rim of this new city    the woman here scribbling    bright black in my new house its white walls white carpets white painted sofas glass tables white lamps    she holds out    in a black hand sprays of white gladioli says a poem is a distraction    a wild    comfort    we need more than poems    or hymns    she expects me to agree    dressed all in white    I reach for the flute fade to the window    look down on roofs riverbanks trees dressed in a thin rime of ice    I might if I weren't so tired but she drifts away    I begin to play something pale    a red Honda pulls up    Adam in denim jacket and jeans    with neon yellow sweater waves at me    I lean against the white sill watching Julie    her beautiful hair chopped into purple green & pink quills    white coat open on brown sweater and tight jeans stride the walk    a gleaming metal belt clanging as she moves    she does not look up    I hear a knock    pounding    shrill calls    a white seething of breakers boils around rock    I find a smile... I have not practised my l...

# Cecil Foster

## Going Home

Jerome rested on his elbows, trying to compose himself. He looked down into her face, the eyes lightly closed and fluttering. Light reflected from the outside through the window with the storm shutters and flimsy thin curtains to cast a haunting reflection on her face. The features he thought so beautiful mere minutes earlier were now almost as white as the February snow outside. He was so angry.

Only moments earlier, he had seen the same face flushed with excitement as her pleasure peaked. Only then did he allow himself to indulge in the purely physical gratification. No sooner was it over than the guilt struck. It manifested itself in debilitating anger. Starting at some point near his ass, it ripped up his spine as if someone had attached an electric wire to his balls and, at that very moment of least resistance, found the socket in the wall. The anger, the guilt were almost uncontrollable. Every fibre and nerve in his body shook and rebelled.

But the stinging jolt did something else. It petrified him, forcing him to slide off her. He sat on the edge of the bed, naked and ashamed, his head hanging as low as his pride, his lust tepidly satisfied but his heart hollow. His spirits were defeated and deflated like an empty balloon. Every statement of the conversation he had overheard earlier in the night came flooding back. Every word pounded in his head like a reggae bass drum, taunting him. Nothing he could do silenced the voices. They had moved into his head and taken over. He could no longer ignore their accusations of betrayal.

In this daze, Jerome heard a loud sucking of teeth, the way West Indians show disgust. To his horror, he realized he was making the sound. Of all the responses possible to assuage this bolt of anger dashing through his body, all he could offer was a sickening sucking of the teeth — an act that would be deemed the epitome of bad manners in polite society. A society like the restricted community into which he was now so openly welcomed; the one that only a few hours earlier had fêted him as one of them: a natural achiever who had so much to give; who, despite his skin colour, so easily met its rigid qualifications for adoption.

This society had rewarded him well. Earlier in the evening, it had not only marked his acceptance and arrival with the social event of the year, but had not frowned when he chose for his trophy the most eligible female executive from among them, a woman who had gone out of her way to be seen standing at his side all night.

Jerome stared through the window. Somewhere in the distance was the pinnacle of one of Toronto's tall buildings. On top of it, partly hidden by the low flying clouds, was a red light, warning of poor weather. It was shining through the winter storm outside. Jerome had reached his pinnacle, something he had worked and suffered so long to achieve, but there was nothing to signal how he really felt. There was no red light to indicate the furious storms raging inside him.

Who was he angry with and why? Jerome tried to reason. Himself, or the white body nestling in the bed? He glanced at the woman, who was resting in the serenity of satisfaction. Contentment enveloped her, like the sheets she was pulling over her shoulders. Such restfulness could only be the testament of inner fulfilment, of her happiness and approval of his performance. Jerome wondered if it occurred to her that he might be tormented, fighting a conscience that chose to be too active on this very night. A conscience that kept taunting him for being used, like a piece of meat, for reducing himself to nothing more than a symbol.

Maybe he shouldn't care so much what other people were saying. He had paid his dues. He was entitled to the fruits of his success. Nobody was going to live his life or put restrictions on him. Nobody had any right to tell him with whom he should choose to share his well-earned achievements. Nor did anyone have any right to look on him as a symbol of their success, to claim his ascension as their achievement, to demand that he share his personal accomplishments communally. Nobody had the right to anoint him as a social role model, to demand that he be responsible for the success of any particular race. He would not bow to any peer pressure. He would choose for himself, socialize with whomever he wanted.

But this reasoning did not wash. He still could not explain his torment. If he enjoyed his personal success so much, why was he so angry at this moment of absolute and supreme triumph—a moment that ordinarily should be so soft and reassuring? He should have quietly fallen asleep, sweet success and acceptance rocking him in their arms.

Instead, he was furious. He had heard other men who had gone with whores swear how, at such critical moments, they too had to fight to control the urge to strike out, to repel, reject.

How they felt unclean, like someone sacrificing everything to get a cherished victory only to discover, at the very moment of receipt, that what was purchased was phony and vacuous—a mere Pyrrhic victory destroying the soul. He never thought it would happen to him. The men who told him such stories were unsophisticated. They were not like him. They had not climbed to the pinnacle and looked back down on the people they had risen from among. They did not know that the mere act of reaching such lofty heights numbed the sensibilities that caused such regrets. Now that he was facing his own crisis, the violent emotions were unexplainable. He was no longer the type of man who had to deal with such misgivings! Yet all he knew was how angry and defiled he felt, as if he had auctioned his very soul.

"What's the matter, dear?" she whispered, turning on her side, displaying the smooth hump of her hips under the sheet. She ran her hand casually along his thigh and across his broad back. The touches seemed no different from earlier. Yet they made him feel as if, by touching him this way, she was laying claim to him, as if she really possessed him. As if she wanted to talk to him, to be caressed or even to be with him for the rest of the night as promised. He chose not to answer. She continued to massage his back. Anger consumed him.

"Upset?" she persisted. Her voice was low and stealthy. The other voices conspired to drown it out, the way the immune system leaps into action at the first sign of a virus. His conscience struggled to decipher what the voices were saying, to ask them why they were spitefully tormenting him. "Is something wrong?"

"Um." Jerome did not know if he was answering Joanne on the bed or the nagging voices beating his conscience into submission.

He got off the bed, steadying himself as the water swished around in the leather mattress. He picked up his pants and underwear from the floor beside the chair. In the shadowy light, he was reminded of all the trappings and trimmings of the good life that the woman on the bed offered: the easy credit, the name recognition, the absence of worry over how the expenses for the lifestyle he so badly craved could be met. A divorce could be arranged so easily. Then everything he wanted, had worked for, would be waiting for him in this very room, with all its enticing perfumes.

This was an address to enhance his curriculum vitae, the ideal one to go with the new title and address on his business cards. Around him was luxury: the Jacuzzi mere steps away, the well-stocked bar waiting to serve guests, the elaborate home-entertainment system, the condo without one cent's mortgage outstanding. They were all his for the taking. One of the perks for having finally achieved his proper status in life. This was the kind of place to which he could willingly invite important friends and associates without being ashamed or apologetic. He wouldn't have to explain that the living room was too small, the basement too rough for people who lived in Rosedale or along Bayview. And Joanne would be the ideal person to stand by his side, to chit-chat knowledgeably with the important guests and to help him say and do the right thing. Then, the next day, he would stand by her side as she did the entertaining. They would be such a team. She would be the perfect social coach. She was willing to teach him, to sandpaper his edges.

He should be rationally, unemotionally comparing these things against what he had at home. The small house with the big mortgage. The fact that he must be the one to pull his partner up the economic and social ladder. He had to do it by himself, not knowing when he made a mistake, unsure of his social graces. His wife was even more ignorant than he of this new culture into which he was being immersed, into which he was seeping. She could not tell him if he was doing right; she was even too frightened to encourage him to entertain his clients and colleagues at home. A few minutes into a conversation she would start doubting herself, glancing at him with pleading eyes to rescue her. She had not kept pace with him.

She might have been the right woman when he was starting out, struggling. As a nurse, she enjoyed a secure salary by the standards she had set herself. And she knew how to get him to relax. She knew which pills soothed his throbbing headaches after a long day at the office. Her trained fingers readily found the deep knots in his shoulders and back and released them so skilfully. But beyond that she was not much help, certainly not in the areas he needed assistance, where Joanne stood head and shoulders above her.

They had outgrown each other, the same way he had outpaced the men who had complained of feeling so hollow after tasting the forbidden fruit. It should be more than tempting for him to want to stay in this cosy bedroom so high above the city. He should be counting his blessings, trying desperately (or at least a bit harder) to extinguish the anger. At least he should be willing to pretend, to hide his disgust. He should settle back and enjoy, knowing that daylight would bring him to his senses when he faced the outside world.

Silently, he slipped one leg into the underpants, suddenly becoming aware of the excruciating stillness in the room, of Joanne's breathing, of the cars struggling to negotiate the treacherous snowbound roads outside, of the snowploughs passing with feverish noises. The storm was still raging. Chances were some of the very men cleaning the streets down below were once his closest friends, his people. He could almost hear them laughing and swearing at the weather, even though in their hearts they were glad the heavens had opened up because the storm provided them with jobs, work the elite of the city never considered for themselves. In his mind, he could hear them loud and clear, even from this perch on the thirtieth floor in the heart of the business district. Earlier in the night, the lobby security was ready to throw him out until Joanne appeared and took his arm. Now, from this foreign land, he could hear the noises below. He wanted to be anywhere except in this bedroom.

Joanne must have sensed his mood. She was saying nothing, just watching him, resignedly not moving. He could feel her eyes boring into him with the kind of sixth sense a bird relies on to detect an approaching cat.

"I'm going home," he said laconically.

"What about the snow and the rain?" she whispered, sounding sleepy. Perhaps she was not really concerned. Just going through the motions. Having sensed his aloofness, maybe she was just pretending to care. "It's too slippery to drive and you've been drinking."

"I'll be okay."

"Take a cab. Get the car in the morning."

"No, I'll be okay." He glanced out the window at the eerie skyline. The way she spoke in commands irritated him. Millions of tiny snowflakes were fluttering through the light, forming a white blanket on the roofs of the houses in the distance. Somewhere down there in the snow, his brand-new, company-provided BMW was parked. It would take him a good twenty minutes to clean the three hours of snow off the car and clear a path through the pile of ice deposited by the ploughs at the entrance. And yes, he shouldn't be driving. But somewhere else in the city peace and quiet were irresistibly beckoning. Jerome knew he had to get out. There was no way he could keep his promise to stay with this woman for the entire night and possibly beyond.

He glanced again at the light on top of the building in the distance. It was still red, but with more of a pinkish hue. He did not know if his eyes were playing tricks. Maybe they were tired from such a long day. Or maybe the light was in fact changing. He was weary. He had to go to his bed.

A few hours earlier, if anyone had told him, even as a joke, that he would be turning his back on the woman in the bed Jerome would not have believed it. Nobody worked and schemed to achieve a coveted prize simply to walk away from it. Dreams were to be treasured, the sweet taste of such achievements savoured. Anyone who knew Jerome Downes knew he was not one to miss opportunities. He would do whatever was necessary to succeed.

But something had happened during the night.

He left home dressed in a rented tuxedo in time to make an entrance on the banquet floor of the swanky Four Seasons Hotel, purposely alone and looking dapper. Only two things were on his mind: having a good time while being officially inducted as a member of what his friends in business school called the "captains of industry" club; and at the end of the night leaving with the sexy Joanne Delores, chief operating officer for Comex Industries, and touted as the company's next president and chief executive.

Joanne had called earlier in the day, supposedly to ask if it was still all right for her to turn up at his party without an escort. As if she really expected him to believe a woman headed for the chief executive suite of a multibillion-dollar company would have trouble finding a male companion for the night. Jerome took this question for what it was—and told her he too would be single for the night.

"Do you have any plans for after the reception?" he asked.

"Not really."

"Maybe we can spend the night getting to know each other a little better," he offered.

"All night?"

"If you want."

"Is that a promise, Mr. Downes?" she teased.

"You betcha," he said into the phone. She laughed and hung up.

When he got off the elevator, Joanne was waiting for him. She was impeccably dressed in one of the most exquisite and revealing dresses he had ever seen. She came straight towards him. Instead of the standard firm business handshake, she planted such wet kisses on his cheeks that she had to use his handkerchief to remove the red lipstick. Her action was a clear signal to everyone: Jerome Downes had arrived in more than one way.

She stayed at his side while he made the rounds and the introductions, signalling to all other women to stay clear of her possession. This was a woman who, according to rumours, was so busy climbing the corporate ladder that she could not find time for matters of the heart. She had turned down more than one well-heeled suitor, if the rumours were correct. She had told the business magazines she didn't find men in business attractive. If she had time to choose a date, it would be someone in sports, not the businessmen she dealt with every day. Yet, she chose to be with him. What more could he want? Jerome asked himself.

But usually, it's the small things that matter. He was standing by the table with the gift, getting ready for the speeches. They were talking, perhaps not knowing he overheard them. Every word from the two black women, the only other black faces in the room, was enough to cut his heart out. He was glad he did not meet them. From what they were saying, he could not look these women in the face and not feel guilty. For the rest of the evening, their voices haunted him.

"I guess there is no hope for our people," the tall slim woman was saying. "I really wonder why I would bother to come to a celebration like this."

"Me too," the other woman said. "Isn't it strange? I tell yuh: strange things happen in this world. A man being fêted for his achievement as a black man trying his hardest not to appear to be black."

"That happens all the time, doesn't it?" the first woman said. "Take the fellow that is the U.S. Supreme Court judge. The same thing. I guess I'll never understand why, as soon as one of the brothers reaches any level of success, he always has to look for a white woman to make him feel accomplished. They simply become a toy, a possession of these women. What's wrong with our sisters that the brothers treat them so? As soon as they become successful they become a traitor to their people."

Jerome kept his head straight. His wineglass was empty, his lips were now parched. He was tempted to refill his glass before the presentations started. But the conversation had caught his ear, particularly the word *traitor*. He had never heard anyone talk about him in such a manner. He had grown accustomed to the praise, so bountiful of late, as if he was now faultless. Something more than the obvious criticism grabbed his attention, struck a chord deep inside him. He wanted to hear more.

"What a fine hunk, too," the other said. "What a pity he couldn't find a sister to help uplift. But he'll soon learn his lesson. As soon as he stumbles or screws up, the very people he's so wrapped up in, they will be the ones to knife him in the back. Mark my words, he'll have to come back home to his own people, just like any old Joe. He'll soon find out how lonely it is at the top; to be the only black face, too. His biggest mistake will be to trust these people. Any sister with his interest at heart can tell him that. But you know how blind the black men are sometimes."

"It's not only a question of uplifting just any sister," the first woman was saying. "I'm sure at one point or another there must have been a sister in his life who helped him to get where he is when he was nothing. But now the brother's riding high. He has to accept all the trappings that society tells him a black man needs to look successful—the white picket fence, the blond wife, the two-and-a-half curly-haired kids and a white dog. I tell yuh, I don't think there is much hope for us as a people."

Suddenly, Jerome doubted himself. Was he hearing correctly? Maybe the alcohol was numbing his senses, making him hear things that were only inside his head. Nobody used those clichés any more. Such language was a relic from another era, thirty years ago or even longer. Could it be that his conscience, loosened by the vintage French wine and the anxiety of the evening, was dredging up bits from all the speeches he had heard and the books he had read when he was in the vanguard of the now-dead black-consciousness movement?

Of course, he was still a pioneer. The newspapers and magazines acknowledged that he was the highest-ranking black business executive in the country, and his company chairman had stressed that his promotion had nothing to do with his colour. Still, appointments to the executive suites were such a rarity for people like him that this one had to be celebrated as another black breaking through. In fact, his appointment was a coup for someone with no established roots in Canadian business and no long family ties. Even if his company pretended otherwise, his promotion had to be celebrated for its symbolism. Maybe his confused mind was merely putting one night's celebration in the context of a historical struggle.

"That's the way this society toys with us," the second woman said. "It preys on our insecurities; makes us feel we have to measure success according to their benchmarks. Destroys everything we built up over the years. For me, the sorrowful thing is the brothers. They are so psychologically beaten down, they're the ones most vulnerable. No matter how strong and boastful they appear, no matter how smart, they're always the weaker ones, the exposed and vulnerable flank."

Joanne brought over the glass of wine. She took her position at his side. Jerome thought he heard one of the women suck her teeth, or perhaps both of them did it at the same time.

The conversation was a time-release capsule placed in his mind. Gradually, it sapped his enthusiasm over the night as the implications continued to haunt him. By the time he and Joanne left the reception, it was snowing heavily. But they still decided to go through with plans for a quiet dinner, her treat to him. She ordered the champagne and they drank, indulged and flirted. From very early, it was quite clear he was totally in control. Nothing could go wrong. She was like putty in his hands, so malleable. Yet he felt she was the one shaping him into something hideous, a distorted figure he might not want to see the next time he passed by a mirror.

By the time they left the restaurant, the snow had piled up. Cars were skidding on the roads. The earlier conversation was racking his brain, vying so much for attention at times that he didn't hear what Joanne was saying. Outside the restaurant, she wrapped the fur coat around her and held on to his arm, once again as if she possessed him. Once again, in his mind, Jerome heard the women sucking their teeth. He drove to her condominium. He parked the car in front of the building, even though she had suggested he use the underground parking since he was staying all night.

"The car will be warm and dry," she said. "We can have breakfast at my club. You'd be surprised at the amount of business I complete over croissants and coffee. But it's crowded and you have to get there on time. Park the car underground."

"No, I'll leave it here." This should have been the first sign to both of them he might not be spending the entire night away from home. Neither of them took the hint.

Jerome had never thought of himself as weak or a traitor. But now, as he sat in the BMW, encapsulated in the fresh leather smell of the interior, he could still hear the women in his mind. What they had said did not apply to him. He knew that for sure; he could pick apart the logic in their arguments if he cared enough to think at all about the foolishness they had said. Anyone who ever met him knew absolutely he wasn't one to be trapped that easily; he was independent in mind and spirit; nobody could force him to accept their standards. Nobody who knew him would dare say he was betraying some racial pride. If he changed, adopted new friends and lifestyles, it was because he wanted to, because he saw the way to a better life. Because he didn't want to feel he was the property of anybody, not even of the people he came from, the same people whose sons and daughters were writing him almost daily asking for jobs and for advice on what university courses they should take if they wanted to be as great a success as he.

At the same time, he could acknowledge the small bit of truth in the women's conversation, but only if they were talking about men generally and not about him specifically. He knew how difficult and frustrating it was coming from the other side and pretending to be part of the business class, knowing most of the executives genuinely believed he didn't belong among them.

There was a time when every morning, on leaving home, he felt he was putting on a mask, or, he reflected on his way up the elevator, that he had to step across a gulf to get to his desk. For the next ten or twelve hours, he pretended to be who and what he wasn't. He pretended to share, understand and care about conversations about spending weekends at cottages in the country as his colleagues did, all the time knowing his activities had been restricted to the city life he could hardly afford. Or he pretended he had thousands of dollars to invest in registered retirement plans, that he too had the monstrous problem of trying to find the right accountant or tax planner. He too would talk glibly about buying stocks at discount for his personal portfolio, discuss favourable commission rates he was paying stockbrokers, knowing full well he could not afford one. Then, at the end of the day, he took off the mask, stepped back over the gulf and became himself again.

But because he had come from people struggling like himself to get ahead, no law said he had to remain among them. He had worked hard and mastered the other man's lifestyle. When he went to business luncheons and receptions, he could now mix freely, not feeling out of place and resented. He had successfully negotiated the crossover as well as could be expected. This final elevation was his chance to submerge himself totally in this culture so that the mask would become his permanent features.

Driving conditions were worse than he thought. The road was reduced to one lane and the defrosters were working overtime to clear the windshield. Jerome wanted so much more in life—things he could not get, no matter how high he rose as a business executive, if he did not change his lifestyle, if he did not start associating with people from whom he could learn. The self-doubts had returned. In his head he could hear Joanne talking softly, whispering they should talk again soon. He would definitely have to set up a new home if he really wanted to get ahead. If not with Joanne, certainly with someone else, but preferably with a business woman. In the morning, he'd call Joanne first thing. Croissants and coffee sounded great.

Jerome felt the warmth of familiarity as soon as he walked in the door. The heavy load on his shoulders lifted instantly. He was on familiar turf; in the darkness and without searching, he knew where to find every cup, fork and spoon; where every chair and table was, the VCR and television, and the framed pictures and university parchments.

Not bothering to take off his coat, he tiptoed upstairs and peeked into the room where the kids were sleeping, blissfully unaware of their father's plans and his interrupted night. Going to each bed, he pulled the blankets over the kids and kissed each of them. He knew he was going to miss them so much if he went through with his plans for another home. So often he had tried to form the right words in his mind; to have the speech prepared, so it would be easy to explain why he had to leave for his fulfilment, to achieve his dreams, to go after his destiny. He hoped they would understand. Closing the door quietly behind him, he tried to dismiss those thoughts from his mind. He tried to smother the disapproving lecture from earlier in the night.

From the hallway, he could hear the quiet snoring coming from his bedroom. She was asleep, perhaps unaware of the night and the big reception. He hadn't told her. Yet it was hard to think a woman who had spent so many years with him didn't know what was going on. Purposely, he had chosen not to tell her. He didn't want her at the reception to cramp his style. In any case, he had told himself, she wouldn't want to be there anyway. She always complained she didn't like hanging out with boring business people, as she called them. She didn't have to put up with them as she didn't have to cross that gulf every day to make a living. "I like being myself," he heard her say in his head. "I'll always be me. I can't be anybody else. I hope people will accept me as I am or to hell with them."

So he hadn't told her and she knew not to wait up for him as he was late most nights. That was why it made so much sense to latch on to a woman like Joanne, who was so much like him, who enjoyed the same people and business events and who, at his side, was such a beautiful enhancement, like the final piece of a jigsaw puzzle.

No matter what those women at the party thought, his choice, although painful, was nonetheless inevitable. In a few hours, he would be at the club in time for one of those power breakfasts. He might never return to this home. Maybe his lawyer would make the arrangements. He'd ask her to make an appointment for him to see the kids so he could explain his actions to them face to face.

Jerome pushed the door open and slipped in, hoping to undress in the warm light reflecting through the window from the snow piled high in the backyard. She must have heard him or maybe, after all these years, even in sleep her senses were so attuned to him that she was instantly aware of his presence.

"You're home," she muttered, turning on her side to make room for him in the bed.

"Yes. I'm home. Tonight I..."

But he didn't finish. She was already snoring peacefully. He looked at her, clothed in the warmth of the room, her hair in long, controllable braids. The clock on the bureau ticked softly. The anger in him dissipated. Jerome looked at his own perfectly shaped shadow across the bed, cutting his wife at the waist. The mask had slipped again. He wondered what colour the light on top of the building was, the light he could no longer see from this part of the city. The voices in his head reminded him the shadow on the bed was also naked and vulnerable.

# Makeda Silvera

## Her Head a Village

Her head was a noisy village, one filled with people, active and full of life, with many concerns and opinions. Children, including her own, ran about. Cousins twice removed bickered. A distant aunt, Maddie, decked out in two printed cotton dresses, a patched-up pair of pants and an old fuzzy sweater, marched up and down the right side of her forehead. Soon she would have a migraine. On the other side, a pack of idlers lounged around a heated domino game, slapping the pieces hard against her left forehead. Close to her neck sat the gossiping crew, passing around bad news and samples of malicious and scandalous tales. The top of her head was quiet. Come evening this would change, with the arrival of schoolchildren; when the workers left their factories and offices, the pots, banging dishes and televisions blaring would add to the noisy village.

The black woman writer had been trying all month to write an essay for presentation at an international forum for Third World women. She was to address the topic, "Writing As a Dangerous Profession." This was proving to be more difficult as the weeks passed. She pleaded for quiet, but could silence only the children.

The villagers did not like her style of writing, her focus and the new name she called herself—feminist. They did not like her choice of lovers, her spending too many hours behind her desk or propped up in her bed with paper and pen or book. The workers complained that she should be in the factories and offices with them; the idlers said she didn't spend much time playing with them and the gossiping crew told so many tales that the woman writer had trouble keeping her essay separate from their stories. Some of the villagers kept quiet, going about their business, but they were too few to shut out the noise. Maddie did not often side with the writer, but neither did she poke at her. She listened and sometimes smiled at the various expressions that surfaced on the woman writer's face. Maddie stood six feet tall with a long, stern face and eyes like well-used marbles. The villagers said Maddie was a woman of the spirits, a mystic woman who carried a sharpened pencil behind her ear. She walked about the village all day, sometimes marching loudly, and other times quietly. Some days she was seen talking to herself.

"When I first come to this country, I used to wear one dress at a time. But times too hard, now you don't know if you coming or going, so I wear all my clothes. You can't be too sure of anything but yourself. So I sure of me, and I wear all my clothes on my back. And I talk to meself, for you have to know yourself in this time."

The villagers didn't know what to make of her. Some feared her, others respected her. The gossipers jeered behind her back.

Plugging her ears against spirit-woman Maddie, the black woman writer sat in different places she thought would be good to her. She first sat behind her desk, but no words came. It was not so much that there were no words to write down—there were many—but the villagers were talking all at once and in so many tongues that it was hard for her to hold onto their words. Each group wanted her to feature them in the essay.

Early in the morning, after her own children left for school, she tried to write in her bed. It was a large queen-size pine bed with five pillows in a small room on the second floor. The room was a pale green and the ceilings a darker shade of green—her favourite colour. She was comfortable there and had produced many essays and poems from that bed. Its double mattress almost reached the ceiling. She felt at peace under the patchwork blanket. It took her back to her grandparents' wooden house a mile from the sea in another village, the tropical one where she was born. Easter lilies, powder-puff trees, dandelions and other wild flowers circled the house. She saw a red-billed Streamertail, the a yellow-crowned night heron and a white-bellied Caribbean dove, their familiar voices filling her head. "*Quaart, Tlee-oo-ee, cruuuuuuuuuu*," and other short repeated calls.

She wrote only lists of "To do's":

washing
cleaning
cooking
laundry
telephone calls
appointments.

At the edge of the paper birds took flight.

Nothing to do with writing, she thought. On days like these, convinced that she would get no writing done, she left the village and lunched with friends. She did not tell her friends about the village in her head. They would think her crazy, like Maddie. When she was alone, after lunch, scores of questions flooded her head.

What conditions are necessary for one to write?
What role do children play in a writer's creativity?
Is seclusion a necessary ingredient?
Questions she had no answers for.

Sometimes she holed up in the garden shed at the edge of the backyward. She had cleared out a space and brought in a kerosene heater. The shed faced south. Old dirty windows ran the length of it and the ceiling's cracked blue paint threatened to fall. There she worked on an oversize ill-kept antique desk, a gift from a former lover. She had furnished the space with two chairs, a wooden crate stacked with a dictionary and a few books, a big armchair dragged from the neighbour's garbage, postcards pasted on the walls to remind her of Africa. There were a few things from her village: coconut husks, ackee seeds, photographs of birds, flowers and her grandparents' house near the sea.

One afternoon, however, the villagers discovered the shed and moved in. The idlers set up their gambling table. Gossip-mongers sat in a large area and Maddie walked around quietly and read everything written on every piece of paper. Soon they all wanted to read her essay. The idlers made fun of her words. The gossip-mongers said they had known all along what she would write. Offices and factories closed early, as the others hurried into the shed to hear what all the shouting was about.

They were all talking at once, with varying opinions.

"Writing is not a dangerous profession, writing is a luxury!" shouted one of the workers.

"Many of us would like to write but can't. We have to work, find food to support our families. Put that in your essay."

"What's this?" another villager asked, pulling at the paper.

"Look here, read here, something about woman as a lover and the danger of writing about that."

The black woman writer's head tore in half as the villagers snatched at the paper. She shouted as loud as she could that there was more to the paper than that.

"See for yourselves—here, read it, I am also writing about the economics of writing, problems of women writers who have families." Almost out of breath, she continued, "See, I also wrote about cultural biases."

"Cultural biases," snarled a cold, grating voice. "Why not just plain old racism? What's wrong with that word?" Before she could answer, another villager who was jumping up and down silenced the rest of them. "This woman thing can't go into paper. It wouldn't look right to talk about that at a Third World Conference." They all shouted in agreement.

She felt dizzy. Her ears ached. Her mouth and tongue were heavy. But she would not give in. She tried to block them out by calling up faces of the women she had loved. But she saw only the faces of the villagers and heard only the sounds of their loud chatter.

"No one will write about women lovers. These are not national concerns in Third World countries. These issues are not relevant. These," they shouted, "are white bourgeois concerns!"

Exhausted, the black woman writer tried again. "All I want to do is to write something about being a black lesbian in a North American city. One where white racism is cloaked in liberalism and where black homophobia..." They were not listening. They bombarded her with more questions.

"What about the danger of your writing being the definitve word for all black women? What about the danger of writing in a liberal white bourgeois society and of selling out? Why don't you write about these things?"

She screamed at them to shut up and give her a voice, but they ignored her and talked even louder.

"Make it clear that you, as a black woman writer, are privileged to be speaking on a panel like this."

"And what about the danger of singular achievement?" asked a worker.

"Woman lover," sniggered another. "What about the danger of writing about racism—police harrassment—murders of our villagers?"

Many times during the month the black woman writer would scream at them to shut up. And when she succeeded in muting their voices she was tired because they refused to speak one at a time.

On days like these the black woman writer escaped from the garden shed to play songs by her favourite blues singer, drink bottles of warm beer and curl up in her queen-size pine bed. she held on to the faces of her lovers and tried to forget the great difficulty in writing the essay.

The writer spent many days and nights staring at the blank white paper in front of her. The villagers did not ease up. They criticized the blank white paper. It was only a few days before the conference. "You have to start writing," they pressured her. "Who is going to represent us?"

Words swarmed around her head like wasps. There was so much she wanted to say about "Writing As a Dangerous Profession," about dangers to *her* as a black woman, writer, lesbian. At times, she felt that writing the paper was hopeless. Once she broke down and cried in front of the villagers. On this particular day, as the hour grew close, she felt desperate—suicidal, in fact. The villagers had no sympathy for her.

"Suicide? You madder than Maddie!" they jeered. "Give Maddie the paper and let her use her pencil," they heckled.

"I'm not mad," she protested with anger. "Get out of my

head. Here"—she threw the blank paper on the ground—"write, write, you all write."

"But you are the writer," they pestered her. They were becoming hostile and vicious. The woman writer felt as if her head would burst.

She thought of Virginia Woolf's *A Room of One's Own*. She wondered if Woolf had had a village in her head.

She took to spending more time in bed with a crate of warm beer at the side. Her eyes were red from worry, not enough sleep and too much drink. She studied her face in a small hand-mirror, examining the lines on her forehead. They were deep and pronounced, lines she had not earned, even with the raising of children, writing several essays and poetry books, cleaning, cooking and caring for lovers. She gazed at all the books around her and became even more depressed.

Interrupted by the angry voices of the villagers, overwhelmed by the force of their voices, she surrendered her thoughts to them.

"Well, what are you going to write? We have ideas to give you." The black woman writer knew their ideas. They were not new, but she listened.

"Write about women in houses without electricity."

"Write about the dangers of living in a police state."

"Write about Third World issues."

"Write about...about..."

"Stick to the real issues that face black women writers."

"Your sexuality is your personal business."

"We don't want to hear about it, and the forum don't want to know."

They accused her of enjoying the luxury of being a lesbian in a decaying society, of forgetting about their problems.

She tried to negotiate with them. "Listen, all I want is a

clear head. I promise to write about your concerns." But they disagreed. "We gave you more than enough time, and you've produced nothing." They insisted that they all write the paper. She was disturbed by their criticism. She would never complete the paper with so many demands. The black woman writer was full of despair; she wanted to explain to the villagers, once again, that what makes writing dangerous for her was who she was— black/woman/lesbian/mother/worker... But they would not let her continue. In angry, harsh voices they pounded her head. "You want to talk about sexuality as a political issue? Villagers are murdered every time they go out, our young people jailed and thrown out of schools." Without success, she explained that she wanted to talk about all the dangers of writing. "Have you ever heard of, read about lesbians in the Third World? They don't have the luxury of sitting down at an international forum and discussing this issue so why should you?"

Her head blazed; her tiny tight braids were like coals on fire. The villagers stayed in her head, shouting and laughing. She tried closing her eyes and massaging her forehead. With her eyes still closed, she eased her body onto the couch. Familiar footsteps sounded at the side of her head. Maddie appeared. "All this shouting and hollering won't solve anything—it will only make us tired and enemies. We all have to live together in this village." Not one villager joked about her two dresses, pants and sweater. Not one villager had anything to say about the pencil stuck in her hair, a pencil she never used. Maddie spoke for a long time, putting the villagers to sleep.

The black woman writer slept late, dreaming first of her grandparents' village and then of her lovers. Now Maddie's face came. She took Maddie's hand and they set out down the village streets, through the fields of wild flowers, dandelion and Easter lilies. Maddie took the pencil from her head and began to write. With Maddie beside her, she awoke in a bed of wild flowers, refreshed.

# Frederick Ward

## Kitten Face

**I'M WAITING** to be punished. Mama says she's "HAD ENOUGH!" She's been "TRYING TO TEACH" me "SOMETHING"——I thought I'd learned it. Anyway, I'm waiting here in Mama's computer room, hoping when Papa comes home he find me at the computer and think I'm learning something. But I'm also waiting to be punished...waiting for Papa to come home so she can tell him——and he'll punish me, all right.

I tried to figure out how he'd do it, and I been practising. I stood in the corner for a few minutes. I spanked my hand with the other——he might do one of those. I spoke scary to myself, all the things he'd say to my sister when he's mad at her and all the things he's say to me when he's mad——some of them, the things I heard him say when he'd talk back to Mama, and I say some things the way Gramma Shu says them, *ghost-like*. I say them under my top lip, wrinkled my eyebrows and dipped them from the middle of my bow'd head into my chin so I could "*pour forth*" the "*madness in my mind*" down through my nose, same as Papa do: "YOUUUuuuuuuu..."——say it all to myself, just to see if I could scare myself into "*preparedness*."

"YOUR PAPA GONNA GET YOU TWICE FOR YOUR DAY...AND GET YOUR EYEBROWS OFF THE TOP OF YOUR HEAD, YOU AIN'T THAT INNOCENT."

Mama's voice were little through her teeth, echoed in me from this morning——have her finger focused right tween my eyes, she says:

"YOU THINK YOU'RE SMART, DON'T YOU? WHAT THE HELL YOU THINK YOU WERE TRYING TO DO, MISTER EDISON?"

I'm in trouble twice cause I discovered I could unscrew the wall socket. I discovered, when I put my finger into the wall socket, it made me jump and feel funny all at the same time. It hurt my finger a bit but the hurt went away when I sucked at it. Then I'd try the new discovery again——all in the last week I done it. This week Mama caught me...she ran me around the house shouting:

"CAUGHT YOU/CAUGHT YOU!"

I'm in trouble again cause I tried to shorten my prayer to God. You see, Mama grabbed me up from the floor when she "caught" me. It scared me, and we both went to screaming. She run through every room in the house, hugging me till it hurt, and her shouting:

"My to mercy, not my baby/my baby my baby child! O Lord! Please...O hold Your wrath gainst me and my guilt. That stranger *talked* his way into my bedroom. Not my baby, my baby boy. No, no, no."

Everything vibrated in her neck and head, chattering her teeth. She grabbed my head and pressed it gainst hers and her vibrations come'd onto me, the same nearly as the buzzing I got when I put my finger into the light socket——but not the hurt. Mama bent quick, sucking in air, come'd up at the silence——maybe The Lord, weren't that mad at her——and swallowed it.

Mama let me down-slide to the floor. I smeared tears and snot on her tween her breasts. She pressed a hand there and drawed it up on her fingers:

"You got a snout full of slop, boy. Go blow your nose. Wash your face." She say this calm as what nothing never happened——say it with her fingers making slow circlings in the tears-n-snot, then wiped them dry in the palm of her other hand——staring. Gramma Shu spoke ghostly once of Mama's staring, say Mama:

"*...at the blue and golds chilowi widgeons mongst wild parsley wallpaper... Staring, plaintively.*"

Mama closed her eyes and looked at me——I could tell it were me cause her eyes rolled up under her eyelids in my direction——She said:

"Get on in there at that table, after, and eat something—— and say your blessing before God, afore you eat. Hear?"

Her

"Answer me boy!"

bumped into my

"Yessum."

I washed! I were hungry and "*Too anxious you were*" to eat fast. I got over the breakfast bowl and says,

"O God, O God, this is a recording, this is a recording, this is a recording..."

Mama broke my prayer with,

"YOU MOST BOUND TO MAKE TROUBLE FOR YOURSELF THIS DAY, AIN'T YOU? AIN'T YOU, BOY!?... WHEN YOUR PAPA GETS/I SWEAR..."

(I ain't say nothing.)

She shout,

"HUSH YOUR BACKTALK TO ME BOY! You f-o-o-l."

She stepped my way but thought on it——had enough. Mama say she had had enough of me.

She sent me to my room but I sneaked in here to the computer. The computer talks to me and I tell it things. You see, when my mama doesn't want me to know what she and the neighbour-woman are talking about, they spell it out. Mama alerts her, says, "Important," and she spells the rest out. I can't read yet, but I can, and do, collect the letters to my memory and I run here to the computer and tell it. Some times the computer knows.

"Computer, what is *f-o-o-l*——huh?"

**COMPUTER:** F-O-O-L: British cookery. A dish made of fruit, scalded or stewed, crushed and mixed with cream or the like...

"Mama didn't say it that way, computer."

It's a good thing Sister's acting funny these days cause I'd be in real trouble tonight. I reasoned that Sister and the dog were eating together cause she never eat nothing at the table and her stomach were swelling——more often she never come'd to the table to eat with the family. I took to following her about but I were afraid. The safe thing to do were just be around her shadow. Whenever her shadow be around I'd go sit next to it, walk with it——I kept my distance with her ceptin for my eyes and ears. I put her shadow in one, its echo in the other. It's fun watching her shadow talk——caused a staring to occupy itself in me. I even crawled inside of Sister's shadow once——after Sister were crying——a "*lonesome spot*" come'd in on Sister's shadow, took its place in droops and sags. I were sitting next of it——when Sister's shadow say to its stomach,

I am so ugly
I can't tell if I am sick
The only tears I can manage for myself
Come when I think of you

I moved with the shadow outside onto the porch where it sit on the steps. Sister planted her elbows on her knees, "*rest her life*"...rest her forehead on the back edge of her palms stretched——cupped towards "*The WHERES.*" Her head were covered and bent over her right shoulder——

"*...forgetful under the weight of a large towel...*"

Gramma Shu say:

"*The crown Shaw of a boxer after losing.*"

I imagined Sister's eyes, if opened, black holes with the worrisome buzz-passing, in and out of, then landing of a greenfly, its hind legs scratching its wings, itching up a few blinks in Sister's stare neath the towel.

"*Such an eyeless face lie next of her,*
*torn out of a round loaf of brown bread*
*dropped in the dirt by the steps.*"

I were most attracted to Sister's feet: swollen, wrinkled and mud chooked. Mama, later, telling my image of Sister to the neighbour woman, say,

"Sister having (Important): M-O-R-N-I-N-G S-I-C-K-N-E-S-S."

Mama say I musn't struggle with Sister when she's this way.

"Computer, what is struggle?"

**COMPUTER:** S-T-R-U-G-G-L-E: to proceed with difficulty or with great effort.

"Effort?"

**COMPUTER:** E-F-F-O-R-T: a positive replacement: a serious attempt to TRY.

"Mama always says to me, 'Don't you try me, boy,"

Sister come'd home lumpy and huddled in her own arms, near quiet ceptin for grunts, moans and swallows chewed behind her lips and the *cries*, give'd off her coat, come'd through the smell of tears on the fur. It might be thought that the *smelling of tears* gives off no cries, but you'd have to know Sister more——cause she doesn't make so many sounds, yet, in everything she do, her voice is locked in it——even the tears on her fur coat. Gramma Shu tell me that I should remember all the things she say to me cause "*they're dying out mongst us.*" And as best, I try. I'm good at remembering voices. Sister don't say much, and I ain't come'd onto her voice that much, but Gramma Shu's voice I got down near enough to fool folks on the telephone. You want to hear it, computer? Computer?

**COMPUTER:** Please wait! (*no response*)

I went and stood in my doorway.

"*Fur coat smelling of tears!*"

Gramma Shu mumbled that passing me...

"Pardon me?"

(I weren't thinking.) She shout,

***"HER FUR COAT SMELLING OF TEARS!"***

...on her way to the bathroom from Sister's room.

I tipped in on Sister whilst her back were to her door and me. She stood by her dresser, wrist-wiping her nose, eyes and lips——her fur coat lying across her bed, curled up. She held a paper in her hand staring at it——soundlessly mouthing the words from it till she lifted then, in weepings, on re-reading them:

"Dear Baby,

Have you got two hearts or one?
If you only got one heart, is that
heart big enough for two pair of
size-13 feet? I think not.

Bye, Baby."

Sister were know'd to have many boyfriends——but this one... Gramma Shu were coming back, so I hid in a tiny place neath Sister's bed, chin-in-my-knees. Sister crumpled the paper and dropped it——missing the waste basket——onto the floor and kicked the paper under the bed. Gramma Shu come'd——entered the room. I got dizzy——scared. I scrunched up my face, forced blinking my eyelids cause Gramma Shu stood afore me in a blue haze——she were, somedays, "A *Three-Legged Praying Mantis*," come'd after us. Sister called her, *Mama Knots*. *Mama Knots*, she were: with speckled, knotty hands, palmed over, and she walked on a knotted old cane that *lived!*——wiggled out from her knotted hand like a long, extended knotted finger. She pointed, urged, spelled out and disciplined us with it, marked time and put memorable periods after her words with that knot.

"Oh, Gramma Shu..."

Sister say:

"I don't want to see nothing ever again, no more. He's leaving me."

Gramma Shu don't want to hear it, say:

"*You ain't saying nothing, girl...saying the wrong thing. Hush!*"

Gramma Shu were trying to wipe Sister's face when Sister snatched herself away to go stand and look into the sun, but her eyes so full of tears——

"*You ain't blinding even your own heart, girl! Get your eyes out of the sun!*"

Gramma Shu shouted at whatever Sister trying, "*Ain't gonna work.*" Then Sister run from the sun, say she "leaving," and Gramma Shu grab up Sister's fur coat, following her, quick-tipping on the *echo* give off from the *smelling of tears*. I come out from under the bed and run to my room——hid again. I wanted to cry, but I didn't want nobody to hear me. I talked to myself

——everything felt crazy. I were crazy. Gramma Shu's blue-haze voice fussed within my thoughts:

"*Crazy! No, you ain't crazy, Kitten Face. I been talking to myself…mymymy…*

*There is a THRONE!*

*In this world*

*What we might*

*Circle around*

*Clap your hands on it!*

"*That's why we talking to ourselves.* **A Throne!** *child. You might burst out anytime the Throne be on your mind, singing or crying to yourself, forgetting that people are around——like when you got something in you whilst you walking in the streets singing inside your mouth and you get to a high point in your feelings and you blurt it* "**OUT!**" *Well now. How people know you ain't crazy when they hear that from you? They don't——and they do.*"

I moaned. Gramma Shu stepped my thoughts:

"*I moan——lots…*

*Moaning is the mule to heaven*

*Long laboured and pure from hollerin'.*

*The women that come'd for tea could catch their breath on my moaning——would rest you up.*"

She moaned for Grandpa Chas:

"*Cold were the tears stuck your Grandpa Charley's hair neath my chin. Muh. Charley twists all the covers about him, wrapped himself into a husk. Called out, in all manner of fever, called out names——some ancient——some knowed: a brother, an uncle, old aunt, his papa's and the neighbour girl's name….*"

She wandered on this…lost me in her thoughts, lost me in a blue haze, and in the haze:

An old man got on a bus and sit down across from Gramma Shu and me——on the long front seat——sit down burying a stare in the floor, and singing a very low, deep "**O**"...holding it an ever! Little old ladies moved away from the area, waving their hands from their wrists like they were scooting flies. Gramma Shu told me not to look at the man. He wouldn't look up, so I thought he were crazy——then he smiled at the floor, the smile jumped off onto it, and the man followed his smile right up into my face.

I giggled——cause Gramma Shu know'd I would——giggled 'Out!' over my thoughts, over her fussing voice within me——blue.

I wanted my sister's note, and when the coast were clear, I sneaked back under her bed and got the bunched-up paper... sneaked with it out of the room and come'd running to Mama's computer, cause I can't read and talks back when you talk.

"Oh, computer..."

I tried to press the paper flat as I could, but my self were as wrinkled as the paper.

"I...tried to press out the wrinkles for you, computer. If I press the paper up against your face, will you read it for me? Computer? Computer?"

**COMPUTER:** I cannot read. (*repeat*) I cannot read.

Scream-touched, trouble took up with Gramma Shu whilst she and I were seated peeling potatoes——discouragement come'd on her lips. To get *trouble* to pass, she called on *little ancientnesses* in herself. She come'd steadfast, have sayings on it: *House cleaning for the spirit*...she mumbled it to herself and to whatever she acknowledged to be about her——empty chairs, opened cupboard doors and talked to the shelves——the potatoes. A pink baby rattler with a baby-blue handle lie afore her on the kitchen table what she grabbed——rattling and stood up shouting: 'Happyhappyhappy!'——pat her breasts, her breath sucked up *hesitations*, and sang in fits around the table, she done. She shout:

"*Sing all the voices what oppose in your bosom. Mighty movement'll come. Sing out your fears and night-slurred yelps for even not the Gramma Shu you and your sister ignore someday'll no longer be here for you to hide behind.*"

Her arms flailing a remembered gesture...smeared it on her apron and she strut a long neck what held up a *countenance of reflective beam*. Her eyes have an agreement in them——grabbed at a sudden movement. She swallowed the *beam*...and, seeing nothing further of the movement, continued peeling potatoes, with grey glances towards the corner every now and then where she seen it——till a meanness straightened her into a squinting stare. She say:

"*Charley Tate, is that you?*"

She let her stare drift about the kitchen, left it in the air when her head dropped. Finished the potatoes. She dumped ground beef into a bowl on the table, then, breaking an egg on the bowl's lip, added it.

"*You picked me out for your girl, Charley.*"

She punched the ground-meat-and-egg mixture, squeezed it tween her fingers:

"*Why you do that, Charley?*"

She determined, without measure or count: dusted the meat with Parmesan cheese, dry mustard, bread crumbs, salt, ginger and marjoram——black ground pepper.

"*I were a silly girl, Charley...Loved music——grow'd up with katydids, fireflies, night mists and loons' songs in my ears——but never a man's till yours. I went with your song.*"

She peeled an apple onto the mixture, tinincy cut garlic, onion, crushed pineapple and added a fistful of raisins. This she squeezed tween her fingers again, made a mound in the bowl, then punched a bit off and rolled the meat into round shapes. Says:

"*A man's song might pluck any girl, but a girl ain't supposed to be plucked by any man's song.*"

She placed the meatballs in a dish and spread chutney over it:

"*She fourteen years old, that girl.... Sister just fourteen, and any man sung for her——it ain't right, Charley. I've lived long enough to see everything I been taught, every right I learnt, disappear through the generations!*"

Gramma Shu turned to me:

"*Son?*"

She swelled on it: "*Your Grandpa Charley Tate...mymymy...*"

Her talk sprang after itself:

"*Contagious man——played trumpet, brought us an echo of The Promise!——Contagious man!*"

Her voice freed itself from her in hicupped laughter similar as fallen leaves do whilst you sweeping them——*they skips the broom:*

"*Charley...Mmmmm!*"

She put the meat dish in the oven...and when it was cooked, Gramma Shu set the table with the food and shook the rattler around it——the family sat——she walked around the table shaking the rattler and humming whilst we ate, stopping back of Sister occasionally and rolling her head in figure eights.

Sister carried a secret thing. At first I thought she stole some of Mama's food the way she'd rub at her stomach...but Mama never say a thing. Nothing about missing food. Mama counts everything——it weren't food. Besides, Sister talked to her stomach. It were a fascinating secret cause it were everywhere about her...has a walk to it: stiff-shift and wobble——had a smell to it too, and she'd sneak off to a quiet place with it——a quiet place inside herself. Across the table from me, she were gone to it. Her eyes give nothing back to you...whatever come'd by them, her eyes give nothing back. Even not when I waved in her face——nothing.

I imagined her without eyes: I imagined tiny purple martins flying in and out of her eye sockets, and chirping echoes come'd from the inside holes——all kind of echoes. I imagined the birds flying with worms in their beaks and perching on the ledges of her eye sockets...leaving the worms inside them, then flying away so fast they leave loose feathers floating about Sister's nose——it tickled me. She sneezed but didn't even blink——she so private. Mama talked down through the holes, say:

"You eating like a bird again, girl. I'm gonna have to give you a physic you keep this up. You can leave the table now."

Sister got up from the table as if summoned from some place, yet been told to leave. I slid from my seat...followed her to the kitchen doorway and watched her stiff-shift wobbling her secret away to her room. Mama reminded me:

"Robert Alex, Jr.? You weren't excused from nowhere, boy." I turned to Mama, and as I sat back down, asked her if I could HAVE WHAT SISTER LEFT ON HER PLATE? Papa put a firm squeeze on my shoulder whenever I tried to ask for something too loud.

Everyone kept bowed as we ate. I were jittery in my chair cause in my plate I saw Papa in my room punishing me. His chewing come'd his footsteps, his hollering at me. I fought gainst his "YOUUUuuuuuu!" Closed my eyes on him, I closed off my hearing to all but Gramma Shu's rattling about the table. I tried to "*Ponder pleasant platitudes and attributes*," by centring her voice in my thinking: her rattling were an antenna tween me and my memories of stories she made up: "*Muffin and the Blueberry*"——"*Andrea and the Bird Song*." I liked that one. Gramma Shu made that up out of a bird on the wallpaper in my room, what her voice took up with and told whilst I stared at it.

*"Now you listen, Kitten Face, and don't you go to sleep afore I finish. You might be a reciter one day and I want you to understand how you're to do it. First, you anchor yourself in some great symbol and pour forth."*

She told the story once and requested,

*"Now you liked that, didn't you? We storytellers in this family. You see how to do it?"*

I scooted back to my chair, squinted up that I were *born of an oak tree and tween tree roots!* I relaxed/were there, and told her the story back:

> In the morning of my life there were a very strong want. I would come to this place of my birth and sing of all the things I thought were very nice and special. All the birds would sing with me and I thought that I were the one who controlled the birds. But of course I couldn't control the the fact that the birds would all go away in the wintertime.
>
> Some of the birds didn't go and I were always trying to get them to sing with me but in the winter that is very hard to do, especially if the birds are cold and unhappy because of the weather. I tried very hard to make the birds happy. I danced——which I couldn't do too well cause my legs were too fat. And my jaws wiggled and shook me onto blurs when I danced a stomp or hopped.
>
> The birds would twitter and giggle over the branches at me but never sing. I would throw rocks at the branches *to wake them up!* But that didn't work. I blew my police whistle at them——threw streamers at them, and I stuck out my Halloween tongues at them. But no use! Then the winter were over and the other

birds returned. WELL! The birds began to sing again. "*GLORIOUSLY SING!*" I sang as well with them. I composed a spring gesture: went bird-wild, flinging my wings to my music, and the birds all joined in...I were in control once again.

But it didn't work. A ghost breath in me broke up my squinting...

In the centre of my plate, *Papa were standing in the doorway to my room, surrounded by fire and smoke*, and wiping his eyes on fist-knuckles. I could handle it——put my eyes on the case.

I say through spit-sprinkles, through Papa's pointing at me, grunting and wired pupils:

"Papa! I were having a scary dream!"

——And he softened,

"It's all right...What were your dream about? Tell your papa."

"It were a giant computer, Papa...wanted to talk to me and I were scared as when you tell me 'NO!'"

"Now I don't say 'No' to you that much. You a good, boy——most of the time. And don't shout. Your sister's trying to sleep. What the computer say, Son?"

"It ask me what I want to be. And I say, I won't tell it."

Papa come'd to acting all the time, act like he the computer, say:

"T-R-U-S-T me."

"I ain't telling you. I can't tell you."

"Why?"

"C a u s e you gonna laugh at me."

"No I will not...Try me. Trust me. Respond please. Please respond."

"I got to be dead to be what I want to be."

"Meaning...What do you mean?"

"You won't laugh?"

"Can I laugh?"

"Oh, Computer, I ain't never heard you laugh. To laugh is...laughing...Computer?...Papa, stop teasing!"

"T-R-U-S-T me... Please respond...What do you want to be when you grow up?"

"I want to be a Jedi pilot——and there ain't no one alive like them until the future."

"Growing up is the future."

"Jedi's is farther up-beyond of the future."

"Farther up-beyond of?"

"Yes. So I got to die, and wait until their time to live comes around."

"Where will you go to wait?"

"I'll go be with Grandpa Tate...He said I could...could come and live with him wherever, with him always...live with him even not in the 'WHERES.'"

"Farther up-beyond OF?"

My fork fell off my plate onto the floor. I never heard it. Papa's fist come'd crashing down on the table:

**"BOY, WHAT YOU DREAMING IN THE FOOD FOR!?"**

Purple martins perched on and pecked at Sister's plate——took it off with them when I slide down off my chair to pick up my fork. Gramma Shu rattled out of the room after that...left Papa staring at Mama's bowed head——staring at her and chewing like he were eating cold Crisco.

——Gramma Shu, rattling echoes.

I were sent directly to my room after dinner. Papa were to come up and *see me*. I went to thinking about Sister. I reasoned that the thing secret, she had, she wore neath her dress. She were lately placing hands on it and giggling to herself. When her secret weren't neath her dress, it were in her gazing, were cuddled in her arms, were in her hair as she ran her hands through it holding it up to the 'WHERES' for viewing——she smelled of it. Mama told her:

"You smell of something secret, Sister. You'd better be careful."

And when Gramma Shu noticed,

"*Sister been removing herself!* "

...I tried to talk with Sister...asked her questions:

"What's your secret...won't you tell me, please——huh?"

I'd climb her knees and fuss hug-over her stomach, put my ear in Sister's mouth,

"Will you...?"

...hear her sucking stuff off her gums, and I'd ask her again:

"——Huh...what's your secret?"

I made fists and stuck them in her jaws like earphones. I stuck my eyes just short afore her lips...watched a fish looking pout take shape in them. Sister say,

"Were his words, Robert Alex."

She say it *echosome*, like she ain't have a face to put with him.

Echoed Gramma Shu,

"*Heart-searchings! Feelings in the dark's what you got left. You ain't in no struggle, girl. She never seen him——feeling around in the dark'll get you heart-searchings!*"

Sister tried to hold her off,

"*Were* his words! He moistened my mouth so I could soft-say——suck in my breath on it——Yes. I were in his hands. It were big on my heart."

Gramma Shu ask me to testify,

"*You hear any struggle in that, Robert Alex?*"

Sister let loose her *struggle* in my eyes, say, with no blinking in it, say,

"I giggled when I heard his words, and hiccupped on the echo of Mama's warning."

"What words, Sister?"

Then Sister tried me,

"Robert Alex," she say, "When the moons rise in my fingernails to their tips, I'll give you an answer."

Gramma Shu grunted,

"*Mmmm! Not whilst I'm around, huh?*"

Sister lift me down off her knees——moons rising in my fingernails——walk off from me...slow-rocking stiff-shift wobbling most like she were gonna fall foward and squish.

For weeks I went around watching my fingernails. Gramma Shu say, my fingernails come with moon crescents——*rising*. Computer, what is a crescent?

**COMPUTER:** Please wait. C-R-E-S-C-E-N-T: 1. a shape resembling a segment of a ring tapering to points at the end. 2. something, as a roll or cookie, having this shape. 3. the figure of the moon in its first or last quarter, resembling a segment of a ring tapering to points at the end...

They're right at the bottoms of my fingernails. Gramma Shu says:

"*Little crescents, moons rising.*"

She sometimes holds my whole face in her hands, says,

"*You got such beautiful eyes, Kitten Face. They are great planets, Honey, surrounded by moons, and big enough to keep you out of trouble, boy.*"

I wondered.

Papa seen my eyes as two raisins in a muffin——called me Muffin after the neighbour Lea's twins, Muffin and The Blueberry. I remember:

When I were little, my Papa come'd to tuck me in one night...pushed me over in my bed, he done, so he could sit next of me. For the longest while he sit, look at me and look away...look at me and look away/look at me...like he hiding-'hind his look-away...and I'd giggle into his "Shush, your sister, stop it." And he'd close his eyes, meaning for me to be silent——have a face, bright as the sun you'd see it. I called him: Chief Smile Sit With No Eyes Silent. He shift-scrunch-up close to me and the covers pinched at me. My "OUCH!" scooted him off a bit, pulling the covers loose from my back, what he straightened, asking: "Would you like to say a prayer tonight, Muffin?" My Papa's eyes shined, "Say it, won't you," they asks of me. And I crawled out of bed, got on my knees, next of his sitting, I placed my elbows on his knees and put my hands together. He dipped his head and I stared up into his eyes, what Papa closed, and I closed mine——went into closed-eyes squinting:

"I forgot!"
"Forgot what, Muffin?"
"I forgot His Name!"
"Whose name?"
"I forgot it!"
Papa's hands folded around mine,
"Whose?"

I closed my eyes so tight, trying to remember, it hurt around my nose. A trembling roared in my ears and I burst:

"O! I remember it!"
"Whose?"
Papa say it like, "That's it, go on," and I shout it:
"GOD'S!...I remember It! I remember His Name. I remember."

Papa hugged me up hard to himself, but I pushed-slipped through his arms back to my knees, elbows on his knee and hands clasped together, remembering:

*O God,*
*I pinched up a flower*
*Neath my nose today*
*And smelt You.*

Papa's jerk, "UMH!" jerked me, and I fast-climbed his knee. He hugged me harder...put me back to bed and tucked me in. He had tears in his eyes. Maybe Papa will remember this when he comes/Oh-oh...

"YOUUUuuuuuu..."

# Dany Laferrière

## Why Must a Negro Writer Always Be Political?

First of all, is it essential for a writer to be identified by colour? I have to deal with this kind of question all the time. In the subway, in a restaurant (the bastard eats!), during a match at the stadium, in a taxi.

The cab driver presents himself as Nigerian. That's how he begins the conversation. Of course he hasn't visited his homeland in twenty years. To be more specific, he's African. He wants to make that perfectly clear. If Africa is now made up of disparate pieces, it's because of the colonialists. They're the ones who divided up the land. Needless to say, he's against this division. If he introduces himself as Nigerian, it's because people are always asking him where he comes from exactly. At first he held his ground. He explained that Africa was made up of a single people. The expression *Black Africa* was not only redundant, he would insist; it was politically stupid, a dirty trick, something the Western mind concocted to confuse Africans. In Africa, colour does not exist. When everyone has the same colour, colour disappears. Differences cease. And South Africa? He'd rather not discuss South Africa. This topic makes his blood boil. Each time the subject comes up, he flies into a white rage (*colère noire*). This play on words makes him chuckle. He recalls a client who spoke out in favour of apartheid. He turned without warning, gave the fellow a swift blow in the mouth. The jerk complained, which resulted in a month's lay-off. But he's glad he did it. The judge told him that, in America, we live in a democracy. Everyone has a right to his opinion. He told the judge it wasn't an opinion, the creep's just a bloody racist bastard. He began to scream blue murder. He was tossed out of court. He got a month off, a severe warning. The next time he would lose his licence. If he hadn't created such a ruckus, his lawyer told him, he would have gotten off with a week. He can live with it. He has no regrets. He's got to be careful, though, not to engage in any sensitive conversations with his clients (I rather doubt he tries very hard. I don't say a word). However, if some jerk comes into his cab and makes racist remarks, he can't be expected to keep quiet. He can't let things like that pass. Anyway, if you lose your job you can always find another one. But if you lose your dignity, you've lost everything. It's not because you're forced to work like a slave that you become less human. I am a Negro. I'm proud to be one. He spoke without practically ever turning his head. I'm under the impression he tells this story all the time. It doesn't matter who his passenger is. He eventually turns in my direction. He looks me over. He seems surprised when he sees me.

—I read your book.

He spoke dryly. Expect the worst when a cab driver turns to you and wants to discuss your book. More than likely, he's read it while at the wheel. If this is the case, books with short chapters, lots of dialogue, are advisable. The kind of book I also like to read.

—I'd like to ask you a question.

— Go ahead.

— Why did you write the book?

The question shot out, a projectile dangerously aimed at my forehead. I wasn't expecting it. Normally, when a book's out, it's out. You either like it or you don't. I remain calm. He pretends to look straight ahead. His ears are outrageously cocked. He is obviously listening.

— You don't want to answer. I know how you feel.

He knows bugger-all! Every single Negro in this bloody town thinks each one of his questions strikes like a bomb and will wreak destruction on all of America.

— I wrote the book I was in the mood to write.

His look implies, That was a cute answer; now say what's really on your mind. Instead I ask him a question.

— What's wrong with my book?

My question throws him off. I notice a slight quiver in his neck. He turns towards me. The cab nearly climbs onto the sidewalk.

— It's a traitor's book.

He rams his palms against the steering wheel. He pumps the accelerator pedal. The panel clock shows 2:49 a.m. He remains silent for a while.

— Sometimes I think I know why you wrote that shit. For the money. It's tough out there. I know. Real tough. You get nothing for free, unless you're willing to sell your soul. There'll always be a buyer for that.

— In my case, no need for a buyer...I did it willingly.

— That's it. You've learned the ropes. So no one can tell you what to do.

— There's another way of looking at it.

He looks at me threateningly. He's not the kind of guy you like to contradict. That's quite clear.

— What do you mean?

— All writers are traitors, on some level.

— That's bullshit.

— I mean it's tough for everybody (I hate to use those words). Competition is fierce. When you can't woo them with your know-how, a good striptease will sometimes do the trick.

— Does that mean you have to sell your race?

— Yes.

He eyes me while stepping on the accelerator. He wants to scare me. Where are the cops when you need them?

— I write to gain power. Just like what you're doing right now. You're driving like a madman to scare the shit out of me. It's the same for me. It's a matter of who gets leverage. I'll do anything to gain the advantage.

He's a bit puzzled. I've used his own words against him. He's a violent man. Violence is the only language he understands. He changes his tune a little. I notice something softer in him, almost invisible to the naked eye.

— Why not work in tandem with the reader?

— I don't consider the reader a friend. It's all an illusion. The reader would ask for nothing better than to tell his life story. He's got a story to tell, one he'd like to shout from every rooftop. So, if you want to glue him to a seat for hours while you tell your tale, you'd better come up with a good line. Nothing fancy. It doesn't even have to be very good.

— That's where I disagree.

— I'm listening.

I was in fact listening.

— Why not use all that energy for the benefit of your race?

— That goes against everything that literature stands for.

Talk about hyperbole!

— How's that?

— You don't write to do someone a favour. You must have something to say, you have to want to say it, you have to find ways to say it. In other words, style.

— You mean you don't feel like defending your people, humiliated for centuries!

— Of course I do. It's obvious. But you have to use the right tool. And it won't be literature. At least it won't be good literature.

— Africa has a rich history. Negro writers have a responsibility. They have to convey this knowledge.

— Exactly. I'm a writer in the present tense. I search for traces of the past in the present. Maybe you're right. There are surely Negroes out there quite suited to the task. Let them talk of the beauty that's part of our race. Not me. I don't have the qualifications. I'm only interested in man's fall, his decrepitude, his frustration, the bitterness that keeps men alive.

— Why don't you just admit you're out to make a buck?

— Like everyone else. For me, writing is just something I do to earn a living. Like everyone else. Why aren't engineers, doctors, lawyers ever asked to justify their choice? I'm telling you: I write because I want to make a name for myself, with all the benefits that go along with it. I also write to get laid by luscious young girls. Before, they wouldn't even give me the time of day.

Now he's on the same wavelength. A vein puffs up in his neck. His blood is obviously pumped up.

— But why not meld the two...I mean, make money and pay homage—I know you hate this word—to your people.

— These are irreconcilable opposites. Commercial sense versus good intentions.

— Some people do it.

— You mean Soyinka and his Nobel prize?

— Yes.

— I don't have his talent. That guy'll wind up in all the school books. I'd rather be read by those who despise me. If you beat a horse, I'm not convinced he'll like you; but anytime you're within striking distance, he'll be aware of your presence. Do you know what I mean?

— Yes, but why do you continually fall back on clichés about Negroes?

— It's an open mine. Everyone has a right to work the soil.

— You exploit...

— Just like anybody else. Don't you think all writers do the same thing? A writer is usually a cannibal. He eats people up, digests them, spews them out in words. White, black, yellow or red.

— What a cynical view of things!

— Not really. An ordinary view of things.

— Does that mean you would have preferred being a white writer?

— Not at all, and this has nothing to do with politics. Practically speaking, it's quite interesting being a Negro right now. People are ready to listen to us. It's a new voice. People have had it up to here with the love triangle (you know: the husband, the wife, the lover). They're so hungry for new stories, they'll beg for them. Even the old machine "adultery" needs oiling. Look at the job Spike Lee did in *Jungle Fever*. The same love triangle, except in different colours. The married couple is black, the mistress white. Any change is welcome. We beg you: change something.

— Yeah, but there's a difference. Spike Lee makes films for blacks. You give the impression you're writing for the whites.

— I write for readers rich enough to have the luxury to read. It's easy to forget: reading is a luxury. Three-quarters of humanity has no clue this pastime exists. When Spike Lee says he's making films for blacks, that's bullshit. How can we know in advance who will be interested in our books, our films? There's no way of knowing. It's likely Spike Lee's film touched more whites than blacks.

— Why do you talk about him so much? Jealous?

— I envy his success, not his talent.

— Why, then?

— I've told you. He interests me. His energy. We're different, though; we don't share the same enemy. For him, it's the white race. For me, it's all of America.

— Paranoid?

— Not enough.

He laughs for the first time. Rich laughter, tight at first, than reaching a strident pitch before following a joyful descent, grave, vibrant. Laughter from the pit of the stomach.

— It's quite simple. Why should I love you? You don't love me. It's not because you're black that I should love you. You, the blacks, are the first to scream for my hide.

He turns. He has a serious look, as if he's just understood something.

— I understand. You're going through a bad patch. You'll see. It'll come back.

— What'll come back?

— Well...(he looks a bit embarrassed)...humanist feelings... fraternal...we blacks don't know how to truly hate.... We're deficient in hate chromosomes....

That's the best he can do. The cab stops on the side of the road. I pay, get off. Someone else gets in. The cab jerks forward, speeds away. I watch. The driver starts up a conversation.

— I'm African. More specifically, I'm from Nigeria. If you want my opinion, all blacks are African, we all come from the first Negro, from the first Negress.

Bullshit.

# *ACKNOWLEDGEMENTS*

## *FIERY SPIRITS*

Thanks to all the authors, literary giants, translators and friends, for offering abundant advice, little notes, and suggestions. With special mention and affection to Cecil Foster, Roberta Morris, Judith Fitzgerald, Vancy Kasper, Professor Nkiru Negwu, Greg Gatenby, Mrs. Étienne, Jill Robinson and Paul Savoie.

To Keith Walker who generously and lovingly translated the excerpt from Gérard Étienne's novel "La pacotille."

To Iris Tupholme for her vision. It is she who insisted that I do a second anthology of
African-Canadian writers. To Maya Mavjee, my other eye, for her incredible insight and sensitivity (that have contributed so much to the birth of this book). And to Ed Carson — who instigated the first collection, *Voices* — for his continued support. I couldn't have done it without all of you. Also to Rosslyn Junke and her publicity team for putting up with my crazy ideas, and to everyone at HarperCollins and CAN:BAIA for their support.

To Nicole Peña for her incredible image on the cover. Perfecto!

My sincere apologies go to those writers whose works I had the opportunity to read first-hand; but, for lack of space, had to leave for the next collection.

*VOICES*

To each author, thank you for your trust and the opportunity to edit this collection. I wish to thank Austin Clarke, who encouraged me to do this book after I had organized a 1991 series of readings for Canadian Artists' Network—Black Artists in Action (CAN:BAIA). Thanks to Paul Savoie for translating Dany Laferrière's work, and Pat Jeffries for nourishing the computer with texts till the wee hours of the morning. Also, thank you to Barbara Berson, Maya Mavjee, Rebecca Vogan, everyone at HarperCollins, and everyone at CAN:BAIA. To Roberta Morris and Judith Fitzgerald, thank you for your suggestions, support and humour when I needed it most, just before the alarm sounded: Deadline.

*FIERY SPIRITS & VOICES*

For this reissue, thanks to all the writers for updating their bios. My apologies to those writers who we could not locate. To Eckehard Dolinski, my good friend, for his keen eyes on Berlin's history and transformation. To Linda Abrahms, Cecil Foster, Roberta Morris, and Penny East for their support. To my writing group for their suggestions: Vancy, Sylvia, Lorraine, Heather, Pricilla, Barbara and Irene. To Karen Hanson, Associate Editor, for her patience and keeping me on my toes. To Shawn Skeir for his wonderful image on the cover, and Alan Jones for his beautiful cover design.

From *Fiery Spirits*:
Introduction © 1994 by Ayanna Black; "The Crystal Cave" © 1994 by Carol Talbot; "Dryland: In My Village" © 1994 by Pauline Peters; "Lamentations: A Letter to My Mother" © 1994 by Kuwee Kumsaa; "The Woman in the Pit and the Elephant's Trunk" © 1994 by Jane Tapsubei Creider; "A Woman Is a Child" © 1994 by Yvonne Vera; "Canopus," "Nocturne for Roots," "Africa — Guyana!" © 1994 by Jan Carew; "My Grandfather and I" © 1994 by Rudolph Allen; "Living Out the Winter" © 1994 by John Hearne; "La pacotille" © 1994 by Gérard Étienne; English translation of "La pacotille" © 1994 by Keith L. Walker; "Affirmative Action" © 1994 by Archibald J. Crail; "Foggy Seasons" © 1994 by Paul Tiyambe Zeleza; "Catharsis/One" © 1994 by Courtnay McFarlane; "Listen to the Language" and "Shoes" © 1994 by Sylvia Hamilton; "Why" © 1994 by Stefan Collins; "Moonface" © 1994 by Richardo Keens-Douglas; "Atavism," "Between Destinies" and "Daydreaming About My Father" © 1994 by Charles C. Smith; "Grief," "Weight of War" and "In a Breath" © 1994 by Dee September; "Town" and "Every Goodbye Ain't Gone" © 1994 by Leleti Tamu; "The Brown Moth" © 1994 by Minister Faust; "Three Passages from Elizet" © 1994 by Dionne Brand.

"Daydreaming About My Father" first appeared in *Sad Dances in the Field of White*, published by Is Five Press.

"La pacotille" by Gérard Étienne (Chapter 11) was originally published by Éditions de l'Hexagone. Copyright © 1994 by Éditions de l'Hexagone. Payment: nil.

From *Voices*:
Introduction, "I Write Imaginary Stories" © 1992 by Ayanna Black; "Letter of the Law of Black," © 1992 by Austin Clarke; "Casualties," "April in Paris," "April 19, 19__," "April 3–4, 1968," "To Milton Acorn," "Marina: The Love Song of Lee Harvey Oswald," © 1992 by George Elliott Clarke; "Memories Have Tongue," "And I Remember," "Lovetalk," © 1992 by Afua Cooper; "Multiculturalism," "Phoenix," "I Am Not," © 1992 by Cyril Dabydeen; "Winter Stroll in Tipaskan," "The Oracle of Babylon," "Conceiving the Stranger," © 1992 by Nigel Darbasie; "Going Home," © 1992 by Cecil Foster; "Little Abu, The Boy Who Knew Too Much," © 1992 by Norma De Haarte; "Under Black Light," © 1992 by Claire Harris; "So What Are You, Anyway?" © 1992 by Lawrence Hill; "Why Must a Negro Writer Always Be Political?" © 1992 by Dany Laferrière; "Conceptualizing the Immaculate," © 1992 by Rozena Maart; "Because We Are Mad," "Garlands to the Beheaded One," © 1992 by Molara Ogundipe-Leslie; "Her Head a Village," © 1992 by Makeda Silvera; "Kitten Face," © 1992 by Frederick Ward.

## *About the Authors*

**Carol Talbot** was born in Windsor, Ontario. She has been teaching English at Sir Wilfred Laurier Secondary School for several years. Her poetry has appeared in several anthologies, the most recent being "*...but where are you really from?*" Talbot has received a New Playwright's Award from Theatre Fountainhead for *The Gathering*, a recent version of which was performed by her students before the whole student body to celebrate black history month. Subsequently, it was aired on the local cable station. Other published works include *Growing Up Black in Canada*. Her current work in progress, *Keepsake*, is a multi-faceted study of the links between quilting, creativity, spirituality and the experience of being a black woman in North America.

**Pauline Peters**, originally from England, has lived in Canada for over 20 years. She received her B.A. in Literature from the University of Toronto. Peters is a writer and storyteller. "Dryland" is a work in progress that has been produced by Nightwood Theatre and the Vancouver Women in View Festival.

**Kuwee Kumsaa**, also known as Martha Kumsa, is an Oromo who was born and raised in Ethiopia. She worked as a journalist in Ethiopia from 1975 to 1980 when she was thrown in jail. After ten years of incarceration without trial, she was released with the help of Amnesty International, PEN International and PEN Canada. She fled persecution in Ethiopia and came to Canada in 1991 as a refugee under Canada's Women at Risk program. She is now a Canadian citizen and a full-time student at the University of Toronto.

**Jane Tapsubei Creider** was born and raised in Kapseret, near Eldoret, Kenya. At the age of 12, she was initiated and, while in seclusion for the following three years, received instruction in the ethical principles, laws and traditions of her people. She now lives in London, Ontario, where she works as a writer, artist and scholar. She is currently working on a dictionary of her native language, Nandi, and on a sequel to the novel *Shrunken Dream*. Other published works include *A Grammar of Nandi*, *Two Lives: My Spirit and I*, "The past in the present: living biographies of the Nandi" and scholarly articles and presentations on the interpretation of female initiation. She is married and raising two children.

**Yvonne Vera** is the winner of the Swedish Prize "Voice of Africa 1999." Her most recent novel is *Butterfly Burning*, published by Baobab Books in 1999. She is the author of *Under the Tongue*, which won the Commonwealth Prize for Literature, Africa Region, 1997. Her other two novels, *Without a Name* and *Nehanda*, were both shortlisted for the Commonwealth Prize. *Why Don't You Carve Other*

*Animals* is her collection of short stories. Her work has been translated into Swedish, German and Danish. She is the editor of *Opening Spaces* — an anthology of contemporary writing by African women. She is a graduate of York University in Canada and currently works as the Director of the National Gallery of Zimbabwe in Bulawayo.

**Jan Carew** was born in the village of Agricola Rome on the Guyana coast. He was educated in Guyana, the United States and Europe. After living for years in Britain as a writer, he entered academia and is now an Emeritus Professor at Northwestern University. A lecturer at institutions such as London University, Princeton and Rutgers, Carew has also served as an advisor to the heads of state of numerous nations on the African continent and in the Caribbean. He is once again a full-time writer and artist, living in Pennsylvania.

Other published works include *Ghosts in Our Blood, With Malcolm X in Africa, England and the Caribbean, The Rape of Paradise, Black Midas, The Wild Coast, Green Winter, The Last Barbarian, Moscow Is Not My Mecca, Cry Black Power, The Flight Streets of Eternity, Sea-Drums in My Blood* and *The Third Gift*. His current work in progress, *Seasons in an Ebony Tower*, is a documentary novel set in Princeton in the early '70s.

**Rudolph Allen** was born in Jamaica, West Indies, and has been living in Canada for many years. He received his B.A.

from Sir George Williams University and his M.B.A. from McGill University. Prior to writing, he worked in business at the Bank of Montreal, for the federal government in Ottawa and for Computer Science Canada in Montreal. Allen's writing has appeared in *Revue Noir '97*, *Koala '92*, *The National Review of Poetry '91*, *Midwest Poetry Review '91* and *The American Poetry Annual '90*. He has read at schools such as the University of Toronto and Humber College Creative Writing School. Presently he lives in Toronto. Forthcoming work includes *The Peoples of Exile*.

**John Hearne** was born in Montreal to Jamaican parents in 1926. He grew up in Jamaica and, after service in the Royal Air Force in World War II, he was educated at universities in Edinburgh and London. Hearne lived between Jamaica and England in the '50s and early '60s. During this time, he published five novels: *Voices Under the Window*, *Stranger at the Gate*, *The Faces of Love*, *The Autumn Equinox* and *Land of the Living*. He was awarded the John Llewellyn Rhys Memorial Prize in 1956 for his first novel, *Voices Under the Window*. Hearne returned to Jamaica permanently in 1962. He taught at the University of the West Indies and worked as a journalist until 1992. His last novel, *The Sure Salvation*, was published in 1981. John Hearne died in 1994.

**Gérard Étienne** was born in Haiti, W.I. After being imprisoned and tortured under the Papa Doc Duvalier regime, he went into exile in Canada in 1964. He has worked as a reporter at *Metro Express* and *Quartier Latin*, as well as being an editor at the daily *Le Matin* and the weekly *Le Voilier* in New Brunswick. He studied linguistics and literature at the University of Montreal, and earned a doctorate from the University of Strasbourg, France.

In 1989, Étienne was awarded a prize for excellence as the best editor in Canada. He is the author of 18 books (poetry, novels and essays) that have been translated into five languages, including Russian, Spanish, German and Chinese. He has also published 60 studies for specialized periodicals in literary criticism, linguistics, semiology, and more than 400 editorials, plus over 800 articles on various subjects. Presently a full professor in journalism and linguistics, he continues extensive research in semiology and is completing a study on race and racism in the Québecois novel.

**Paul Tiyambe Zeleza** is a Professor of History and African Studies at the University of Illinois, where he is also the Director of the Center for African Studies. He has taught at the Universities of Trent, Malawi, the West Indies and Kenyatta University in Kenya. He was educated at universities in Malawi, England and Canada. Zeleza is the author of several scholarly books and three books of fiction, including *Smouldering Charcoal* (1992) and *The Joys of Exile: Stories* (1994). He has also published dozens of scholarly articles and is the recipient of numerous fellowships, research grants and literary awards. He received the 1994 Noma Award for Publishing in Africa, Africa's most prestigious book award, for his book *A Modern*

*Economic History of Africa. Volume 1. The Nineteenth Century* (1993). He has also received the 1998 Special Commendation by the Noma Award for his book *Manufacturing African Studies and Crises* (1997).

**Courtnay McFarlane** is a visual artist, community worker and poet. His poetry has appeared in the anthologies *Word Up* and *Plush.* He also co-edited the anthology *Ma-Ka Diasporic Juks: Contemporary Writing by Queers of African Descent.*

**Sylvia Hamilton** is a filmmaker and writer/researcher who was born in Beechville, Nova Scotia. She holds a B.A. in English and Sociology from Acadia University and is currently pursuing an M.A. at Dalhousie University. Her lectures, films and published works explore the social and cultural history and experience of African Nova Scotians. Her film work includes the award-winning *Black Mother Black Daughter, Speak it! From the Heart of Black Nova Scotia* (winner of a 1994 Gemini Award), *Against the Tides: The Jones Family* (part of the Hymn To Freedom Series) and *You, Me and the CBC.* She is also a published poet and essayist. She is a contributing author of *We're Rooted Here and They Can't Pull Us Up: Essays in African Canadian Women's History.*

She is presently working on several film projects, one of which will explore the historical and contemporary links between black women in Nova Scotia and Sierra Leone, West Africa. She lives in Halifax.

**Stefan Collins** is originally from Nova Scotia. His poetry has appeared in *Rites Magazine*, *Queer Press Publication*, *Sir Ian Mckellan* (England), *International Lesbian and Gay Association* (NY), *Sojourner* (NY) and *Black Press* (LA). He tested HIV positive in May 1982 and has been involved in AIDS education within the black community, buddying outreach and public speaking and workshop facilitation. He now lives in Amsterdam.

**Richardo Keens-Douglas**, a writer, storyteller, motivational speaker and actor was born in Grenada in the West Indies. His play, *The Nutmeg Princess,* won the Dora Mavor Moore Award for Outstanding New Musical of 1999. Since 1991, he has received national recognition as the host of the CBCs acclaimed storytelling radio talk show, "Cloud 9." As a storyteller, Keens-Douglas has thrilled audiences across Canada, the USA, aboard the *H.M.S. Britannia*, the Caribbean and at international storytelling festivals. His storytelling play *Once Upon An Island* was a Sterling Award nominee in Edmonton in 1991. His stories have been anthologized and recorded in Canada. His children's books have won many awards, and they include *The Nutmeg Princess*, *La Diablesse and the Baby*, *Freedom Child of the Sea*, *Grandpa's Visit*, *Miss Meow Pageant* and *Mama God, Papa God.*

**Charles C. Smith** has worked as Projects Editor for the *New York Quarterly* poetry magazine, edited three collections of poetry and been coordinator of the Black

Perspective Cultural Program. In 1985 he won the Black Theatre Canada Anti-Apartheid Playwright Contest for his one-act play, *Last Days for the Desperate*. He is the editor of three books: *Bantu*, *Teeth of the Whirlwind* and *Sad Dances in a Field of White*. Other published works include *Partial Lives*, *A Piece of Twisted Steel*, "Racism and Community Planning: Building Equity or Waiting for Explosions" and a contribution to the "The Canadian Caribbean Issue" of *Descant*.

**Dee September** was born in Cape Town, South Africa. She immigrated to Canada with her family and settled in Winnepeg, Manitoba. Her poetry has been translated into 15 languages and published in 21 countries. September has appeared on educational radio and television programs in Winnipeg, Toronto and Vancouver. Her poetry appeared in various publications, including *Soviet Women* (Russia), *Forward* (Zambia), *Fireweed*, *Landscape* (Canada) and *Sage Eye* (England). Dee has read her work at numerous venues in Canada, the United States, Tanzania and England. Other published works include *Making Waves*. She is a multi-media artist presently residing in Vancouver, writing poetry and short stories.

**Leleti Tamu** was born in Jamaica and immigrated to Canada in 1971. Her poetry has appeared in *Fireweed* and *Dyeworks*. She now lives in Toronto with her son, Jonathan, and their cat, Bulla.

**Minister Faust** obtained his B.A. with Distinction in English Literature and Political Science in 1991 and his B.Ed. in English Literature and Social Studies in 1993. His poetry has appeared in *Dead Tree Product*, *Power to the People* and *The Gateway*. He has read his poetry widely across Canada and has appeared at various times on radio, including CBC-FMs "Brave New Waves" and CBC Alberta. Faust lives in Edmonton.

**Dionne Brand** was born in Trinidad and has lived in Toronto for over 20 years. She studied English and Philosophy at the University of Toronto and did her post-graduate work at OISE. Brand's poetry and other writings have appeared in various magazines and journals, including *Fireweed*, *Prism* and *This Magazine*. In 1997, she won the Governor General's Award for poetry and the Trillium Award for *Land to Light On*. Her novel *In Another Place, Not Here* was shortlisted for the Chapters/*Books in Canada* First Novel Award and the Trillium Award. Her most recent novel is entitled *At the Full and Change of the Moon*. Other published works include *Fore day morning*, *Earth Magic* (children's poetry), *Winter Epigrams and Epigrams to Ernesto Cardenal in Defense of Claudia*, *Primitive Offensive*, *Chronicles of the Hostile Sun*, *No Language is Neutral*, *Sans Souci And Other Stories* and *Lives of Black Working Women in Ontario — An Oral History*.

**Molara Ogundipe-Leslie** is a Nigerian-born writer, poet, scholar and literary critic. She is a founding member of the

International Women for a Meaningful Summit and co-founder of the Association of African Research and Development and Women in Nigeria. She has been a major figure in academia since the '60s, a leading scholar in women's studies and women-in-development. Ogundipe-Leslie's biography and poems have appeared in several authoritative anthologies, including *The Penguin Book of Modern African Poetry, Voices from 20th-Century Africa*, the *Heinemann International Book of African Poetry* and *African Women Poets,* edited by Frank Chapasula. Her collection *Sew the Old Days and Other Poems* was published in 1985, and her work has appeared in various magazines and anthologies.

Ogundipe-Leslie has innovated a new-yet-old type of poetry that harks back to the traditional performance modes of her Yoruba culture: the call and refrain, the play with sound at its many levels as the mind rises naturally from speech to incantation to song (a style surviving in the black sermon); and the active participation of her audience in the creative process. She sometimes calls this form "living poetry," not only because it is a vibrant tradition in Africa, but because it is also a form that draws on the immediate vitality of her audience.

**Norma De Haarte** was born in Georgetown, Guyana. She graduated from Guyana's Teachers' College in 1968. After graduating with two bachelor's degrees in Teaching and Education, she returned to Guyana and worked with the Ministry of Education as a guidance officer. In 1982 she returned to Canada and worked as an elementary school teacher. Her first novel, *Guyana Betrayal*, was published in 1991. Other published works include *Little Abu, The Boy Who Knew Too Much* (1992) and *Mr. Jimmy, the Black Pudding Man* (1997).

**Afua Cooper** has published four books of poetry, including the acclaimed *Memories Have Tongue* (1992) and her compilation of female dub poetry, entitled *Utterances and Incantations: Women, Poetry, and Dub* (1999). Her poetry has also appeared in anthologies worldwide. She completed her doctoral dissertation in African-North-American history and has published critical works on African-Canadian gender history. She co-authored *We're Rooted Here and They Can't Pull Us Up: Essays in African Canadian Women's History* (reprinted in 1999), which won the prestigious Joseph Brant award for history. She currently teaches history at the University of Toronto.

**Cyril Dabydeen**, who originally hailed from Guyana, has been living in Canada for the past three decades. He is the author of three novels, four collections of short stories and eight collections of poetry. His work has appeared in numerous magazines in Canada, the United States, the UK, Europe, the Caribbean, New Zealand, India and elsewhere. His latest books include, *Black Jesus and Other Stories*, *Berbice Crossing*, *Discussing Columbus*, *Stoning the Wind* and *Coastland: New and Selected Poems.* He edited *A Shapely Fire: Changing the Literary Landscape* and *Another*

*Way to Dance: Contemporary Asian Poetry in Canada and the US.* A former poet laureate of Ottawa, he has been appointed one of nine international jurors to adjudicate the Year 2000 Neustadt International Prize for Literature. He ended his formal education at Queen's University, Ontario, and has taught at Algonquin College and the University of Ottawa. He has also worked for many years in human rights for the federal and municipal governments. He has read widely from his books across Canada, in the US, Europe, the Caribbean and Asia.

**Lawrence Hill** is the author of the novel *Some Great Thing* as well as *Women of Vision: The Story of the Canadian Negro Women's Association* and *Trials and Triumphs: The Story of African-Canadians*, a children's history book. His second novel, *Any Known Blood*, was published to much acclaim in 1997. A creative writing instructor at Ryerson Polytechnic University in Toronto, his short fiction has appeared in numerous anthologies and magazines including *Toronto Life*, *Descant*, and *Exile.*

**George Elliott Clarke** was born in Nova Scotia, a seventh-generation Canadian. He is a graduate of both the University of Waterloo and Dalhousie University. He has worked as an editor, researcher, journalist and parliamentary aide. Clarke is the author of three books of poetry, *Saltucher Spirituals*, *Deeper Blues* and *Whylah Falls* and the editor of *Fire on the Water*, an anthology of black Nova Scotian writing.

**Austin Clarke** was born in Barbados and came to Toronto in 1955, where he attended the University of Toronto. He has had a varied and busy career as visiting professor at many American universities, as the organizer of a broadcasting system in Barbados, as a member of the controversial Canadian Immigration and Refugee Board and as the recent host of the TV book show *Literati*, where he interviews leading writers from around the world. Since 1964, Clarke has published eight novels and five short story collections in the United States, Canada and England. He has been honored with many awards for his writing, and his novel, *Storm of Fortune*, was shortlisted for the Governor General's Award in 1973. Recently the winner of the 1999 W.O. Mitchell Prize, awarded each year to a Canadian writer who has produced an outstanding body of work and served as a caring mentor for other writers, Austin Clarke has just published his memoir, *Pigtails and Breadfruit: The Rituals of Slave Food.*

**Nigel Darbasie** was born in Trinidad, West Indies. In 1969 he moved to Canada, settling in Edmonton. His poetry has been published in several anthologies and high-school text books and has also been broadcast on the CBC.

**Rozena Maart** writes both fiction and non-fiction. She is widely published in magazines and journals in Canada and abroad, and her work explores black consciousness, psychoanalysis, Derridean deconstruction and political philosophy. She is a founding member of the first black feminist organization in Cape Town, Women Against Repression. She was nominated as Woman of the Year in 1987, at the age of 24, for her work in the area of violence against women and her work in Women Against Repression. Among her most recent publications is a work entitled *The Absence of the Knowledge of White Consciousness in Contemporary Feminist Theory.* She received her Ph.D. from The Centre for Cultural Studies in Birmingham, UK.

**Claire Harris** came to Calgary from Trinidad in 1966. Today she lives the itinerant life of a full-time writer. Her poetry, prose and fiction have been widely anthologized and there are editions in German and Gudjarati. Her new book, *She*, will be published in the year 2000 by Goose Lane Editions. She has won numerous awards: the Commonwealth Regional Award for *Fables from the Women's Quarters* (1984), The Writers Guild of Alberta Poetry prize, the Alberta Culture Poetry Prize for *Travelling to Find a Remedy* (1986) and an Alberta culture Special Award for *Conception of Winter* (1989). *Drawing Down a Daughter* was shortlisted for the Governor General's Award in 1993 and *Dipped in Shadow* (1996) was shortlisted for the WGA prize.

**Cecil Foster** is the author of *A Place Called Heaven*, a controversial look at the reality of the Black Canadian experience, which won the Gordon Montador Award. He is the author of three acclaimed novels: *No Man in the House*, *Sleep on, Beloved*, and *Slammin' Tar*. He is a freelance columnist for the *Toronto Star*, as well as the host of "Urban Talk" on CFRB Radio. He has taught journalism at Ryerson Polytechnic University and Humber College in Toronto, has worked at the CTV network, and has contributed regularly to *The Globe and Mail*, *The Financial Post* and CBC Radio and Television. Cecil Foster lives in Toronto.

**Makeda Silvera** was born in Jamaica and spent her early years in Kingston before immigrating to Canada. Writing has always been a major interest. She began in journalism, working with Toronto's *Contrast* and *Share*, and was a former editorial collective member of *Fireweed*, a feminist quarterly. Her stories, articles and essays have appeared in numerous journals. She is the author of two books, *Silenced*, a collection of interviews with Caribbean domestic workers in Canada, and *Remembering G*, her first book of fiction. She also edited *Piece of My Heart*, writings by lesbians of colour living in North America. Silvera is co-founder of Sister Vision Press, the first press for women of colour in Canada, where she works as managing editor.

**Frederick Ward** is an author, playwright, composer and actor. He studied music in Los Angeles and has taught at Dalhousie University. His published works include *Riverslip*, *Nobody Called Me Mine*, *A Room Full of Balloons* and *The Curing Berry*, a collection of prose-poetry. Ward's compositions, poetry, plays and theatrical performances have won him international recognition. In May 1992, Dalhousie University awarded him an honourary LL.D.

Born in Kansas City, Missouri, he now lives in Blockhouse, Nova Scotia, and Montreal.

**Dany Laferrière** was born in Port-au-Prince, Haiti, where he practiced journalism under the dictatorial reign of Duvalier. When a friend, also a journalist, was found murdered in 1976, Laferrière took the hint and went into exile in Canada in 1978, where he wrote his first novel, *Comment faire l'amour avec un nègre sans se fatiguer* (How to Make Love to a Negro Without Getting Tired), which has been translated into several languages. The film version of the book was released in 45 countries. He is also the author of *Eroshima*, *L'odeur du café*, *La chair du maître* and *Le charme de après-midi sans fin*. Nine of his books have been translated into ten languages. He lives in Miami and Montreal.

### *About the Editor*

**Ayanna Black** was born in Jamaica and lived in England before immigrating to Canada in 1994. Her poetry has been anthologized in various books such as *SP/ELLes*, *Women and Words*, *One Out of Many* and *Daughters of the Sun, Women of the Moon*. Her non-fiction writings have appeared in *Fuse Magazine*, *Fireweed*, *The Best Writing on Writing* and *Siolence: Poets on Women, Violence & Silence*.

She is one of the founding members of *Tiger Lily*, Canada's first magazine by women of colour. She is author of the poetry collection *No Contingencies* and co-author of *Linked Alive*. Black is editor of two collections of poetry and short fiction, *Voices* and *Fiery Spirits*. She has read and conducted poetry workshops in public schools, universities, libraries and art galleries in Canada, the United Kingdom, the United States and Italy. She is presently working on a new book of poetry, *The Berlin Poems*. She lives in Toronto.